T0354497

ALEUT PRINCESS

LORETTA SANFORD CUELLAR

iUniverse

ALEUT PRINCESS

iUniverse books may be ordered through booksellers or by contacting:

iUniverse
1663 Liberty Drive
Bloomington, IN 47403
www.iuniverse.com
1-800-Authors (1-800-288-4677)

ISBN: 978-1-5320-2108-4 (sc)
ISBN: 978-1-5320-2109-1 (e)

Library of Congress Control Number: 2017941803

Print information available on the last page.

iUniverse rev. date: 06/13/2017

For Mary Ann

and

in loving memory of Benicio Cuellar

(December 21, 1946–July 4, 2016)

CONTENTS

CHAPTER 1

Linda Kolvalski was screeching, a high-pitched sound that hurt the ears. "Anna, are you in there?" She'd been pounding on Anna's door for the last five minutes. It seemed like much longer. The small tenement room Anna Hasson lived in for the past few years had at least kept a roof over her head. Linda hadn't heard from her cousin in a few days and once again was having anxiety attacks that Anna had drunk herself into a stupor. Where had Anna said she'd hidden that extra key? Under the dirty, frayed hall carpet? She squatted down, and reaching her hand under the hall carpet that ran directly in front of the door to Anna's room, she fumbled around, feeling on her hand the dirt and grime of many years. Sweeping her hand back and forth, going farther under the rug, she finally felt something hard that felt like a key. When she pulled it out, she gagged at the sight of the black slimy grime now covering her hand.

Opening the door, Linda's stomach uncontrollably retched at

the smell. Linda shook her head and teared up. The room itself was old with the strong moldy, musty smell that consumed an old room that hadn't been cleaned in years. The smell of dried urine combined with the fresh vomit was overpowering. The room had been occupied by too many lost souls with broken dreams, and it made the room feel oppressively claustrophobic. The two small windows had yellowed, torn pull-down shades. Cracks ran down every wall. Cobwebs hung from the corners and down the gray ceiling like hundreds of dirty, fuzzy, sticky threads. The once green paint was so dull and dirty that one had to look close to recognize the color, half of it peeling off the walls. Whatever life the room may have had at one time had been sucked out for lack of care and the hopelessness of its tenants.

Anna was lying in her bed on sheets that had several yellow stains and obviously hadn't been washed in a long time. Blood had dried on Anna's chin from earlier when she had bitten her tongue. Dirty clothes and trash lay scattered over the small room, which only had a bed, one wooden chair, and canned goods sitting on a small table in one corner. A small sink was filled with a few dirty pots, and dishes sat next to the table. A bathroom with a toilet and shower was down the hall, and she shared it with other tenants on the same floor.

Linda could see Anna was still breathing, so she slapped her face back and forth and yelled, "Anna, Anna, you're killing yourself with your drinking. Who gave it to you this time?"

Linda felt sorrier for herself than she did for her cousin. Anna wasn't even her real cousin. They were related through some marriage to someone way back when. Linda didn't even remember their names anymore. From the beginning of Anna's arrival in Juneau, Linda had tried to help her, giving her a place to live in one of the small Quonset huts built by the military on the tide flats of Juneau. She lived there with her new husband, Willie. Money had been scarce, but they'd managed on the small salary her husband made as the night janitor at the post office and the money they made from selling some of the baskets that Anna weaved.

Linda was Creole, half Russian, and half Aleut, as so many of the Aleut race were. Anna's mother, Anuuk, was related to Linda's through marriage, and Linda had felt obliged to take her in when she'd arrived in Juneau. It was the Aleut way. Aleuts took care of one another, even if they were only one-eighth Aleut.

At the time of initial Russian contact in 1741, there was an estimated fifteen thousand Aleuts, but that number drastically declined in the late 1700s and 1800s because of many Russian men marrying Aleut women and the brutality of the Russian fur traders, who treated the Aleuts like slaves. By the time both Linda and Anna were born, full-blooded Aleuts composed less than 1 percent of the population.

Anna finally moaned and slurred as she said, "Hospital. Please get me to the hospital."

"I swear, Anna, this is the last time. I'm not going to watch you kill yourself any longer. I'm done finished. No more. Period!" Linda yelled in her high-pitched screech. She had enough problems of her own. It seemed like her teenage boys were getting into trouble daily, and her husband, Willie, was back drinking hooch again.

Linda couldn't help but tear up and shudder at the sad condition Anna was living in. She'd been diagnosed with cirrhosis of the liver some ten years earlier. Now Anna had a yellow tinge to her whole body, making her once beautiful bronze skin look a sickly green. Her body was covered in bruises, and her once long, shiny black hair was dull and badly matted now.

Once upon a time, Anna had been stunningly beautiful. She had been petite at only five foot one—and with a perfectly shaped body, neither too thin nor too heavy. Most of the time, she would braid her hair in one thick french braid, pulling her thick hair away from her high cheekbones and dark brown eyes that looked like two pieces of black coal. When Anna Hanson looked a person straight in the eyes, the depth of her stare would produce such discomfort that often the person would lower his or her eyes and look away. The kind of intimacy and depth in her eyes could strip a person of hidden sins.

Anna awoke the next morning in the small St. Ann's Hospital in Juneau. How many times had she been admitted in the last few years? Too many times to remember. Not that she wanted to remember—not now, not ever! It didn't matter anymore. She'd probably be leaving in a coffin this time, taking all her secrets with her to the grave. She was filled with shame—things she didn't want anyone to know, secrets built on top of more secrets until the only way to numb the pain was drinking herself into oblivion with hooch. Too much hooch for too long. She had been warned some ten years earlier, warned by the doctors and nurses of St. Ann's Hospital. In the last five years, she'd been warned specifically by Sister Mary Kathleen, who'd spent many hours praying for her and talking her through all her physical, emotional, and spiritual pain. Anna wanted to believe her, wanted to believe that prayers were answered; however, every time she left the hospital, life and the pain that went with it had overwhelmed her, and within days she would be back to drinking hooch, back to the place where she could numb all her emotions and hide from the shame that consumed her very being.

The small St. Ann's community hospital in Juneau was founded in September 11, 1886, by the Sisters of St. Ann. In the late fall of that same year, the St. Ann's Hospital Society was established. The object of the hospital society was "mutual relief and gratuitous charity." Miners and other members of the society were required to contribute $1.00 a month to qualify for free admission to the hospital and free medicine and treatment while in the hospital. For a fee of $2.50 a day, the hospital would provide patients with private rooms and special attention. Patients with no means to pay were treated for free. And anyone in good health was eligible to belong to the society regardless of age, sex, religious affiliation, or ethnicity.

Over the years, St. Ann's Hospital continued to grow, adding new wings in 1916, 1933, and had just laid the foundation for new week. It went from a frontier hospital to a modern medical facility with a growing staff of skilled physicians and nurses.

Sister Mary Kathleen, although young for such responsibility, was the administrator, and now Anna wondered why she hadn't come to see her yet. She'd been admitted late the night before, and it was now the middle of the afternoon. If Anna trusted any human being, it was Sister Mary Kathleen. She was the only person who even had a hint of the secrets Anna carried within her.

But now Anna was so consumed with shame she couldn't think of one single thing she'd done in her life that was a source of pride. Well, maybe one. She was 100 percent Aleut, and she'd once been known as an Aleut princess. Still, it wasn't anything she'd done. It was her birthright. Her brain felt like scrambled eggs. She couldn't think straight. She wondered if maybe Sister Mary Kathleen was as fed up with her as Anna was with herself. Or maybe Sister was just weary of hearing her rage against God?

"Oh, God," she cried out. "If You're real, show Yourself to me." Was there eternal life? If there was, she was going straight to hell, and Anna Hasson was terrified.

Anna thought she knew all about God. She had been raised in the Russian Orthodox church after all. She had begged for His help every night during that long boat ride from her village to Juneau. It was so many years ago. She had been only fifteen years old. Like a broken record, the memory replayed over and over in her head. It was as if it had happened only yesterday. She had staggered off that fishing boat and onto the Juneau tidal flats, enraged at a God she neither understood nor cared to understand. If—and that was a big *if*—He really loved her like she'd been taught, where was He? He certainly had not come to her rescue. Over the years she had from time to time and in the depth of despair begged Him to rescue her. Always nothing, just a dead, dark silence that devoured her soul.

A nurse entered the room; she was there to give her another

injection and ease her pain. "How are we doing today?" she asked in a sing-song voice.

"How do you think I am?" was Anna's sarcastic reply. Dear God, how she hated being treated like she was a stupid child.

"Well, aren't we little Miss Haughty today," the nurse replied. Anna just wanted to slap that huffy, smug look off her face.

"Actually, I'm a princess, an Aleut princess!" Anna cried out.

"That sounds delusional Miss Hasson." the nurse said still in her sing-song voice. It was a dead-end conversation because Anna knew that although that had been her status at one time in her life, it was so long ago, so far away that even she had a hard time remembering how it felt to feel happy, safe, and secure.

Anna changed the subject. "Do you know if Sister Mary Kathleen has been told I'm here?" Anna quietly asked.

"Sister has been told," the nurse abruptly answered. Anna nodded her head in acknowledgment and closed her eyes in an effort to shut out the nurse's patronizing words.

As the nurse left the room, she added with a huff, "Sister Kathleen has more to do than check in on you, Ms. Hasson. You were just here a couple of months ago with the same problems." And she marched out the door in her crisp white uniform and nurse's hat.

Anna Hasson had been addicted to hooch since she was sixteen.

Hooch is an extremely potent and distilled with molasses or sugar, flour, potatoes, and yeast. The term *hooch* was at one time a popular slang for liquor. During 1920s prohibition it became common parlance for any illegal liquor, and the term still has a connotation of an illicit or at least cheap distilled spirit. By the time Anna was born in 1926, there were maybe fifteen Aleuts who out of the 130 in the village—drank hooch on a daily basis. The rest of the villagers just called them drunkards and gossiped about them. And here she was—once an Aleut princess but now nothing more than a drunkard.

There was only speculation on how the Aleut Indian's learned how to make liquor. One story told that it all began when the United States purchased Alaska from the Russians in 1867. Soldiers were dispatched to the Alaskan wilderness and manned remote posts where they had no easy access to alcohol. Many thought that one group of these soldiers began to brew their own extremely potent spirit out of molasses, yeast, berries, sugar, and graham flour. The liquor became a trade between the Indians and the solders. The Indians subsequently learned how to make it for themselves and began trading it with their neighbors.

Other accounts said that the liquor from the Hudson Bay Company and the Russian traders furnished to the Indians was very weak and expensive. A deserter from a Russian whaling ship taught the Aleuts how to distill liquor from molasses or sugar with flour, potatoes, and yeast, and they distilled the vilest and most powerful of spirits.

Anna's eyes were red and burned from salty tears. The pillow was soaking wet from her tears. Whatever family members she'd once had were now gone. Sven, the one man she had loved, had left her because of her continued drunkenness, and the three children she'd given birth to had all been taken from her at her own request.

Anna's black despair was too much for her to bear. Her life held no meaning. Why had she even been born? She was now sobbing uncontrollably, rolling her head back and forth, back and forth on the pillow

It was in that moment she heard her mother Anuuk's soft voice coming from somewhere deep inside her. "Remember, Ahha (her Indian name), you are an Aleut princess. Your father, Chuuyugis Takuun, was what the invading Russians call an Aleut, but we are really *Unangan* which means 'we the people.'" Anuuk's soft voice grew stronger in Anna's mind. "You are full-blooded Aleut, and there are only a handful of us left. You must fight for your race and see that it doesn't die with you. It is your destiny. You are and always will be an Aleut princess. Hold your head high, and never forget who you are."

Anna had forgotten, and it had led her into a self-destructive life that had brought her to this place, dying alone in a hospital with no family or even friends to comfort her.

She squeezed her stinging eyes. Shutting them tightly, she drifted, drifted back to the time when she had been safe, happy, proud, and even a little puffed up to be an Aleut princess.

CHAPTER 2

On this early evening, Anuuk sat with her seven-year-old daughter, content and happy. She smiled down at her only daughter, Ahha, given to her late in life. A true miracle in Anuuk's mind, not only because she had birthed her late in life but also because Ahha was one of the few left with a pure Aleut bloodline. Ahha was a true Aleut princess. Ahha's father was the chief of the village with almost two hundred Aleut people.

Initial Russian contact in 1741 with the Aleuts who occupied the Aleutian Island changed the destiny of the Aleut race forever. The Russian fur traders brought brutality, cruelty, and disease. In the 17 hundreds they killed many of the Aleut men and kept the women for their own comfort.

In 1867, the second-largest real estate deal in the history of United States of America occurred, bigger in scope than anywhere in the Old West. The US government bought Alaska for a meager $7.5

million. Alaska was considered "Seward's Folly" since Americans were unaware of its true riches of fur-bearing animals, timber, coal, copper, gold, and the richest salmon fishing grounds in the world. So for decades Alaska lived in state of limbo, and lawlessness was the norm.

Some of Anuuk's family bloodline escaped marrying or being raped by Russians through deceit and lies. One of Anuuk's favorite stories was of her great-grandmother and how she had dressed her daughter (Anuuk's mother) as a boy and kept her hidden much of the time. But that was long ago, and life for Anuuk had been safe and happy for a long time.

Anuuk did not know that within eight years it would all be gone, and the federal government would order American soldiers to burn her village to the ground. Anuuk's life would tragically end far from the island she loves. Her husband, Aalux, and two grown sons, Chuuyugis and Tixlax, would never return to her, and her only daughter, Ahha, would be kidnapped off the beach just a few feet from their seaside house. Almost a year would pass before Anuuk found out her daughter was even alive. Worse yet, Anuuk's whole Aleut race would fall just short of complete annihilation through genocide.

It was early evening, Anuuk's favorite time of day. She sat on the wooden floor, cross-legged, by the oil stove, chanting softly. Anuuk was weaving one of her many baskets from birch bark, puffin feathers, and wild rye grass, which grew along the volcanic rolling hills of Atka Island, her island.

The main method of grass basketry, called *qiigam aygaaxs* by the Aleuts, was false embroidery (overlay). Strands of grasses or reeds were overlaid upon the basic weaving surface to obtain a plastic effect. It is an art reserved for Aleut women to this day.

Atka Island is the largest island in the Andreanof Islands of the Aleutian Islands. More than one thousand miles from Anchorage, it is one of the most isolated native villages on the Aleutian chain, and in the 1800s, it became an important trade site and safe harbor for the Russian fur traders.

However, for now Anuuk was safe and happy, and her seven-year-old daughter was sitting at her feet, smiling up at her. Anuuk whispered in prayer to *Agugux* (the Creator), "Thank you for this beautiful daughter." It had always baffled Anuuk how she could have given birth to such a beauty. Anuuk was only four foot eight, with chubby cheeks, wild black hair, and short legs that gave her a squatty look. He skin was weather-beaten and looked like leather from the years of harsh climate, and the joints on both her hands were knobby. She had kept her thumbnail long and filed to a fine point, preserving the old way. It made ripping apart old leather pieces to resew much faster.

Today had been an especially good day. Early that same morning while out picking berries, Anuuk saw "her bird," the puffin. The bird was a spiritual sign to her, her own personal totem, even though she was Russian Orthodox like most of the village and most of the Aleut race. Anuuk still believed in some of the old ways of the Aleuts—animistic mixed in with totems. The puffin had a penguin-like coloring and a colorful break, and the Aleuts had given it the nickname "sea parrot." From the time Anuuk was a young girl, whenever she saw a puffin, life seemed to go easier. It was a sign of spring and summer, when food was in abundance, the wild fireweed covered the hills, and you could hear laughter throughout the whole village.

As a young girl, Annuk once carved a puffin out of driftwood, and it was displayed on the same shelf where several of Aalux's carved figures of ivory (from walrus tusks) also sat.

The house is the biggest house in the village, a hundred feet by sixty.

The partially subterranean houses roofed over with rafters of Driftwood and whalebone, covered with a layer of sod. They were called *Barabaras*. The *Barabaras* were gone with so many of the old ways of the Aleuts that had sustained them for thousands' of years.

All of the houses were now built above ground from wooden planks brought in by the various barges. The villagers paid for it all through trading their furs, carvings, and baskets. Any cracks or holes were filled with moss. The village had electricity, and two bare lightbulbs hung from the rafters of Anuuk's home. Anuuk still used the whale oil lamps since the electricity was off more than it was on.

The house was only three rooms. Two of the rooms were partially walled off and used for sleeping. The long living and kitchen area had wooden benches along one wall. Shelves were filled with handwoven baskets and carvings from wood and the ivory. Hanging on one wall in a place of honor were her husband and son's ornate wooden hunting hats (*chaguda-x*). They were colorfully designed and trimmed with sea lion whiskers, feathers, and ivory. They looked somewhat like large sun visors with feathers and whiskers shooting out the back. By the time Ahha was born, many of the old ways of the Aleuts had been dropped, and now the beautiful chaguda-x was only used in ceremonial dances. A hand pump for water was installed on a small wooden counter, and they used it for washing and cleaning. Anuuk even had a flushing toilet. A person could flush it by pulling the chain hanging from the ceiling. It was in a corner of the house hidden only by an old leather blanket hung over a rope.

The oil stove that Anuuk and her daughter now sat by provided them with much-needed warmth, and they also used it for cooking. On this night they had *alutiqqutigaq*, a mixture of berries, fat, and fish. Their bellies were full, and they felt warm and cozy.

Anuuk was teaching Ahha how to weave both baskets and mats. Ahha was trying to delay her bedtime and begged, "Mama, tell me again how I came to be." Anuuk smiled. She knew it was a ruse, but she never tired of telling her daughter about the miracle of her birth.

"Well," Anuuk began in her soft voice. "I had my two sons, and they were getting older. I asked God for a daughter, but it never happened. I just kept asking Jesus to please, please give me a daughter. I was afraid I was getting too old as *my time* of the month didn't always come every month like it had since I was a young girl. I thought maybe the time for me to have another child had passed like so many of the other older women in the village. Then one day I felt a flutter inside me as if a butterfly was in my belly. The flutter got stronger and stronger, and I knew you were there and growing because my belly got bigger and bigger."

A quizzical look was on Ahha's face, and she asked, "Did God put me in your belly, Mama."

17

Anuuk smiled and replied, "Yes, with the help of your father." The answer seemed to satisfy Ahha at least for the moment.

There was a comfortable silence between them as the mother assisted the daughter in her weaving. Small fingers sometime weren't strong enough to pull the weaving tight, and sometimes the edge of the dried dune rye grass had razor-sharp edges and could leave stinging small cuts on the fingers and hands. Ahha was a precocious child who could drive an adult to distraction with her why questions, so the silence only lasted for a minute or two.

"I never see God, Mama, do you?" Ahha asked.

Anuuk thought for a moment and answered, "Not exactly, but I see His work. Like you. You are one of His works, Daughter. Or when I look in the sky and see the moon and the stars. Or when I see the snowflakes falling. Remember how I told you that of all the thousands of snowflakes that fall, there isn't one alike? Just like there isn't one Aleut person who is the same. Jesus tells us that we are wonderfully and uniquely made. There will always be only one Ahha."

Ahha didn't think she was so wonderfully made. She made lots of mistakes. She couldn't weave well, her fingers fumbling all over the place, and she often stumbled over her own feet. Besides she didn't always do exactly what her mother told her. Just today she had

18

eaten some of the orange salmon berries right off the bush when her mother had told her not to and to save them for dinner. And yet she was an Aleut princess, and everyone she knew treated her with love and respect. It was confusing. Maybe they didn't see her mistakes.

So she asked "Mama, does Jesus still love me when I'm naughty?"

Anuuk smiled. "Ahha," she said in her soft voice, "we believe in Jesus, and we don't believe God will love us because we are good. God will make us good because He loves us." Ahha looked up at her mother. Her dark brown eyes were wide and filled with uncertainty. Anuuk looked deep into her daughter's eyes and understood her daughter at only age seven did not comprehend the concept of God loving the individual so much that He made a person good because he or she chose to follow His Son, Jesus. She cupped her daughter's face in her hands and told her, "Don't worry yourself about it, Ahha. Jesus will show you when you get a little older." And now my little princess, off to bed with you."

Ahha ran to her bed. It was made of straw with logs for a small frame, and it waited for her in the back of the house in the corner of the same room where her two older brothers also slept. The straw was covered with a green cloth that came from trading with the many trading ships that docked in the port.

Ahha took off her leather dress, which her mother had made

from the skin of many different birds. She climbed into her bed and under the covers made from fox furs. She was happy, and she drifted off to sleep, listening to her mother chanting about the puffin.

In the late 1800s, the population of the sea otter, which had sustained the village for decades, had declined because of overhunting by the Russian fur traders. Both reindeer and fox farming was introduced to the island, and the village became relatively affluent when they started trading the furs. Certainly, they were affluent enough to provide blankets made of fox fur for the chief's daughter, their own Aleut princess.

Anna's thoughts snapped back to the present, if only she could go back and do it over again. Anna was in that strange twilight place, only half aware of her surrounding but lingering in the dream of her mother. Her mind was foggy, and from far away she heard the clicking sounds from the nuns who had long brown wooden beads hanging from their waists. The sound was comforting to Anna. She opened her eyes, and Sister Mary Kathleen was standing next to the bed, smiling down on her.

CHAPTER 3

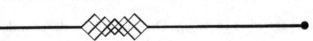

Desiree Lajour was running, stumbling over the many roots in the path that led to Swan Lake. It was twilight, and the sun had just set, leaving it its wake a deep pink glow on the horizon. She was numb, blocking out reality of the consuming pain just below the surface. She couldn't ... she *wouldn't* cry. She was terrified of crying because she knew there would never be enough tears to heal the feelings she had at the loss of her mother.

Desiree's father had come home from the hopital less than an hour ago, knelt down in front of her, and holding her shoulders, gently choked out the words "Your mother died tonight giving birth to your new brother." It was the first and last time she would ever see her father cry.

She'd just stood there, staring at her father until she'd finally whispered, "Can I go to the lake?"

Her father nodded his head yes. He well understood his daughter, and her need for space when confronted with conflicting emotions. There was a smidgen of freckles across her nose and with her emerald green eyes so like her mothers. Her similarity wrenched at his heart. At age nine she was a small replica of her full-blooded Irish mother. Ferociously independent and free-spirited from birth, he and his wife had agreed to encourage Desiree's independence with just enough love and discipline to keep her safe.

Her father's words had just bounced from her as if they weren't real. They were surreal, not touching her spirit. There was a complete disconnect. She was astute enough to understand that her world had just changed from a happy and safe nine-year-old to … what? Desiree didn't know, and she was terrified of all that unknown.

It was the image of her father's face that hurt her the most. Desiree had never seen his face so contorted. His eyes red and filled with tears, with sadness, even despair. It was an image that would remain with her for the rest of her life.

Desiree was born in Vernon, British Columbia, a providence of Canada. The site of the city was first discovered by the Okanagan people, a tribe of the interior Salish people who initially named the community *NintalMoos Chin*, meaning "jumping over the place where the creek narrows," which referred to a section of the Swan Lake that passes through downtown Vernon. When Desiree was first born, the population of Vernon was around five thousand, give or take a couple of hundred. It was still small but big enough to provide water, electricity, schools, a volunteer fire station, and its own hospital. The favorite sport was skiing—downhill and cross-country. At age nine Desiree was already a skilled cross-country skier, using it in the wintertime to get around the hundred-acre ranch her parents owned.

Swan Lake's shores were less than a half of a mile from her house, and Desiree had her own special spot where she often went. She loved to read or just sit quietly, dreaming and fantasizing about the many wonderful things she just knew were going to happen in her life. Her favorite fantasy was to become an Olympic ski champion.

Desiree had started reading when she was four and had an insatiable appetite for books and knowledge. She was already two grades ahead of her peers. Not that there were many children her age in the school. In fact, there were only six in her class, three boys and three girls. Desiree knew she was the smartest in her class, but her parent constantly warned her not to get too "puffy" about it. They told her that it was a gift from God and that with that gift came responsibility. Her father had written out Luke 12:47–48, which said, "That servant who knows his master's will and does not get ready or does not do what his master wants will be beaten with many blows. But the one who does not know and does things deserving punishment will be beaten with few blows. From everyone who has been given much, much will be demanded; and from the one who has been entrusted with much more will be asked."

Desiree knew patience was required of her, but it was difficult and frustrating, especially with her siblings. Still, her father had tacked the scripture to the wall right over her bed, and she read it every day. Her parents were consistently sending her to the room she shared with her four-year-old sister and telling her to "think about it." She wasn't allowed to come out until her parents felt "she was thinking straight."

Thinking straight? She couldn't think at all. Her mind was like a whirlwind with words and images going around and around in head so fast it almost made her dizzy. Desiree sat with her knees tight against her chest. With her arms tightly wrapped around her legs, she rocked slowly back and forth, back and forth. She had been raised a strict Roman Catholic, and the only thought screaming in her head was, *Where are You, God? Why? Why? Why?*

She had gone to catechism classes every Saturday morning along with the other local Catholic kids in the area. The catechism said, "God was a spirit, and He was everywhere." Desiree thought she had understood, but now she wasn't so sure. Her mother dying in childbirth made no sense to her. Who was going to take care of her new baby brother? Her four-year-old sister? Her seven-year-old brother? Desiree instinctively knew it was going to be her, and her shoulders slumped with the weight.

Her parents weren't rich, but they weren't poor either. They had never gone hungry. They had always attended to their basic needs, and the kids had never been without Christmas presents under the tree. Her parents were a good team. Now what? Desiree knew her dad had all he could do to take care of the ranch. It was a cattle ranch with more than a hundred heads of cattle. There were chickens, pigs, and horses too. There was also a humongous vegetable garden that her mother tended along with the three-bedroom house they all lived in.

In an instant Desiree's freedom and innocence were gone. Her life would never be the same. She sat frozen in time, staring with burning eyes at the reflection of the sunset on the water. This was the lake she loved, the place that had always brought her such happiness, the place she always felt close to nature, close to God. Now she felt nothing, absolutely nothing!

It was early spring. The regal black and white loons were nesting, and their haunting, eerie mating calls began as they always did in the sunset of the evening. Desiree jerked out of her trancelike state. The loon was her favorite bird, their calls sending chills up and down her spine. The loon was her personal totem as she always felt the presence of God around them. Or rather, she felt that God was talking to her through their haunting calls.

The tears finally began to fall, streaming down her face cleansing her as the pain of her mother's death was released. The loons' shrill mating calls spoke to her, blowing away the chaos in her head. The pink sunset was gone, and the moon's light was now reflected in the water.

Desiree was young enough to believe, young enough not to have been scarred by the world and life, and she was open and trusting. So she listened, trusting her spirit, trusting God. Slowly, she stood up, shaking the sleep out of both her tingling feet.

Walking slowly back toward her house, the call of the loons followed her till all she could hear was the haunting echo of their *eeeeeewoooooeeeeeeeeewoooo.* She was comforted by their mating calls.

CHAPTER 4

The years had flown by quickly. It was hard to believe her mother had been gone for seven years. Desiree was now sixteen years old, and she had just gotten her high school diploma. Tomorrow her father would drive her to Victoria, where she would be trained to become a nurse. She wanted to serve God, and she thought that one day she'd like to become a nun.

Her mother's face was still clear in her mind. Every day she missed her just as much as she had the day before. It wasn't like the pain of losing her was any less. It was just that she accepted it as part of her life. Desiree was sure there would never be anything else in her life that would test her faith like her mother's death Of course, she had no idea there would be another time in her life when her whole world would be turned around and she would fall into the depth of despair.

The first year after her mother's death had been the hardest.

Desiree's quick understanding of concepts would help. But she would struggle daily whenever she became frustrated and impatient with others who took so much longer or just plain didn't get it. Impatience was her worst fault, and her father was constantly quoting to her what he called "the love" scriptures. "Love is patient, love is kind. It does not envy, it does not boast, it is not proud. It is not rude. It is not self-seeking. It is not easily angered. It keeps no records of wrongs. Love does not delight in evil but rejoices with the truth. It always protects, always hopes, always perseveres. Love never fails." Sometimes it rambled around in her head over and over again like a stanza from a piece of music or a chorus from the latest popular song.

Desiree had found her father that raw, painful night sitting in the old wooden rocking chair next to the large rock fireplace where the simmering coals flickered off the walls, providing the only eerie light in the room. She had never seen her father cry until that night. He was sitting there with his head in his hands, uncontrollably weeping. He had not been aware of her presence until she had reached out and gently touch his shoulder.

"Daddy?" she said as more of a question than a statement.

His head had jerked up, and his eyes had connected with hers. "My daughter, Dessie," he had whispered. Her dad had always called her Dessie. However, when she did something he disapproved of, he called her by her full name, Desiree Ellen Lajour, usually followed by some scripture verse just to make his point.

"What are we going to do without Mom, Dad?" Desiree choked on her own words.

He still held his head in his hands, shaking it back and forth before finally replying, "I'm going to need your help with your new brother and, well … everything."

Her heart had started pounding out of her chest, and she felt like she was going to throw up. "But I don't know how to take care of a new baby!" she blurted out.

Her dad maintained eye contact, boring a hole straight into her heart and soul. He had reached out and pulled her close to him and firmly said, "You'll learn. I'll get Miss Elsie to show you how."

Miss Elsie lived on the neighboring farm. She had three children of her own about the same age as her seven-year-old brother, Gabriel. Miss Elsie's husband had lost a leg in a farming accident the year before, and her father was always helping him out. After the accident Desiree had overheard her mother and father talking about how hard it was for the Dungans to keep body and soul together. Desiree wondered how Miss Elsie was going to find the time to help her.

The hospital had kept her new baby brother till after her mother's funeral. In Desiree's memory that day was at best foggy and filled with chaos. In fact, the whole first year after her mother's death was foggy. It seemed like all she did was repeat the love scripture over and over. All she could remember of that first year was how she'd felt like crying or screaming or hiding out at her favorite spot on Swan Lake. Everything she did she did to honor her mother's memory. It was the only thing that got her through each day.

Her father had named her new brother Patrick because her mother's name had been Patricia. In that first year, Patrick was the only person she never was impatient with, not even when he woke up in the middle of night hungry and wet. Desiree would sit rocking with him in front of the stone fireplace and feel at peace.

Her father had arranged with the Dungans to help on their farm on a daily basis in return for Miss Elsie helping Desiree learn some of the new chores she now had. Like making homemade bread or learning to can all the vegetables from the vegetable garden but, most importantly, how to care for a newborn baby.

The first time Desiree had done the family wash in the old wringer washer kept in the enclosed gray wooden porch in the back of the house, she had run her arm through the wringer. She hadn't broken any bones, but her arm had turned black and blue and was sore for more than a week. She had used a wooden box to reach the clothesline until late one night after a fourteen-hour workday when her father had lowered all the lines to fit her height. She and her father had managed. On her tenth birthday, her father had pulled her close, lifted her face toward his, and told her how much he loved her and how proud he was of her.

There wasn't any time to feel sorry for herself in the next few years. Desiree learned to take it one day at a time, tackling each chore that was before her, including going to school, taking care of her two brothers and sister, and managing the household. There were times when she would find herself crying, the tears rolling down her freckled face for no reason. Her brother Gabriel, who was only two years younger than her, would always ask the same question, "What's wrong? Why are you crying?"

Desiree would always answer in the same way. "Just missing Mom, Gabe. Just missing Mom."

Gabriel would always choke up and whisper, "Me too, Sis." And then they would always pray together, asking God to please help them with their pain that went with losing their mother.

Although close, Desiree and her father didn't speak much in the next few years. There was reason other than the fact that they simply never had enough time. They did, however, remain in sync with each other, sensing by a look or a gentle touch the next task they needed to finish. The only time the family really had any time together was

Sunday morning Mass and Sunday dinner during which her two brothers and sister relentlessly scrambled for their father's attention.

It got to be routine as the years passed, but it was a little easier for Desiree as her brother Gabriel took on some of her chores. Patrick became a toddler, and her sister, Karen, started school. It was a blessing that Desiree was a quick learner because she could often get her homework done during school hours. Her father always seemed tired, but he smiled often at his children and would roar into the house at dinnertime, always complimenting Desiree on the meal she had prepared.

When Desiree was fourteen years old, Ms. Elsie's husband died from an infection he had gotten on the stump of his amputated leg. Her father had tried to work both farms with the help of a hired hand, but the physical and financial strain became too much on Miss Elsie and her father. It was inevitable with both her father and Miss Elsie being about the same age, one year after her husband's death Miss Elsie sold her farm, and they were married. With the money from the sale of Miss Elsie's farm, two more bedrooms were added to the three-bedroom home Desiree had lived in all her life, because now there were six children under one roof.

Miss Elsie was very different from Desiree's mother. She was a strong woman almost as tall as Desiree's father, who stood exactly six feet tall. With brown sharp eyes and waist-long brown hair that she kept up in big bun on the back of her head, she could easily intimate a child without saying a word. She had a sweet shyness about her that Desiree both respected and was drawn to.

Shortly after the marriage, her father pulled her aside and told her, "It's okay to care about Miss Elsie Dessie. It doesn't mean you're being disloyal to you mother. No one can or will take your mother's place in your heart." Desiree just looked at him and blinked away the tears forming in her eyes. She'd shaken her head yes, letting her father know she understood. What confused her was how he had known how guilty she felt about all the feelings she had for Miss Elsie.

Desiree's mother had been petite and animated, and she had always had something to say about everything. She'd also had a quick temper that matched her fiery red hair. Her new stepmother was quiet even shy, but Desiree could see that she cared about her father, adored her youngest brother, Patrick, and obviously cared about her brother Gabe, sister Karen, and even her.

There were now seven children in the home, and the last year that Desiree was there, it was difficult to find a private space to be alone for praying, reading, and thinking. Often she would walk to her place at the edge of Swan Lake, and it was there in the cool of the evening and listening to the call of the loons that she discovered she wanted to be a nurse and maybe even a nun. She wasn't sure about being a nun because she felt that anyone who committed their lives to serving God must have a great deal of courage. What if she failed? What if she couldn't control her impatience? What if God didn't want her to be a nun? The questions in her mind were too many, and the answers were slow in coming.

One night when all her siblings and stepsiblings were in their rooms sleeping, she crept out into the living room, where her father sat in the rocking chair, smoking his pipe. Ms. Elsie was hemming a dress for her sister, Karen, and the two were quietly talking.

"Excuse me." Desiree was always hesitant to interrupt them. Her father smiled up at her. Desiree loved the way he always called her Dessie. It always made her feel so loved.

"Well, I've been thinking that since I graduate in four months, I should talk to you both about my plans." Desiree hesitated for a moment, waiting for their response.

Her father reached over and shut off the radio program they had been listening to, and both of them looked at her quietly with expecting eyes. "We've been waiting until you were ready to talk with us," her father stated.

Desiree stated slowly, carefully choosing each word. "Well, I know I want to help people, and I think the best way for me to do that is to study nursing." Her father nodded in agreement, which gave her the courage to go on.

Desiree continued, "I've been reading about St. Ann's Academy in Victoria. They have scholarship program I'm sure I can qualify for. I'd just have to have your written permission since I'm only sixteen."

"There's more, Father." Desiree could see the questioning look in both their eyes. "I've been praying about possibly becoming a St. Ann's nun." There, she'd said it out loud, and she felt herself turn flush, starting at the bottom of her feet and going all the way up to her head. It was like she was a rubber band pulled tight to the breaking point, and once she acknowledged her private thoughts, her whole body wasn't so tight.

Desiree's father knew his oldest child was devout in her prayer life, and mature beyond her years because of the early death of her mother. She had taken on the chores of a grown woman at age nine and taken care of her siblings as any mother would have. Still, making such a serious decision to become a nun at the young age of 16 he felt was too young to make such a serious commitment.

"Dessie," he said in his fatherly tone, "why don't we just get you into the nursing program, and after two or three years, you can decide if you want to become a nun?"

Desiree sighed, relieved because she knew she wasn't ready to make that decision. Not yet. Desiree closed her eyes and vividly remembered the first night when her mother had died and she'd heard the call of the loons. She had known somehow with God's help her family would be okay. And so they had been. Over the next couple of years Desiree continued to seek God, confident He guided her. She had learned to listen for Him and to follow His leading. She had read somewhere that the desire for God's will in an individual life is written in the human heart. Desiree believed the desire for God was written in her heart. "Be still and know that I am God."

CHAPTER 5

I n August 1957, in their old Chrysler Saratoga Coup, Desiree and her father drove the 528 kilometers to St. Ann's Academy in Victoria, BC. Desiree had received a scholarship at her graduation, enough to pay for all the schooling she would need to become a registered nurse plus her board and room at St. Ann's Academy. She was sixteen years old, mature beyond her years, and ready to march forth into her future like a warrior going into battle. Little did she know that the battle would send her into the depths of despair.

On the long ride to Victoria Desiree asked her father "Do you think Mom would be proud of me?"

Her father was quiet for so long she wondered if he was going to answer her. "You know, Dessie, you're so like your mom. You remind me of her every day. The way you tackle any tasks with that little scowl on your face. Your impatience with life itself and that wild, curly red hair of yours that always looks like it needs combing.

Desiree unconsciously ran her fingers through her hair. She'd never taken the time to try to tame it. She'd never had the time. She guessed it just wasn't important to her.

Her father had hesitated as if he was trying to form the right words before he finally went on, "Your mother was smart, Dessie, like you. She would always say it was a gift from God, and it could also be a curse. The curse being the smarter a person was, the more responsibility a person had. And sometimes … well, sometimes an intelligent person just wanted to be free of the responsibility and have someone take care of them instead of them always taking care of others. Remember, Dessie, Luke12:47–48. "That servant who knows his master's will and does not get ready or does not do what his master wants will be beaten with many blows. But the one who does not know and does things deserving punishment will be beaten with few blows. From everyone who has been given much, much will be demanded; and from the one who has been entrusted with much, much more will be asked."

Desiree turned in the passenger's seat of the car and looking directly at her father protested. "That just doesn't seem fair. Why should the people who truly love God be punished more than someone who doesn't know or love God?"

Her father answered slowly, "Dessie, Dessie, you're only sixteen and leaving your home with enough money to follow your dream of helping people. Most other sixteen-year-olds still aren't thinking about their future. You understand more than most of your peers thus you are more accountable for the decisions you make. Think about it, Dessie. If a two-year-old puts their hands on a hot stove and gets burned are they as responsible as an eight-year-old? But to answer your question, yes, I'm sure your mother is proud of you every day just as I am, Dessie." Tears welled up in Desiree's eyes. That was all she needed to hear.

They arrived in Victoria late that same evening and stayed in a hotel for the night, which was a first for Desiree. In Victoria, the spirit of the Lekwamment people pervaded all of its history, and the place had become the busiest seaport north of San Francisco. St. Ann's Academy was a testament of the dedication of the sisters of St. Ann, who were an integral part of the beginnings of education and health care in British Columbia.

Desiree could not sleep from shear excitement and nervousness. She had never been so far from home and had never slept anywhere but in her own bed. It was an emotional paradox, leaving the only home she'd ever known. It was especially difficult leaving her brother Gabriel, sister Karen, and her brother Patrick, who was now seven. She had been like a mother to Patrick, and as she was leaving, he'd clung to her until Ms. Elsie had gently pulled him away. It was even difficult to leave her three stepsiblings. She had grown to love them as well. At the same time, she was excited to leave and become a nurse. She was thrilled about what the future held for her. More importantly, she believed it was God's will for her life.

Father and daughter pulled up to the wrought-iron gate of St. Ann's Academy at eight thirty the next morning. It was Victoria's first Roman Catholic Cathedral, built in 1858, and they had added the school in 1886. Its appearance was formidable, adding to Desiree's anxiety. *Such beautiful grandeur,* she thought to herself. For the first time, she felt insecure and overwhelmed. After all, she was just a young country girl who had never been away from her home and had led a sheltered protected life.

Desiree and her father had a few moments to stop and pray in the large cathedral. Like the many rural French Canadian churches it was modeled after, the church had an ornate altar and ceiling carvings, gold-leaf detailing, original oil paintings, and stained glass windows, and in 1913, a Casavant pipe organ had been added. Desiree had never seen anything so grand, so different from the little country church she had attended all her life. She felt overwhelmed and unsure of her decision.

The school, offices, living areas for the nuns, and the students had a grand entrance to the seventy-six-thousand-square-foot building. There was a large double oak door in the center of the building with a small wooden hand-carved sign that said, "Please ring for entrance." Her father reached out and pushed the buzzer.

The nun who had opened the large doubled doors to them welcomed them and led them to an office that was located under the grand winding staircase that led to the second floor of the building. There, they were introduced to Sister Mary Assumpta, the mother superior and administrator of St. Ann's Academy. The mother superior spoke gently but with a firmness that left no doubt as to who was in charge.

"Mr. Lajour, I have received the funds from the National Knight of Columbus for Desiree's board and room and for four years of schooling in nursing. Since your daughter has not reached eighteen, I need your signature on the scholarship papers. We also will need you to give us permission to oversee her personal development and her education. You understand, Mr. Lajour, that your daughter will be assigned to St. Joseph's hospital for all her hands-on training?"

"Yes, Sister, I understand." Desiree saw a look on his face she had never seen before. His jaw was firmly set, and she knew his leaving his oldest child at only age sixteen year was not easy.

Sister Mary Assumpta continued, "We will also need to have

your written permission for your daughter for any visits she may have that take her off campus. Of course, this includes any visits to her home and family."

Her father replied with a yes and proceeded to sign the necessary paperwork. Desiree was given permission to escort him to the big double doors, where he silently held her in his arms. Then taking her face in his hands, he whispered to her, "I believe in you, Daughter. I always have, and I always will. I'd like to believe your mother is here watching over you. Always remember where you came from. I leave you in God's hands, Dessie." And with that, he abruptly turned on his heels and was gone, leaving Desiree staring at the large oak doors.

Desiree whole body was shaking, and it felt like her legs were going to give out on her. She felt like a little girl who just wanted her daddy, but the nun who had originally escorted them in was suddenly beside her, gently touching her shoulder. She introduced herself as Sister Mary Bernadette and said, "Come, Desiree. Let me show your room and around the rest of the building."

The next year was a whirlwind of activity with little time left for Desiree to miss her family. The day after her arrival, she'd been taken to St. Joseph's hospital to begin her training. She was on the floor six hour a day for five days a week, and she was taught how to use universal precaution when emptying a bedpan, delivering meals, or giving a bed bath. Chemistry, anatomy, psychology, physiology, and math all started one week late. Desiree absorbed it all. Her innate need for knowledge was driving her.

Along with Desiree's nursing studies, she was required to take a Bible class and attend chapel every morning and evening. During the week chapel was held in the small chapel built for the St. Ann nuns, and she only attended Mass on Sunday in the cathedral. She was called to Sister Assumpta's office several times that first year for being late to chapel. She would often become so absorbed in her studies that she would lose track of the time. Her daily prayer always involved asking God what His plan for her life was. She was sure about nursing, but she struggled with the idea of becoming a nun. Desiree grasped the notion of God coming first in everything she did or said. She wasn't sure of what that meant exactly, but she knew that her consuming love was nursing,

She wrote her father about her confusion. In his return letter, he said to her, "Dessie, ask yourself if you are called to follow Jesus Christ more closely than you are now though the leading of the Holy Spirit." He then quoted scripture like he always had throughout her life. He always told her she could find the answers for her life in God's Word. He had then suggested she read Jeremiah 1:4–9, which said, "The word of the Lord came to me saying; 'Before I formed you in the womb I knew you, before you were born I set you apart; I appointed you as a prophet to the nations.' 'Ah, sovereign Lord,' I said, 'I do not know how to speak, I am only child.' But the Lord said to me, 'Do not say, "I am only a child." You must go to everyone I send you to and say whatever I command you. Do not be afraid of them, for I am with you and will rescue you,' declares the Lord."

Desiree posted the scripture up over her bed and read it every day for the next few months.

There are four steps to becoming a sister of St. Ann's—aspirant (precandidacy), postulancy (candidacy), novitiate, and first vows (or perpetual vows that can be renewed over again) to poverty, chastity, and obedience. Lastly, there are final vows or public vows, which can only happen after many years.

The order of sisters of St. Ann's is based on Ignatian spirituality. It is rooted in the conviction that God is active, personal, and above all, present to us. It is a pathway to deeper prayer, good decisions guided by keen discernment, and an active life of service to others.

At age eighteen, Desiree asked if she could be accepted as an aspirant to the sisters of St. Ann and was accepted. Two years later she received her certificate as a registered nurse and continued on her journey to become a sister of St Ann's. At the age of twenty-two, Desiree Ellen Lajour became Sister Mary Kathleen, SSA. She had taken her perpetual vows, not knowing when she would be ready for her final public vows.

At the age of twenty-five and with almost four years of experience, Sister Mary Kathleen was called to the administrative position at a hospital in Juneau. "And I heard the voice of the Lord saying, 'Whom shall I send, who will go …' and I said, 'Here I am, Lord. Send me.'"

Sister Mary Kathleen arrived in Juneau, confident and secure that she was doing God's will for her life. She had no idea that within six years, her faith would be tested beyond human endurance, and she would find herself back in her favorite spot on Swan Lake, listening to the call of the loons.

CHAPTER 6

Anna had just finished her evening meal when she heard the clickity click, click of the long wooden rosary beads that the St. Ann's nuns always wore hanging from their waist. She knew they had put her on a tasteless diet, and she was going to let Sister Mary Kathleen know that she didn't appreciate it.

Anna stared hard at the door, willing Sister Mary Kathleen to come though. She was so alone, and if she didn't have someone to talk with soon, she was sure she was literally going to lose her mind. Anna thought to herself that Sister Mary Kathleen was the only real friend she had left. Their relationship had started some five year ago in the emergency room of St. Ann's Hospital.

One dark night after heavily drinking, Anna had gone on a joy ride with one of her many drinking buddies. The male driver of the car and his friend had picked the two girls up in the bar, paying for their time and sex. They had gotten in a car accident. The car had flown off of a small bridge over Lemon Creek and landed on the stump of a big tree. It had killed the driver's friend. The stump had pushed his body through the roof of the car, leaving a body that was no longer recognizable. The remaining three had been thrown from the car, which had left them bruised, cut up, and in shock. The next thing that Anna remembered was arriving at the emergency room, where the bright lights had startled her and also sobered her up. Sister Mary Kathleen had been in the emergency room that night and became Anna's confidante in the week she had been hospitalized.

Now five years later, Sister Mary Kathleen knelt in the small nun's chapel, earnestly praying for guidance before heading to Anna's room. As a nun first and a nurse second, she broke all the rules of emotional involvement with her patients. She was aware that with Anna, it went so much deeper than compassion. It was an instant connection from the first time she laid eyes on Anna in the emergency room. Sister Mary Kathleen didn't know why these *connections* happened and with only a handful of people in her life. She only knew they did, and she had no control over it. That person became the first thing she would think about when she awoke and the last thing she would think about before falling asleep. It was like getting some chorus from a song stuck in her head. It just kept going around and around. Sister Mary Kathleen had come to believe that it was God's way of leading her into constant prayer for the person. It wasn't for her to question. It was for her to obey and sometimes even act. She had learned the hard way that it was only when she would yield the control over her mind to God that it would dissipate.

Anna was one of her patients that Sister Mary Kathleen could not get out of her head, and every time Anna had been admitted in the last few years, it was as if she had once again taken up residency in her mind. Sister Mary Kathleen prayed not only for guidance but for objectivity.

How many times had she put her patients before God and certainly before her vows as a nun? How many scheduled prayer times had she missed by putting her nursing skills first? How many times had she lost her patience with some of the lay nurses under her supervision? Sister Mary Kathleen had lost count. She was comforted by the thought that God did not call the qualified but qualified those He called. She looked up at the large hand-carved crucifix that hung above the altar, saying out loud, "*Mia culpa, mia culpa, mia maxima culpa.*" She was saying, "Through my fault, through my fault, through my most grievous fault."

"Sister!" Anna exclaimed as the nun walked through the door of her room.

"Anna, Anna, I'm so sorry to see you back here." Sister Mary Kathleen said as she caressed Anna's forehead.

"Am I going to die, Sister?" Anna asked, coming straight to the point. They had never really discussed Anna's personal life. Anna had been too filled with shame, and it was that shame that controlled her life. Instead they had extensively spoken about her diagnosis of cirrhosis of the liver, and Sister had tried to help her trace the hand of God in her life.

"My dear Anna," Sister Mary Kathleen began. "I warned you the last time you were here three or four months ago that your liver was 90 percent scarred and that there isn't any treatment available that will cure or repair the scarring that has already occurred on your liver. As I told you, your liver is like a filter, filtering the toxic poisons like ammonia from your system. You didn't quit drinking hooch or stick to the diet we gave you, did you?"

Anna's shameful eyes said it all, and barely whispering, she answered, "I tried, Sister. I really did, but it only worked for a couple of days. It's just that I've been so miserable, so unhappy for most of my life." Anna's voice trailed off, and then with a deep sigh, she continued, "I can't stand how I feel. It's like there's this dark, gigantic, throbbing blob in my stomach that never goes away until I drink whiskey or hooch. You have no idea how much I hate myself.

How much I hate my life. When I drink, I just don't care what happens to me. Truthfully, most of the time, I just want to die." Anna closed her eyes, hoping against hope that Sister Mary Kathleen could somehow help her out of the hole she'd dug herself into.

"Anna," Sister said gently. "You've developed what we call encephalopathy, and your liver can no longer filter any of the poisons going into your bloodstream. It also means your mental capacities are being affected. "Have you noticed any difference in the way you think in the last couple of months?"

Anna hesitated before answering. "I don't know. Maybe. Sometimes I forget what day it is or even what I've done the night before. But that's been going on for some time, and I always just thought it was due to my drinking too much."

Sister Mary Kathleen wondered how this tiny woman had survived as long as she had. "Anna," she said firmly, "there's really nothing more we can do for you but try to keep you as comfortable possible. We've put you on a low-protein diet because protein can cause toxins in your system to build up. We are also giving you lactulose, which will help slow down ammonia and other toxins from building up in your large intestines."

Sister continued, "Unfortunately, we can't give you any narcotics like something to help you sleep or to help your anxiety because it will make the symptoms of encephalopathy worse and affect your thinking."

Anna's eyes grew wide as the reality of her condition came thundering down on her. "But Sister, you once told me that it might be possible to get a liver transplant."

"Oh, Anna, I'm so sorry." Sister choked on her own words. Why had she given Anna an unrealistic hope? Taking Anna's hand in her own, she continued, "It's a new procedure, only a little more than five years old. There's a long waiting list and not nearly enough liver donations. Plus finding a match that your body won't reject is a complicated process. I'm so sorry, but it doesn't look like there is enough time for that to be an option for you."

Anna's eyes were downcast. She was overwhelmed by the shame she felt for the kind of life she had lived. She was silent for so long that Sister Mary Kathleen wondered if she was going to respond. "Would you like me to leave and come back later, Anna?" Sister quietly asked.

"No, no, stay with me," Anna cried out as she began sobbing uncontrollably. Maybe it was the reality that her death was imminent, or maybe it was just that she had finally hit rock bottom. Anna began babbling then. Her words tumbled over each other like water flowing from a spring thaw down the side of a rocky mountain.

"When I was a young girl, I was a real princess ... an Aleut princess. My father was chief of the village I lived in. The spring I was fourteen, everything changed. My father and two older brothers along with some other men from the village went to a summer camp on the north side of Atka Island. Atka Island is where I had lived all fourteen years of my life. It has the Pacific Ocean on the south side and the Bering Sea on the north side. My father and brothers went to find the place where the two big oceans come together and where the whales come every spring to feed. They went in three "*baidarkas*," small boats covered in sea lion skin that resemble Yuk'ik kayaks but are aerodynamically sleeker and faster. They were gone longer than usual. At first, my mother didn't really worry because the spot where the oceans meet often moved, and some years they wouldn't even find it. Toward the middle of summer only one of the baidarkas returned with two of the men who had gone with them. They said they had found many whales migrating north in the area where the two bodies of water met. There were more whales than they'd realized, and one of the whales capsized the "*baidarka*" my father and one of my brothers were in. My other brother and the man with him in their "*baidarka*" tried to help them, both just disappeared into the sea. The two men hung their heads low and just kept repeating over and over to my mother, 'There were just too many whales!'"

Sister Mary Kathleen had read about the phenomena. It was called a confluence, and it took place all over the world. The most well-known case happened in the Gulf of Alaska, where the Pacific Ocean and Bering Sea met. A person can tell this is coming by the change and contrast in the color of the water. A slight foam makes a thin white line between the two bodies of water. The heavy, sediment-laden water from the glaciers, valleys, and rivers pour into the open ocean, creating a moving foam line and two different colored waters.

Anna continued, "My life changed that day. It was a long, sad winter. By tradition, my mother would mourn for only thirty days, but because my father and both my brothers had been killed at sea, I think she mourned thirty days not just for my father but thirty days for each of my brothers. In mourning it is the Aleut custom to abstain from food and give away a large number of personal possessions. My mother gave away many of the baskets she and I had woven. Some of my mother's basketry was the finest in the village. She had used only her thumbnail, which she had grown long and then sharpened to use as a tool. She made both large and small *qiigam_aygaaxsii.* They are woven from grass pieces, birch bark, and puffin feathers, and often we inserted polished pebbles, pieces of shells, and Russian beads that we traded for furs." Anna sighed, taking a deep breath.

"You're quite the historian, Anna," Sister said, wanting to validate the story and encouraging Anna to continue.

Anna felt stronger and was now determined to tell Sister Mary Kathleen about her life. "I think the saddest day that winter was the day my mother hung small baskets on the wall where my father and brothers hunting hats had always hung. Aleuts are famous for their hunting hats, which feature elaborate and colorful designs and may be trimmed with sea lion whiskers, feathers, and ivory. At sea Aleut men wore wooden hunting hats. The shape of the headgear indicated a man's rank. A short visor was worn by the young and inexperienced hunters, an elongated visor by the rank and file, and open-crown long-visor one by important and mature men. My father had an open-crown long-visor hat because he was considered the chief of our village. I knew that day that nothing in our lives would ever be the same. We never went outside that whole winter, and my mother spent most of her days sitting next to the oil stove on her knees, rocking back and forth, chanting."

Sister Mary Kathleen could picture Anna as a fourteen-year-old, not yet women but not a child anymore either, confused, scared, and unable to comfort her mother. "Where is your mother now?" Sister asked.

"Dead," Anna answered in a monotone voice. "She died in an internment camp outside of Ketchikan in the winter of 1943."

Sister Mary Kathleen had only been in Alaska for six years and was considered by lifetime Alaskans a "Cheechoko" a person who was not yet considered a true Alaskans. "What do you mean an internment camp?" she asked.

The deep-seeded anger and bitterness was evident in Anna's voice. "Oh, yes, an internment camp. All the Aleut people were taken off the islands at the beginning of World War II, and there they stayed until the end of the war. Many of them died from disease before those who were left were returned to their villages. The village where I had lived had been burned to the ground by American soldiers. No one ever talks about it. It's like this big secret, and some people don't even believe it really happened."

"Were you with her when she died, Anna?" Sister quietly asked.

"No, I was here in Juneau. I didn't even find out she was dead until a few months after she had died. John Charlie wouldn't tell me anything other than that she had died of pneumonia. He still lives here in Juneau and has a room up over the bar/restaurant where he has been the cook for years." Anna's voice changed, and she pleaded with Sister, "Could you call him for me? I need to talk to him. Not only about how my mother died, but there's something important I have to tell him before I die."

Sister Mary Kathleen was now confused about how had she been separated from her mother. Anna saw the perplexed look on Sister's face, and the floodgates opened.

"The summer after my father and brothers were lost at sea, my mother seemed a little better. She and I would pick blueberries and salmon berries that grew wild. We had plenty of fish from others in the village and some canned food my mother had traded for some of the ivory carving from walrus tusks my father and brothers had carved over the years. One early evening just before the sun set over the ocean, I was on the beach, hunting for pebbles and shells we could polish to use for our basket weaving."

Anna paused, and closing her eyes, she relived that time in her life. She had just turned fifteen years old, and in spite of the reality of her father and brother's death the summer before, she was happy—happy because her mother was so much better and had once again turned her attention back to her daughter.

She was chanting softly to herself as she bent down to pick up another small shiny shell. She could see herself in her soft leather moccasins, and her waist-long shiny black hair kept falling over her shoulder and getting in the way of her vision. She felt the soft bird-skin garment she was wearing, which was now a little short and tight on her. Her mother would have to make her a new one soon. The beach she was on wasn't far from the home she shared with her mother, and the setting sun sparkled off the water in colors of pink and gold.

Ahha had not paid any attention to the two men rowing a skiff toward the shore. There were often several fishing vessels moored in the small cove. It was low tide and much easier for the men on the vessels to come ashore when the waves weren't chopping against the rocky coastline. Suddenly, she heard an unfamiliar sound, and as she stood up to turn and explore the cause, everything had gone dark.

The loud, rhythmic chugging of the diesel engine woke her. She was lying on a small dirty bunk attached to the hull of the vessel. She shook her head, trying to clear her mind. Completely disorientated and confused, Ahha thought she must be dreaming. Looking around, she could see another dirty bunk next to hers in which a man was sleeping. He was half dressed and unshaven with stringy dark hair spread out on the filthy pillow. He smelled like diesel oil, rotting fish, and sour sweat. Ahha was terrified. Was he going to kill her? It was then she realized she wasn't dreaming at all, and a very real nightmare began.

Sister Mary Kathleen had sat quietly by Anna's bedside waiting for her to continue. Anna finally opened her eyes, and filled with the shame she felt, she choked out what had happened. "I had just turned fifteen when two men captured me from my village and took me aboard their fishing vessel. They raped and sodomized me every day. One dark night I think about a week later, they came into a boat harbor and left me on the dock. They refueled their fishing vessel and left the harbor. I never knew their names or the name of the fishing vessel. It wasn't until the next morning that I even knew where I was. Someone on the dock told me I was in Juneau. I remembered my mother once talking about some relative named Linda who lived in Juneau. A strange man approached me. He wasn't Aleut, but he was Indian. He took me to where she lived, and Linda took me in. Later he became my friend, and I found out he was a Tlinget Indian. I don't remember much of the next couple of weeks, but one night Linda's new husband gave me a drink called hooch. It tasted awful to me, burning my throat, but I could feel its effect on me. With each sip I choked down, I could feel the tightness in my body relax. It came in wave after wave until my whole body was so relaxed I fell asleep. At first, it was the feeling hooch gave me that I craved, but after a while I also craved the drink. I enjoyed the burning sensation in my mouth and throat. All I knew in the beginning was that when I drank hooch, all the pain inside of me was temporarily numbed, and by the time I realized alcohol could turn on you and control your life, I was addicted."

"Oh, Anna, I'm so sorry!" Sister exclaimed. Instinctively, she knew that there was so much more to Anna's story. Then she checked her pocket watch and saw it was the time when the cloister of St. Ann's nuns went to the chapel for prayer. Once again, she was going to miss it.

Anna went on, "Linda's the one who started calling me Anna. My Aleut name is Ahha. It didn't matter to me because all I wanted to do was forget it ever happened and maybe somehow go back to my village. But then … well, then I realized my time of the month had stopped, and I knew I was pregnant. I was so embarrassed and so ashamed that I tried to kill it." Anna hesitated, and looking up at Sister Mary Kathleen, she choked out the rest of her story.

"Someone had told me that if a woman took a coke bottle, shook it up, and inserted the bottle inside her, it could cause a miscarriage. So I drank hooch until I was so drunk I felt nothing, and I tried it! I didn't care if I lived or died, so I also threw myself down a flight of stairs just to make sure. I had thought it had worked because I cramped up over and over, and there was lots of blood with blood clots I flushed down the toilet."

"It didn't work because a few weeks later, I began to feel life in my belly, and one night Linda took me to this hospital, where I gave birth to a little boy. I never saw him and told the nurses to take him away. The next day the doctor came to my room and told me that there had been two placentas and that it looked like I'd miscarried a twin. He asked me if I'd had any severe bleeding in my early pregnancy. I was too embarrassed to tell him the truth, so I just told him that I'd bled a little. I left the hospital a couple of days later and was just relieved it was all over with. I didn't know that giving up my son would haunt me every day of my life, so I just kept drinking because it killed the pain."

Anna was watching Sister Mary Kathleen closely. Was Sister as disgusted with her as she was with herself? Anna saw only compassion written on her face, and it gave her the courage to go on.

"I thought it would be easy, that I could block it all out, maybe even somehow return to my village. But then World War II happened, and all the Aleut people were taken from their villages and put into internment camps here in Southeast Alaska. One night I was in the bar where John Charlie was the cook, and he told me the American soldiers had burned our village to the ground. I couldn't go back, and I couldn't go forward. It was like I was frozen in time, and every day I thought about the son I had given away. I still think about him to this day, and there's an ache in my heart that never goes away. I once tried to explain it to Sven, but he was so angry with me because I had also given our three-month-old daughter away. He just didn't understand, I just wasn't worthy enough to be a mother."

Sister Mary Kathleen held Anna's hand even tighter, gently caressing it with her thumb. She prayed for the right words and for the Holy Spirit to guide her. She had no idea how to comfort someone who had lost everything she loved in her life. Slowly, she asked, "Whose Sven?"

Anna answered quickly, "Sven was my husband for about three years. He still is my husband. We've never gotten a divorce, but we've been separated for many years. He's the only man I've ever truly loved. We had a daughter together, but I gave her away when she was three months old. He's never forgiven me for that. She's eighteen years old now, and I think he knows where she's at. I have another favor to ask you. He's a fisherman and has his own fishing boat named the *Blue Lady*. If you call the ACS (Alaska Communication System), they will patch you through to him. Please tell him of my condition and say that I need to talk to him."

Sister Mary Kathleen felt overwhelmed. How had this tiny petite lady survived with so much heartache in her life? She had thought there was nothing worse in life than losing her mother when she was only nine years old. Anna had lost her identity, her people, her husband, her children, and her faith. And yet, Sister sensed, there was still hope left in her soul.

"Do you still believe in God, Anna?" Sister asked.

"I don't know, Sister," Anna replied. "I know I prayed every day and every night that He would rescue me from those two horrible men who raped me, and all that happened was I had a son I gave away because I couldn't stand being reminded daily of the circumstances of his conception. It's like every time I've asked God for something, my life has just gotten worse, and sometimes I feel like if there is a God, all He wants to do is punish me."

"Anna," Sister replied, "I don't know why God allowed all those sad things to happen to you. But I do know that Jesus Christ will change us from the inside out if we allow Him. I know that He can take the things that have hurt our spirits and turn them around into something eternally good. But we must trust Him no matter what the circumstances in our life are. I know, Anna, that if you will surrender your will to Him, all that has happened in your life will be made good. I have to leave you for the night, Anna. But I will make those phone calls you have asked, and I'll see you tomorrow."

With that, Sister Mary Kathleen bent down, gently kissed Anna's forehead, and quietly left the room. "Mia culpa, Mia culpa,

Mia maxima culpa," she whispered to herself on the way out of Anna's room.

Anna lay there wide awake. She wasn't sure how right Sister Mary Kathleen was about God. After all, she'd only told her about part of her life. Anna knew that God knew, even if Sister didn't. At this minute Anna couldn't get past the rage she felt about all the mistakes she'd made and the injustices that had been done to her people.

My people! How long had it been since she had called them her people? Maybe it wasn't too late. Maybe if she asked God for forgiveness and help? Maybe if she could find her children, she could still fight for justice for the Aleut people? She'd been so selfish, so self-centered, so focused on her own sad life that she'd almost forgotten her mother's words to her. "Remember, Ahha, you will always be an Aleut princess, and you will always belong to your people."

CHAPTER 7

Anuuk had absently shaken her head yes when Ahha had asked if she could walk to the beach and hunt for shells and pebbles. It rained the majority of the year, but this early evening in May was rare. It was sunny and warm, and the tide was out. In fact, it was at one of its lowest points of the year. The shoreline was rocky and surf-worn, and the low tide provided for some sandy spaces between some of the large black and gray barnacle-covered boulders that covered the coastline of Atka Island. It was perfect for finding shells and pebbles for weaving into their baskets.

Anuuk was aware of the several fishing vessels moored in the small cove off the lower half of the village. There were always a mail boat, fishing vessels, trading vessels, and sometimes barges moored in the spring, summer, and fall seasons. Some of the men from the village would help unload and load in order to trade fox furs for goods and supplies.

Although the Aleuts continued to partially survive by hunting and gathering as well as fishing for salmon, crabs, shellfish, and cod, Russian contact in the late 1700s and 1800s had quickly devastated the Aleut culture, and the sea otter hunting era ended in the late 1800s. For the Aleut people to survive, they subsidized their income by trading with the many vessels that docked on their shores.

The sun had set, and a twilight amber hue hung over the island. It had grown chilly and Anuuk threw a leather-like cape made from the skin of birds over her shoulders. Ahha, she thought, had once again lost her sense of time, when Annuuk became aware Ahha had been gone longer than usual. It was a bad habit she had when she was doing something she loved. As Anuuk approached the shoreline, she became aware of one of the fishing vessels chugging their way out of the cove. It wasn't usual as most vessels preferred to anchor down in the dark of night. Her heart skipped a beat when she remembered that three years back a young girl had been taken off the beach and never seen again. She had forgotten about it until this very moment. Anuuk felt like her heart was going to beat right out of her chest. The hard pounding caused her whole body to shake. Somewhere deep inside she knew. Anuuk just knew her beautiful daughter, her Aleut princess, was gone. She fell to her knees, crying out to the God she believed had deserted her.

"Why? Why? Why? It was so unfair." *My whole family! It can't possible get any worse,* she thought to herself. A part of her had died with her husband and two sons. Now her daughter was gone. Anuuk believed Ahha had been born through divine intervention, but had she been wrong? Had she been living in a fantasy world all this time? Even in the depth of her despair, she called out to God, "Help me. Please help me. I don't want to live anymore."

God knew what He was doing, not giving the human mind access to the future. If Anuuk would have known what the next two years would bring to her life, the pain would have been too much to bear. However, those two years would give her the time she needed to find out if her daughter was alive.

The sun was just coming up over the grassy hills of Atka. It was going to be another rare sunny day, the horizon casting pink and gold hues that reflected off the ocean. Johnny Charles had gotten up early to go bird hunting, and he found Anuuk on the volcanic slopes, sitting with her knees up to her chest, rocking back and forth, mournfully chanting.

Johnny Charles was a young, rather shy man. His father was named Tayagug, meaning *three*. It was a name given to him at birth when his family noticed that he was born minus a small finger and ring finger on his left hand. Tayagug had taken over as leader of the village after the loss of Anuuk's husband and two sons last summer. He was tall for an Aleut, but then he had only a quarter of Aleut blood in him. He was of mixed blood, a little Russian, a little Swedish, and a little Tlinget Haida. He was only a few years older than Ahha, and he had admired and loved her from afar, at first as her protector. Then as she'd developed into a young woman, his love for her had changed into the kind of love that happened between a man and women. In JC dreams, he desired to eventually marry Ahha, but he doubted he would ever be worthy enough.

He knelt down in front of Anuuk. "Anuuk, what's wrong? Why are you out here by yourself so early in the morning?"

"She's gone JC," Anuuk said, sobbing.

"Who's gone? What are you talking about?" JC was seriously alarmed.

Anuuk pointed toward the horizon. "Ahha's been taken. My Aleut princess has been taken!"

"What? What happened? What do you mean?" Johnny's mind was reeling, and without thinking, he shot questions at her rapidly.

Anuuk looked at him, her face twisted in fear and pain. "One of the fishing vessels was leaving the cove when I came out just before dark to call her into the house. She wasn't here, and I just knew she had been taken for perverted, disgusting reasons."

John Charlie felt sick to his stomach. The Aleut princess was the pride of the village. Everyone in the village knew the stories of God's divine intervention that had given them a true Aleut princess. They knew how Ahha's great-grandmother had been kept hidden from the Russian traders. How she had married an Aleut leader, and they in turn had kept the bloodline pure. But everyone believed it had been only by the grace of God. It was a story told over and over again in their ceremonial dances.

John Charlie took Anuuk's hands in his, pulled her up, and forced her to stand. "Come, Anuuk. I'm going to take you to the church and the priest, Father Vladimir." As Johnny pulled her, Anuuk reluctantly put one foot in front of the other. There was a loud buzzing in her ears like white noise, keeping all physical, mental, and spiritual pain far away from Anuuk's reality.

The Christian community that evolved into what is now known as the Russian Orthodox church is traditionally said to have been founded by the apostle Andrew, who is thought to have visited the Scythia and Greek colonies along the northern coast of the Black Sea. According to one of the legends, Andrew reached the future location of Kiev and foretold the foundation of a great Christian city. Thus, the Russian Orthodox church began.

Russian traders settled in Alaska during the eighteenth century.

In 1740, divine liturgy was celebrated on board a Russian ship off the Alaskan coast. In 1794, the Russian Orthodox church sent missionaries—Saint Herman of Alaska among them—to establish a formal mission in Alaska. Their missionary endeavors contributed to the conversions of many Alaskan natives to the Orthodox church.

There was a small Russian Orthodox church at the edge of the village that everyone attended on a regular basis. Anuuk had taken Ahha there since she was a baby and taught her to believe in the Holy Trinity. The Orthodox church followed a doctrine of hypostases, which posited that the Trinity was composed of three distinct divine persons without overlap. But the most central belief was the doctrine of the resurrection of Jesus Christ.

Most Aleuts combined Russian Orthodox beliefs with some of their ancient beliefs, including animism, which states that all life is produced by a spiritual force or that all natural phenomena have souls. They also embraced the belief that each human or each group of humans (e.g., a clan or tribe) had a spiritual connection or a kinship with another physical being, such as an animal or plant, often called a "spirit being" or "totem."

Anuuk was a Christian, and she followed the teachings of Jesus Christ. At the same time, she had her own totem, the puffin bird.

She often felt like it was one of the many ways Jesus spoke to her. There were no puffin birds around on this terrible morning. Anuuk felt as if God had deserted her.

Father Vladimar had just stepped outside and was mediating on the scripture he had just read when he saw Johnny Charles and Anuuk coming up the small hill to the church. Johnny Charles was literally pulling Anuuk behind him. He instantly knew something was very wrong. Anuuk looked disheveled. Her wild black hair was falling into her eyes, and it looked as if it hadn't been combed in weeks. As they drew closer, Father Vladimar could see she'd been crying. Her eyes were swollen and red. What could have possibly happened to this faithful, sweet woman? He'd seen her practically every day since last summer after the loss of her husband and sons. He had been there to counsel her through her grief, denial, anger, bargaining, depression, and acceptance. She'd been in depression for most of the winter, and only in the last month or so had she begun to accept the reality that they were gone.

As the two walked closer to him, Johnny Charles blurted out, "Ahha has been taken!"

The words didn't register with Father Vladimar. "What do you mean Ahha's been taken?" His mind was churning so fast he could barely get the words out.

Johnny Charles told him the story that Anuuk had told him. Father Vladimar was watching Anuuk closely. He could see that she was in shock and still in denial. He gently took her hand. led her into the church, and told Johnny Charles to go and alert the rest of the village.

The Russian Orthodox churches in North America were in complete disarray after World War I. The church building in Atka was badly in need of repairs, and the only finances available came from the hundred or so villagers who faithfully attended Sunday Mass. Father Valdimar's very survival, shelter, and food depended on the generosity of the villagers. As a result of the Russian Revolution, the North American diocese of the Russian Orthodox church (known as the "Metropolia") continued to exist in a *de facto* autonomous mode of self-governance. Between the World Wars, the Metropolia coexisted and at times cooperated with an independent synod that was later known as the Russian Orthodox Church Outside of Russia (ROCOR) or the Russian Orthodox Church Abroad.

Father Valdimar was a true man of God. He had been on Atka Island for so many years that he was not only the villager's spiritual adviser but was considered one of them too. He knew the stories about Ahha and how Anuuk and her husband considered her birth to be divine providence. Her pure bloodline had also led the villagers to honor her as a true Aleut princess.

Father Valdimar had no idea how to comfort Anuuk, so they sat in silence in the front pew, staring up at the altar. The small red votive candle Father Valdimar had just lit only a half hour before traditionally suggested to them that they were in the presence of Christ.

It was Anuuk who spoke first. "Do you really believe that Christ is here with us, Father? Because if He is, why didn't He protect Ahha? Why has He deserted me?"

Father Valdimar was slow to answer. "I don't know, Anuuk. I'd have to be God to answer that question. What I do know is that He has promised He would never desert us, never leave us. Everyone in the village knows you believe that Ahha's birth was by divine providence. Has that changed, Anuuk?"

Anuuk's shook her head back and forth, trying to clear her mind. She couldn't think straight. All of these disconnected thoughts were rapidly firing in her brain. She was surrounded by a bubble of despair and sadness. Finally, she answered, "It had to be a miracle. It just had to be. My time of the month had stopped months before I knew I was pregnant with her, and I didn't even realize I was pregnant until I started feeling life inside me. And then she was born so perfect in every way, and her bloodline was 100 percent Aleut. You know how rare that is, Father? She was a true Aleut princess, and I always believed that through her, the Aleut race would once again be proud of their place in history."

Father Valdimar simply said, "And what makes you think that isn't still God's plan for her, Anuuk?" His question so startled Anuuk she couldn't answer him.

Anuuk was suddenly so exhausted physically and emotionally that all she wanted to do was go home and sleep. Maybe then she'd be able to think more clearly. They walked in silence to the only home Anuuk had known for the past fifty years. Half the village people stood in silence, standing in front of the stick house. No one spoke. There was only the soft sound of chanting as they told the story of the lost Aleut princess.

CHAPTER 8

Astorm warning had come over the two-way radio. For the old-time Alaskans, it was just your run-of-the-mill wind and rain. It was enough though that the waters churned and created three- and four-foot waves, which made the journey choppy for smaller vessels in the open ocean. At thirty-six feet, the Blue Lady was one of those small vessels, and its captain, Sven Hasson, thought if he wanted to get any sleep that night, he'd better make a run for inside waters. *Besides,* Sven thought to himself, *the hold is almost filled with fresh salmon.*

It was late July, and following the migration path of the king salmon, Sven was gillnetting in the Gulf of Alaska. The Gulf of Alaska is an arm of the Pacific Ocean defined by the curve of the coastline of Southeastern Alaska. Gillnetting is a harvesting technique employing fine-filament nets that are set like a giant badminton net. The top edge is held up by floats, and the bottom is pulled down by a heavy lead line, forming a wall in the water that entangles fish by their gills. Drift gillnets are lowered off the stern or bow of a boat and allowed to drift freely in deep water, entangling fish that swim into them. The net is slowly pulled in when the floats along the top begin to jiggle vigorously. The entangled fish are pulled up and shaken out of the net and then thrown into the hold. The net is then reset, and the process begins again.

Sven was regretting not hiring one of the many dock stompers looking for work at the Juneau small boat harbor. Even though he was a big man who was more than six feet tall and physically fit from all his years of fishing, he wasn't that young anymore, and he was dog tired. The Blue Lady averaged seven knots an hour. A knot measured speed equal to 1.15 miles per hour, and it took him about eight hours from the Juneau dock to make it to the open ocean. He'd been in hurry to be one of the first fishing vessels when the season had opened up for migrating king salmon. Working solo had worn him out, and Sven welcomed the small storm that would give him an excuse to dock and sell what fish he had.

The Blue Lady was named after his grandmother, who was Creole, half Russian, and half Aleut, and she was known for the way she turned all her clothing shades of blue by using blueberries that grew wild in Alaska. His grandfather had been Swedish and part of the tens of thousands immigrants who had arrived in the 1850s from the California Gold Rush. His grandfather hadn't gotten rich but had mined enough gold to follow his dream up into Sitka, Alaska, which was only the capital of Alaska at the time, but also the main hub of the Alaska gold rush. Sitka was also where he met and married Sven's grandmother and where Sven's father had been born.

In the 1880s, Tlingit Chief Kowee showed up in Sitka with gold. Joe Juneau and Richard Harris went with the chief back to the area and found gold, lots of gold. Eventually, what was originally called Harrisburg (and then Rockwell) and finally renamed Juneau would become the home of the three largest gold mines in the world. Eventually, Juneau would become the second largest city in the United States by area, not by population.

Sven's grandfather followed the gold and eventually went to work for the Alaska Treadwell Gold Mining Company. It was the first large-scale mining operation in Alaska and would become one of the most bountiful. In 1917, the deep five-hundred-foot hole flooded out and collapsed. The miners had given it the nickname "Glory Hole" because of the unsafe conditions, and numerous miners had gone home to "Glory." It was a name that would stick and go down in the history books.

In 1922, the Treadwell mine closed, and Sven was born. Sven's father had never gotten gold fever, and as a teenager and young man, he had been one of the many dock stompers looking for work on the Juneau harbor dock for small boat. By the time Sven was born, his father owned his own fishing vessel and had named it the Blue Lady after Sven's great-grandmother. From the time Sven was thirteen years old, he spent all his summers on the Blue Lady, fishing with his father. Sven's mother, who was part Tlingit and part Aleut, was a force to be reckoned with, and she demanded Sven get his high school diploma before fishing full-time.

Sven was tall, strong, and quiet. He had always been uncomfortable in large crowds, almost claustrophobic. Even as youngster when he had gone with his mother and two older sisters to varies community events, like the Fourth of July parades celebrations, he would get this nervous energy that caused him to shake on the inside. But when he was out fishing with his father, he was his happiest, even in storms when the boat would be thrown around in the large waves. Fishing was all Sven had ever wanted to do. The ocean was his best friend, and it was there in the early evenings when pulling in the fishing gear, and securing the boat for the night, Sven would feel the presence of God. He had been raised in the Roman Catholic tradition, but as an adult, he seldom attended church. His church was the beauty that came from the emerald green islands sprinkled throughout the coastline of Southeast Alaska, the pristine blue-white glaciers meandered down mountains, the diverse wildlife in their natural habitats, and the freedom offered in the last frontier known as Alaska.

Sven was approaching the Cape Spencer Lighthouse, which was south of Yakutatat at the entrance to Cross Sound and Icy Strait, when the call came over his marine band radio.

"Calling the Blue Lady. Over."

"This is Sven Hasson on the Blue Lady. Over."

"Sven, this is Kyle over at ACS. I'm going to patch you through to a Sister Mary Kathleen from St. Ann's Hospital. Over."

"Thanks, Kyle. I've got it. Over." Sven immediately felt nauseous. It had to be about Anna. Even though they had been separated for almost eighteen years, he still loved her, and all he could do was pray to God she wasn't dead.

A strong female voice came over the two-way radio. "Mr. Hasson, this is Sister Mary Kathleen at St. Ann's Hospital. I'm calling on behalf of your wife, Anna Hasson." There was a brief silence before the nun remembered to say, "Over."

Sven's mind was racing. *She must still be alive!* "Yes, Sister, go ahead. Over."

"Your wife is in critical condition, Mr. Hasson, and I'm afraid all we can do is keep her comfortable. But she requested I get in touch with you as she desperately wants to see you. Over."

Somewhere in the back of Sven's mind, he had known for the past almost eighteen years this kind of call would come. It was one of the reasons he had separated from Anna, even though he had never stopped loving her. He simply could not emotionally handle watching her slowly kill herself day after day. Besides he hadn't been able to really forgive her for giving away their three-month-old daughter. It remained an open wound and one that haunted him nightly.

"Yes, Sister, I can be in Juneau by late tomorrow afternoon. Will that be okay? Over."

Oh, God, he silently prayed to himself, *please just give me a few more hours with her.* There was so much pain between them. There were so many issues that needed to be settled and too many things that had been said in hot anger.

Sister Mary Kathleen's voice came back over the radio. "Yes, we have a little time here. If you could just contact me as soon as you get into Juneau. Over." Sister Mary Kathleen could hear the deep feelings in Sven's voice, and all she wanted to do was give him some kind hope. She knew that only God knew the day and hour of a person's death, and she had to believe that the Holy Spirit was guiding her.

"I'll be in touch then. Sister. Thank you for getting in contact with me. Over."

Sven was in the inland water passage where the small storm had subsided. He turned off the radio. There was too much activity from other fishing vessels during the night, and Sven just wanted to fall into a deep sleep.

He sat on his bunk with his head in his hands. He was so confused. So many conflicting emotions, love, and anger being the dominating emotions. What was it his mother had told him? Emotions were nothing more than energy in motion? At this moment in time he felt overwhelmed and numb. It was like someone had taken a needle and injected his heart and soul with an anesthetic No, that wasn't quite right. He was terrified, terrified that Anna would die before he could get to her. "Oh, God help me," he cried out. Sven believed that the image of God was imprinted in every person. It had been so long since he had asked God to help him. He hadn't asked for more than eighteen years, right after he'd found out Anna had given their three-month-old daughter away. His whole body began to shake, and he sobbed, deep stomach-wrenching sobs.

Sometime in the quiet of the night with only the sound of the oceans water lapping against the boat, Sven's sobs stopped, and he vaguely perceived the presence of God right there in the galley of his fishing vessel.

CHAPTER 9

I t was late afternoon the next day by the time the Blue Lady docked at the Juneau harbor. When Sven was in town, he sometimes stayed with his elderly mother, who lived with his older sister and family. He didn't want to see them just yet. They had been after him for years to divorce Anna and to get on with his life. For the past eighteen years, it was like he was frozen in time. He couldn't move forward, and he couldn't move backward. And his mother and sister were always trying to *fix* him. He knew their intentions were only in his best interest, but he just couldn't handle it. Instead of letting them know he was in town, he grabbed some clothing, rented a small room in a local hotel, and took a long shower to get the smell of fish off his body. It was close to seven in the evening before Sven finally got to the hospital.

Sister Mary Kathleen met him at the main entrance of the hospital and led him into a small sitting room on the left of the reception desk. "Mr. Hasson," she gently said, "all we can really do is keep her comfortable at this point. She's alert and seems very determined to talk with you and someone named John Charlie. I've placed a phone call to him at his workplace, but he hasn't yet returned my call."

Sven knew John Charlie or JC, as everyone called him. He'd lived in the same village that Anna had been born in, and he had lived in Juneau for as long as Sven had known him. He knew JC was the closest thing to a brother Anna had, but ever since Sven had separated from Anna, JC had distanced himself from Sven. It had baffled Sven because he suspected that JC loved Anna as much as he did. So he was a little surprised at Anna's insistence on seeing him. "That's okay, Sister. I'll get in touch with him. I know where he works."

"Would you please tell him to get in touch with me? I need to ask him about how Anna's mother died. Anna told me he knew the details of her death but would never discuss them with her, and well, it just seems important to her to have that information." With that, Sister Mary Kathleen gave him Anna's room number and told him to let her know if there was anything she could do to help, and then she shook his hand before she left the room.

Sven took a deep breath and entered Anna's hospital room. She appeared to be asleep. He stood at the foot of her hospital bed for a few minutes just staring at her. She looked so tiny like an innocent child. It was almost as if the bed was too big for her. Her coal black long hair was spread out around her head almost like a halo against the glistening white pillows. He quietly pulled up a chair next to the side of the bed. He wanted to hold her hand, but she looked so peaceful, so fragile that he was afraid of hurting her by the sheer strength of his overwhelming emotions. His thoughts drifted, remembering with impassioned thoughts the first time he'd seen her.

It was the middle of winter. It had been snowing all day, and Juneau was covered in a blanket of white. The snow crunched under his feet as Sven walked the few blocks from the dock to the downtown area of Juneau. He was strong and young, and he had been working all day on winter repairs for the Blue Lady with his father. He wasn't a big drinker, but he enjoyed a few beers now and then and the camaraderie of the locals in a bar. He was headed for the well-known Red Dog Saloon with its sawdust floors and good old-fashioned honky-tonk. It was a tourist trap in the summer and locals avoided it, but in the winter it was a great hangout for Juneau residents.

Anna was sitting at the bar by herself, a silver seal-skin Alaskan parka hanging on the back of the bar stool. Sven saw her the second he walked in through the swinging doors. He instantly thought she was the most beautiful women he had ever seen. There was a look of innocence about her—not the girl-next-door type but rather a childlike naivety. She had on a pair of handmade mukluks with dark slacks tucked in at the ankles. Her heavy white turtleneck sweater brought out her bronze skin, and her straight black hair hung halfway down her back.

Sven took a seat a couple stools down from where Anna sat and ordered a beer. He couldn't keep his eyes off her. She had ignored him at first, but she finally turned toward him and looked him straight in the eyes. Her almond-shaped dark brown eyes bore straight into his soul. She didn't flinch, and it took Sven's breath away. He stuttered out, "Can I buy you a drink?"

Anna had shyly smiled at him and nodded. They sipped on their beers and talked until the saloon closed. She told him of her childhood in her Atka village. When he asked her how she had come to live in Juneau, she grew silent. Her lips quivered, and she shut her eyes. Her voice shaky, she had said she didn't want to talk about it.

When they finally walked together out of the saloon into the crisp winter air, the snow had stopped falling, and with surrounding mountains in view, Juneau looked like a winter wonderland. Sven had dared to take her hand, and they walked in silence. Two true

Alaskans were caught up in the magic of the Alaskan night. They came to the Quonset hut on the tidal flats of Juneau, where Anna lived with a relative, and they parted after setting up a dinner date for the next evening.

Within two months after seeing Anna every day, Sven asked her to marry him. They were sitting in a local restaurant on their third cup of coffee, and Sven literally blurted it out. "I love you, Anna Ahha. Will you marry me?" Sven would throughout their marriage always call her Anna-Ahha, acknowledging both her Aleut heritage, and her American citizenship.

She looked him straight in the eyes and said, "I love you too, Sven, but there's something I haven't told you." And quickly before she'd lost her courage, she'd told him how she'd come to Juneau, how she'd been raped repeatedly by the two men who had kidnapped her from the shores of her village, how she had gotten pregnant and then thought she had miscarried only to find out she was still pregnant, and how she had given birth to a son she'd given away. Anna left out the part where she had deliberately tried to abort the child. She did tell him how she'd found out later that she'd been pregnant with twins and how a day hadn't passed since giving up her son that she hadn't grieved the loss of him.

Sven felt sad about the pain he saw in her eyes. It had taken a few minutes for him to absorb all she was saying before he quietly said in response, "Will you marry me, Anna Ahha?" She looked at him with those dark eyes that he so easily got lost in and said yes! They married a week later and rented a small one-bedroom apartment in the Channel Apartments only a couple of blocks away from the small boat harbor. It was the nicest place Anna Hasson had ever lived.

"Sven!" Anna's soft voice brought him back to the present. He loved the way that she said his name. She was one of the few people who had pronounced his name right from the beginning. Most people pronounced his name like the number seven.

"Anna Ahha," he answered back, taking her hand in both of his. He had always called her by both her given name and her English name.

Anna looked at him and whispered, "Sven, I'm so sorry, so sorry for everything. Mostly for giving our daughter away. I've never stopped loving you, Sven. Oh, God, I've made such a mess out of my life."

"We've both made a mess out of our lives, Anna Ahha. I should have given up fishing and stayed with you, not signed those adoption papers and gotten our daughter back. We would have been okay. I'm as much to blame as you are, my love."

Anna took a deep breath and pleaded her case for the first time in her life, "Sven, Sister Mary Kathleen said something to me that has helped me. She said it isn't how you begin in life that's important. It's how you end. And Sven, I want to end well. I have one thing I'm really proud of, and that's my Aleut heritage. Even though I haven't acted like it, I am an Aleut princess, and I want to leave that legacy. But I need your help. Could you find our daughter for me? Would you even try to find her? I want to meet and talk to her and tell her of her heritage and that I have always loved her.

Anna hesitated. Sven thought she'd finished, but she hadn't. Looking him straight in the eye, she squeezed Sven's hand tight and whispered, "Is there any chance I could get you to try to find my son?"

Sven had her hand in both of his and was surprised at the strength of her questions. He knew what he was hearing was Anna's impassioned last wish. He had failed her before. He hadn't been there for her when she'd needed him the most. There was no going back, no rewind, and now it was too late. He'd let his stupid pride get in the way. What was it his father had said to him? "Pride goes before a fall, Son." If only he'd listened.

"Oh, Anna Ahha," Sven said, and in one breath he shared one of the secrets he'd kept. "I know where our daughter is. I've known all along. You know, she's just graduating from high school this year, and I plan on being there. She looks so like you. She doesn't know who I am, but her family has allowed me over the years to watch her from afar. But I had to promise to not interfere in her life. Her name is Kimberly."

"Sven, why didn't you tell me before?" Anna cried out.

He lowered his eyes and replied, "Because I didn't think you were strong enough to stay away from her if you knew where she was."

Anna knew he was probably right, and for a few minutes, they both were silent, clinging to each other's hands as salty tears ran down both their cheeks.

Sven was the first to break the heavy silence between them. "There's more, my love. I also think I know where your son is."

"What?" Anna jerked her hand away. "How?"

"Well," Sven began, "you know how I sometimes dock the Blue Lady at the Auke Bay boat harbor? Well, a few years back, I was at the Auke Bay boat harbor fueling up the Blue Lady, and there was a small open boat docked next to me with this young kid loading some heavy supplies. So I offered to help him. He said, 'Thanks, mister.' And then he smiled at me. I could tell he had Aleut in him, and when he smiled, I swear, Anna Ahha, it was your smile. When I asked him how old he was, his age matched the same time your son was born. He also added that he'd been born in Juneau. While loading the supplies and in the course of our conversation, he told me he was the only child of adopted parents and lodged with his father out at Echo Cove. His name is Cayden Jennings, and I've kept track of him over the years. I don't want to give you false hope, Anna Ahha, but I think he's your son."

Sven watched his wife closely, not sure how she was going to take this new information. She had closed her eyes and listened. After a long silence, she replied, "I've kept secrets from you too, Sven. There's one I can't yet tell you, so I can't fault you for not sharing this with me sooner. I can only beg you to try to find both my children and find out if they will see me. Anna was choking up because somewhere deep in her spirit, she suspected divine providence was at work in her life.

CHAPTER 10

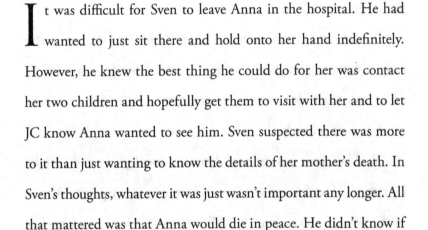

It was difficult for Sven to leave Anna in the hospital. He had wanted to just sit there and hold onto her hand indefinitely. However, he knew the best thing he could do for her was contact her two children and hopefully get them to visit with her and to let JC know Anna wanted to see him. Sven suspected there was more to it than just wanting to know the details of her mother's death. In Sven's thoughts, whatever it was just wasn't important any longer. All that mattered was that Anna would die in peace. He didn't know if that was even possible, but he knew he would do everything in his power to make it happen.

JC was the short-order night cook at a local bar and grill. He'd gotten the job only a few days after his arrival in Juneau. Now it had been almost twenty years. The job provided an efficiency apartment in the same two-story building just over the bar and grill, and he earned an adequate salary. JC was a private person, never saying much about his personal life, but he was the personification of personable. Few were ever invited up to his apartment, but he had been observed on rare occasions allowing a falling-down drunk to sleep it off in his private quarters. When meeting JC, folks quickly knew two things about him. He was proud to be part Aleut, and he loved Alaska. He called tourists or even new arrivals to Juneau "aliens." Most Alaskans would give a hearty chuckle when they heard him.

JC was surprised to see Sven Hasson amble into the bar on the early summer night. How long had it been since he seen him? A good two years! He was even more surprised when Sven asked to speak to him privately.

They had gone out the back door into an alleyway, and both lit cigarettes before Sven spoke. Sven got straight to the point. "Anna's in the hospital. It's serious, JC. All they can do for her is keep her comfortable. It won't be long, and she's asking to see you. Sister Mary Kathleen wants to talk to you. She's saying Anna wants to know the details of her mother's death." Sven began choking on his words and couldn't say anymore. JC reached out and patted him on his shoulder.

Guilt washed over JC like any addiction that controls a person's life. It wasn't just the fact he'd refused to tell Anna how horribly her mother had died. It was so much more. It was the reality that he'd been in love with Anna from the time she was a young girl. He'd found out she was in Juneau, and that was the main reason he'd chosen to live in Juneau. But Anna had never treated him like anything other than a brother, and he'd just gone along with it, hoping she'd feel differently in time. Then Sven had come into her life, and although he'd been crushed, he'd seen how happy she was. He forced himself to become friends with Sven.

The first couple of years Sven and Anna were married, the three of them were together often. JC had even been the first person Sven had called the night Sven and Anna's daughter was born. But then it all went to hell in a handbasket. It was the beginning of the fishing season, and Sven was out fishing within three months after the baby's birth.

Two weeks later on one rainy evening, Anna showed up at the bar drunker than JC had ever seen her. She slurred her words but said that she had given her baby up for adoption. She'd gone on and on about how she couldn't take care of the baby by herself and how she'd begged Sven to give up fishing and find a job where he could be at home every night. Sven told her she was being unreasonable and that fishing was all he knew.

JC was stunned at the news, and he didn't know what to say to

Anna, especially in the drunken condition she was in. He called a cab and had her driven home, thinking he would talk with her the next day. Sven arrived home the next day, and when JC got to the apartment, he found Sven throwing his clothes in pillowcases and Anna sitting on the couch, sobbing and begging him not to leave. JC had tried to reason with them both, and Sven had almost punched him in the face. He approached JC, both his hands balled up in white-knuckled fists, and yelled, "Get out of my way, JC. She gave our daughter away, and I will never forgive her. If I never see her again, it'll be too soon." And with that, he threw the four pillowcase filled with his clothes and personal items over his shoulders and stomped out. After that, JC didn't see him for a couple of years.

JC had seen Anna though, but most of the time, she was drunk. Her personal appearance, which was something she'd always been meticulous about, began to deteriorate. She'd always reeked of that sour smell that came from drinking too much alcohol, too much sex, and poor personal hygiene. JC suspected she had prostituted herself on occasion, and it made him sick to his stomach. She'd moved out of the one-bedroom apartment she and Sven had shared into a run-down boarding hotel. Most of her conversations were ramblings about how wretched men were and how she'd only been used by them, but mostly, she'd talked about herself and what a sinful, immoral person she was, always ending with how the two children she'd had were better off without her in their lives.

One night almost two years after she and Sven had separated, she came into the bar and grill just as JC was closing up the kitchen. He'd tried to get her to eat something. Her gaunt appearance genuinely concerned him. He'd sent her up to his apartment to sleep it off while he finished up in the kitchen. When he'd finally gotten up to his apartment, JC found her passed out on his bed. The bed was a pull-out couch that he seldom put up, even though it took up much of the living space. He took a shower to get the greasy hamburger smell off, plopped down on the bed next to her, and instantly fell asleep.

JC woke up late the next morning. It was routine for him. He never got to bed before four in the morning, and he woke up around noon. Anna was sitting at the small kitchen table in one of the two kitchen chairs. She had on one of his white undershirts that fit her like a dress coming down over her knees. She looked like a little girl, sitting there in the straight-back chair with one leg hanging down, her foot swinging back and forth in a nervous gesture. The other knee pulled against her chest while she clipped her toe nails. Her long black hair was wet and brushed back from her face, falling down her back, and she smelled of ivory soap. This was the Anna he had always loved, and he stood there silent, watching her, relishing in her beauty.

He'd finally blurted out, "Why don't you stay here with me for a few days, Anna? You can rest, eat, maybe put a couple of pounds on, and maybe weave one of those baskets you're so good at?"

Anna had looked at him long and hard, staring at him with her penetrating brown eyes before she'd answered, "Okay."

It had been impossible not to touch her as she lay so close to him, and Anna let him make love to her. He told her how much he had always loved her, and he also told her she could stay with him as long as she wanted. She stayed four days.

On the fourth night, he'd quickly cleaned up the grill before closing. He was filled with hope—hope that Anna would be by his side for the rest of their lives. He opened the door to his apartment only to find her gone. In her place there was a handwritten note sitting on the small kitchen table. The note read, "JC, I cannot thank you enough for the friendship you offer me. But the truth is I still love Sven, and I cannot let you believe there is anything more between us than friendship. I'm sorry. Please don't try to contact me. I will find my way to you when I am ready. Anna."

JC kept the note on the table for months, reading it so many times the words went around and around in his head like a broken record, and instead of the one or two beers he drank every night after work, he drank four or five, sometimes washing them down with a shot of whiskey.

JC had seen Anna off and on over the years. She'd come into the bar and grill now and then late at night, and he'd give her something to eat and sometimes give her money. But they never spoke of the time she'd spent in his apartment.

Now Anna was dying and wanted to see him. She wanted to know how her mother had died. That was another story he'd buried deep in his spirit out of sheer shame, anger, and embarrassment— shame because he'd done nothing to help his Aleut race, anger at a government that had deserted the Aleuts, and embarrassment for the Alaskan people who had turned their heads the other way.

CHAPTER 11

JC was up early the day after Sven's visit was early for JC—10:00 a.m. to be exact. It didn't matter. He'd been unable to sleep anyway. The terrible memories he'd blocked off for so long haunted him. Sister Mary Kathleen met him at the front door of St. Ann's Hospital and ushered him into her private office, closing the door behind them.

"Anna tells me you know the details of her mother's death." Sister Mary Kathleen came straight to the point. "She also was emphatic about talking with you in person. I suspect there's something more than her mother's death on her mind. Do you have any idea what it might be?"

JC couldn't think of what it might possibly be. He had never again spoken of his love for Anna and had buried it deep inside of himself, always blocking it from his emotions when it threatened to surface. Anna had remained aloof after those few days she'd spent in his apartment, and JC had honored her request never to contact her. Over the years, months would go by before she showed up at his work. Their conversations at those times had been only superficial, nothing personal. They were like two strangers meeting for the first time. JC had never told Anna the details of her mother's death for no other reason than she had never asked. He hadn't told her that his own mother had also died within weeks of Anuuk's death or that both Anuuk and his mother had watched as their village was burned to the ground. As a matter of fact, he had never talked to Anna about the whole painful tragedy involving the Aleut race.

He had looked at Sister and simply said, "I honestly don't know," and with that, he pulled out a ragged notebook. I had been years since he had read what he'd written. It wasn't that he was much of a writer. It was just that he'd had been compelled to write it all down. It was catharsis, purging his soul and his spirit of the pain connected to the possible genocide of his people.

"This may take a little time, Sister. Can I read to you what I wrote?" He looked at the nun, waiting for a signal from her to go ahead.

Sister Mary Kathleen nodded her head in agreement, and JC began to read.

How we have suffered. In the scheme of life, I suppose the internment of the Aleuts was a small chapter in the history of World War II. By the time World War II, there were less than nine hundred Aleuts who were interned. Nonetheless, the Aleuts ... or as we like to call ourselves, the Unangans, meaning "the people," called the volcanic Aleutian Islands their home for thousands of years. For centuries the Aleuts' daily activities revolved around the water. We fished and hunted in baidaras, lean traditional kayaks most often made from the hides of sea lions. The ocean provided us with an abundance of whales, seals, salmon, halibut, and shellfish. The island also attracted an annual migration of millions of birds. Even to this day, the bald eagles lounge around the villages and roam the streets of villages. They are as common as gulls.

Before the first Russians explorers in 1741, our numbers were between twenty and thirty thousand. The discovery of the islands' sea otter populations prompted a mad rush for furs and eventually, a bloody Russian conquest and colonization. We, the

Aleut race, were reduced by as much as 80 percent because of the brutality of the Russians fur traders, many of them killing all the men in the villages and keeping the women for their own pleasure. This, of course, translated into many children who were half Russian and half Aleut. The pure blood Aleut was rare and highly respected, even honored. Most of us had been converted to Russian Orthodoxy, and it is our faith that sustained us. The church was the center of our lives by the time the United States bought Alaska in 1867. We lived a kind of hybrid life, seeking subsistence from the sea while readily adopting modern conveniences like plumbing and electric lights.

Under American rule, we, the remaining Aleut people, were classed as wards of the state. Some of the islands were ruled by the Fish and Wild Life Services, while some fell under the Bureau of Indian Affairs. Further confusion arose in 1940 and 1941 when the US military saw the Aleutians as a possible enemy target and the United States initiated a military presence. Soldiers and laborers flooded in from outside. Property values rose, and the liquor flowed. They also used our women, further deteriorating our Aleut bloodline. That's one of the reasons Annuk and Ahha (Anna) were so important to our village. They were both pure Aleut, and for that they were honored. Anna was known as an Aleut princess and treated accordingly. Ahha was taken from us a year before the evacuation, and although we didn't know what had happened to her we, her mother and I were grateful she didn't go through the suffering her villagers would experience.

On December 7, 1941, hundreds of Japanese fighter and bombers struck Pearl Harbor in Hawaii. The United States was at war with the Japanese enemy. Military strategists knew Americans would be eyeing the Aleutians. If there were serious casualties among Aleut civilians, it would leave administrators open to criticism, of course, and it would be easier for the military to operate without a population of wards underfoot. But a mass civilian evacuation was a daunting logistical prospect, and no one knew how far the war might spread. With so many different government entities having a hand in the management of the Aleuts, no one agency was inclined to take the lead on a possible relocation.

Then on June 7, 1942, at the far end of the Aleutian chain, the Japanese invaded Attu and Kiska, 550 miles from our village on Atka. On Attu, the lone Bureau of Indian Affairs was executed, and the forty-three Aleut residents were rounded up and eventually shipped to Japan as prisoners of war, where more than half of them died of starvation and tuberculosis before the end of the fighting.

The invasion triggered the chaotic removal of all Aleut civilians from the islands. On June 12, a naval commander ordered the immediate evacuation of Atka. The residents, myself included, my father, my mother, and Anna's mother had retreated to the hills, and we watched as a military crew burned the village to the ground to prevent its use by the invaders. Then the village people were ordered to board a military ship, and without further explanation, their long voyage east began. They received no warning of their departure and no information about where they were going or how long they would be gone. Some carried a small single suitcase, but most carried nothing at all. We were crowded into a cold cargo hatch. There was no privacy, nothing, and we were treated like animals.

The Pribilovian Aleuts were taken to two camps on opposing sides of Funter Bay near Juneau. The residents of Atka were sent to Killisnoo Island, a small Island located off the central west coast of Admiralty Island and just south of the city of Angoon, about thirty miles from Juneau. We were taken to a defunct herring factory that had been built in 1882 by the North West Trading Company. The conditions were deplorable. Meals were basic. Medical supplies were limited, and medical staff largely absent. Sanitation was nonexistent. The few Aleuts who were able to find work in towns were allowed to do so in part to relieve the overcrowding conditions. I was one of the fortunate ones and found work and a place to live within a couple of days of my arrival in Juneau. It was then that I also found out that Ahha (Anna) was alive and living in Juneau. I was thrilled and immediately found where she was living and was able to tell her mother, Anuuk, that Ahha was alive before she died.

We had come from our treeless islands with their gentle rolling hills and the openness of the sea against our will to a rainy slice of dense, damp forest wedged between mountains and oceans. Although I've personally come to love the mountains and trees, in the beginning it was the trees more than anything else representing the strangeness and terror of our sudden relocation.

My people were without hunting or fishing gear or even boats and could not continue their lifestyles. The bunk houses were tiny with too many people crowded in a small area, using blankets to try to allow for some privacy. Some of the floors were rotting away, and high tides would often flow under the rotting wood. The smell of excretion and waste was so pungent that when I visited for the first time, it made my stomach wretch. There was one outhouse that serviced two hundred people. The garbage cans were overflowing. Human excrement was everywhere, even next to the doors of the cabins, and the drainage boxes into which they were to empty dishwater and kitchen waste were filthy beyond description.

An early order of business in the evacuation camps was to establish a chapel. Orthodox communities in southeast Alaska donated religious icons to help furnish the churches. It was our strong faith in our religion that held us together through the trials that my people endured during their three-year displacement. They believed they were "helping their country," even though to this day, they fight for their rights as citizens of the United State of America.

With that, JC laid down his notebook. He'd had to blink back the tears welling up in his eyes. He'd locked away those feelings of anguish for so many years. He was terrified that if they came out, he wouldn't want to go on living. Between the anguish for his people and the love he'd held for Anna, it was too much for one person to bear.

Sister Mary Kathleen had sat and listened silently. She was

stunned! It was difficult for her to absorb. A whole race of people practically wiped off the face of the earth. But they'd survived. Maybe not well, but where there was life, there was hope. She now better understood Anna's need to connect with her children. They were Aleut, born of an Aleut princess, and they should know their heritage.

Sister Mary Kathleen shook JC's hand, told him Anna's room number, and assured him she was there to help in any way she could.

JC was visibly shaking as he entered Anna's hospital room. There was a hospital table over the top of her bed with an untouched tray of food on it. It hid her face from his view. He stepped further into the room, and he saw she was sound asleep. He was half relieved, his emotions raw after reliving the horror of what had happened to his people. He'd come back later.

He stopped at Sister Mary Kathleen's office on his way out and asked her to let Anna know he'd been there and would come back tomorrow morning. Stepping outside under the cloudy sky, he welcomed the drizzling rain so prominent in Juneau. It fit his mood perfectly.

CHAPTER 12

B etty Jennings lived her life to the fullest, and her log cabin was a reflection of all she cherished. She loved trees, especially the green pine trees blanketing the surrounding mountains, bringing the aroma of pine down the mountainsides. She and her husband, Mike, had remodeled what was once her parents' home, adding a modern kitchen and enlarging the living room. The home sat on the shores of Auke Bay, a pristine lake from the runoff waters of the Mendenhall glacier. It was the same home she had been born and raised in. Betty was an only child, so she and Mike took the home over when her parents retired to Arizona. Betty was sure that she never wanted to live anywhere else other than Juneau. It was in her blood. Mike felt the same way.

A women of serious faith and a bit of a mystic, Betty believed everything happened for a reason. She gauged her days by whatever task or event was put before her. She believed in her soul and spirit that this was the will of God for her. Somewhere in her life as she had matured as a Christian, she came to understand that she was a triune being, a spirit that had a soul and lived in a body. Betty had been raised in the Roman Catholic church as had her husband, and they were comfortable following in that religious tradition.

There had only been one time in her life when the joy she felt for life had been temporally taken from her. Both she and Mike had wanted a large family, and after five years of marriage, they found out that Betty could never have children. She was devastated, and for the first time in her life, she doubted her faith in God. Betty had a couple of joyless years. It was if she was stuck in some kind of time warp. She cried easily, and she felt she was going through the motions of life like a robot. Then one day she became aware that while she had conscientiously and deliberately blocked the painful emotions that went along with her inability to have her own biological children, she had also lost the capacity to feel and experience the happy, positive blessings in her life. It absolutely terrified her, and for the first time in her life, she understood a person couldn't just pick and choose what emotions to block and which ones to feel. Betty had hardened her heart toward emotional pain, and the heart could not differentiate between positive and negative feelings.

Once again, Betty had turned to her faith, and in a short time, she found herself feeling the joy of a bird in the trees, the new fallen snow, the sweetness of her husband, and all the hundreds of daily blessings that came her way. When the moments of emotional pain had come, she stopped fighting them and allowed herself to flow with the sad feelings and to grieve the loss of her dream. It was only then that the miracle happened.

Prior to marrying Mike, she had flown to Seattle, studied for a few months, and received her licensed practical nurse (LPN) certificate. She only worked part-time in the winter months at St. Ann's Hospital, spending the summers as the cook for her husband's small logging operation at Echo Cove. Echo Cove was only a few miles from Juneau's official "end of the road," and so to get to the location, one had to go by boat or plane.

One winter night Betty was working the night shift at the hospital when a newborn baby boy was brought into the hospital nursery. Betty had been assigned to clean the newborn up. He was nameless, and they were supposed to keep him at the back of the nursery because his mother was giving him up for adoption. Betty spent her whole shift that night holding and rocking the baby boy. It had been three years since she and Mike had put in the necessary paperwork for adoption. That night had been more than twenty years ago, but now Betty just knew this small baby boy was to be her son.

They named him Cayden Michael Jennings. They knew very little about his biological mother, only that she was Aleut. The father was unknown, and that it was possible that the mother had been a heavy drinker during the pregnancy.

Betty spent the first two years of Cayden's life holding, rocking, and softly singing to him. He was a fussy baby, often crying for what appeared no reason. Her LPN education had briefly addressed some of the possible symptoms. She had gone back to the one physiology book she had kept from her LPN training and read and reread the one page that addressed fetal alcohol syndrome. Not much was known at the time of Cayden's birth, but the first paragraph pretty much said it all. "The developing fetal nervous system is particularity sensitive to ethanol toxicity, which can come from the maternal alcohol consumptions through the placenta." Betty found her calling in life. She would document each day and fight for her son for as long as it took to counteract whatever damage had been done through alcohol.

It wasn't easy, and there were many times when she went to bed exhausted and discouraged. Cayden had a below average birth weight. He was slow to learn. His motor skills were behind for his age group. He had slow social/adaptive skills, and his hyperactivity was a nightmare, especially during the primary years of his schooling.

Betty homeschooled Cayden until the eighth grade. She quickly learned to follow his lead. When he showed an interest in building blocks, she went out and bought the largest set of Lincoln Logs she could find. It took three years before he could build with the logs by himself, but his motor skills improved as did his ability to stay focused. And he learned how to read and follow the instructions too. Cayden had an affinity for nature and animals, and Betty used the stunning natural environment in and around Juneau to teach him how to read and write. By the time he was thirteen years old, he could identify both the plant and animal life in the area, and he could also tell you their purposes in the environment. Scholastically, he was more than ready for public schooling at that point.

He graduated from high school with honors. Socially, he had learned to interact appropriately with others through snow skiing, a sport he excelled in. He was shy, and he continued to struggle in crowds of people as an adult.

On this early day in May, Betty sat at her kitchen table, drinking a hot cup of coffee as she watched her adult son unloading the truck of the groceries they had spent all morning buying. It was a yearly ritual, supplying Echo Logging camp for the summer. Providing the weather held, tomorrow they would load their one-year-old seventeen-foot "Glasspar" boat and head for the logging camp, where

Mike along with two hired hands were already working twelve-hour days.

When the phone rang, Betty picked up on the second ring. A deep baritone voice introduced himself. "Mrs. Jennings, my name is Sven Hasson. Could I speak to you for a few minutes about your son, Cayden Jennings? I assure you it isn't anything bad."

What on earth? Betty couldn't begin to imagine what this stranger had to say. "Yes, go ahead." Her curiosity aroused, she signaled for Cayden to come close to the phone, putting her arm around his waist.

"Mrs. Jennings, normally, I wouldn't be so bold. But there's not much time left, and I need to ask you if your son, Cayden, is adopted and if he was born in Juneau in February of 1941? I think he's the biological son of my wife, who is dying, and she is requesting to see him."

Betty's whole body began to shake. She had always known that this day might come. Cayden had heard the questions. He knew he'd been adopted. He'd always known, and it just hadn't mattered because he'd always been close to both his parents. The look on Cayden's face was one of alarm and surprise. Betty looked at her son for his lead. He was a grown man, and she knew it was his choice to make. Without really thinking, just reacting, he gave his mother a yes nod.

Betty confirmed Sven's inquiry and waited for his response. Sven went on to say that he wasn't the father, that Anna had her son before he had meant and married her. He apologized for the awkwardness of his position and suggested a mediator, specifically Sister Mary Kathleen. Cayden could call her and talk with her about whatever decision he made.

Both Betty and Cayden had sat in stunned silence after the phone call. It was Betty who spoke first. "I think we should let your father know, don't you?" she asked. Cayden nodded his head yes but remained silent. Betty knew her son well. She knew it would take him awhile to think about and process the information. He reached out and squeezed his mother's hand. Then he went outside and walked the trail down to the lake. Betty knew that she and Mike's relationship with Cayden was solid, but she was still concerned about the effect it might have Cayden. Only once in his twenty-two years had Cayden asked about his biological mother, and she had told him what she knew—that she was Aleut, that she only fifteen when he was born, that the father was listed as unknown, and that she had possibly miscarried a twin to Cayden. That seemed to satisfy him, and he had never brought the subject up again.

Cayden's mind was in whirl. His curiosity was aroused. What did she look like? Why did she give him away? What kind of person was she? The questions kept popping into his mind like arrows shot one after another at a target, the target being Cayden. It took a couple of hours before Cayden realized that if he was ever to have any peace, he needed to ask his questions and receive the answers from the only person who could give them, his biological mother. He went back to the only home he had ever known and the only mother he had ever loved. He draped his arm around her shoulders and called Sister Mary Kathleen.

CHAPTER 13

Sister Mary Kathleen was surprised when the phone call came only a day later after Sven's visit to Anna. The young man identified himself as Cayden Jennings, the biological son of Anna Hasson. He identified Sven as the individual who had contacted him, and he said that Sven suggested that she could act as a mediator between him and his biological mother. Sister Mary Kathleen knew how important it was to Anna to find and talk with her son, so she agreed, and they scheduled a meeting for early the next morning. Sister thought that would give her the evening to prepare Anna, and Cayden thought he'd still have plenty of time to load his parents' boat and make it out to Echo Cove before it got dark. Both would underestimate the dynamics of the meeting between mother and son.

Sister Mary Kathleen finally made it to Anna's hospital room just as the day's light turned to twilight, which was as dark as it would get during the summer months. It wasn't unusual to see children still playing outside, people walking the streets and surrounding trails or still talking with their neighbors at nine o'clock in the evening. Many folks had blackout shades because daylight came as early as five o'clock.

Anna was still awake, lying in her bed and watching the *Ed Sullivan Show* in black and white. Sister turned the TV down and said, "Anna, Sven found your son, and I've talked with him on the phone. He wants to come and see you tomorrow morning."

Anna's lips began to tremble. Her mouth formed an "O" shape, but no sound came out. She began vigorously shaking as if she had the chills, and she was unable to control her bladder. She finally blurted out, "What am I going to say to him?"

"The truth," Sister said firmly as she got her a clean grown and pad for her bed.

"But the truth is so ugly. He's going to hate me!" Anna exclaimed, sitting up and taking off her urine-soaked grown and putting a fresh one on.

While sliding the wet pad out from under Anna, Sister Mary Kathleen firmly said, "Really, Anna? Is it really all ugly? What about the fact that his mother is an honest-to-goodness Aleut princess? What about the fact that you've thought about him every single day of his life, prayed he had a good life, and grieved his loss in your life every day?"

Anna stopped shaking, and looking Sister Mary Kathleen straight in the eyes, she asked her if she would please stay by her side when her son arrived. Sister promised she would.

Cayden Jennings had a thing about being punctual and walked into the hospital at 9:00 a.m. sharp. The most attractive nun he had ever seen was standing in the lobby. The nursing nun was dressed in freshly starched white nursing garment. The flowing skirt ended at the middle of her ankles, only partially covering her spotless white nursing shoes. The habit that encompassed her face only succeeded in emphasizing her delicate features and emerald green eyes. There was just a smidgen of freckles on her lily white skin.

For just a moment, Cayden completely forgot he was there to meet his biological mother for the first time. Instantaneously, he thought, *I bet there's curly auburn red hair under that habit. No wonder nuns aren't allowed to look into mirrors.* He didn't know if that was really true or not, but he'd heard it somewhere. Cayden could feel his face flushing. The last thing he wanted to do was show any disrespect to a nun. He'd always admired them, and he thought that any woman who had the courage to devote her life to God must be very brave.

He reached out his hand to shake the nun's, introducing himself at the same time. "Good morning, Sister. I'm Cayden Jennings. I spoke with you on the phone yesterday."

Sister Mary Kathleen couldn't help but see a handsome young man standing in front of her. She judged him to be close to her age. He had a woody smell about him that reminded her of her father. His dark brown penetrating eyes were exactly like his biological mother Anna's. He was dressed casually in a plaid Pendleton wool shirt tucked into blue jeans. He seemed shy, and yet there was a presence about him that spoke of confidence, and he obviously was well mannered.

"Yes," she said, "and I'm Sister Mary Kathleen." She reached out to return his handshake.

The second their hands came together in a firm handshake, it was as if electricity passed between them. Both hurriedly pulled their hands away, flustered for what felt like a long time. In reality, it was only a few seconds.

Sister Mary Kathleen quickly gained her composer and ushered Cayden into the small waiting room. In her most professional manner, she gave him a brief summary on Anna's health condition. She told him that it was one of Anna's dying wishes to meet and talk with her son in person and that Anna had asked her to be in the room during the meeting.

Cayden was comforted knowing that Sister Mary Kathleen would be in the room. She brought a calmness with her that Cayden did not feel at this moment. He couldn't remember the last time he had been so rattled. Between the instant attraction he'd just had for a nun, a reality that was absolutely taboo in his world, and meeting the biological mother who had given him away at birth, he was having an anxiety attack. Cayden was a slow, methodical thinker, and everything was moving way too fast for him. What had his mother Betty taught him? "Breathe, Cayden. Deep, long breaths."

St. Ann's Hospital was a small hospital, and it only took a few moments to reach Anna Hasson's room. Wishing she hadn't made the promise to stay with Anna, Sister Mary Kathleen went into the room ahead of Cayden. He stood just outside the door, slowly taking deep breaths.

CHAPTER 14

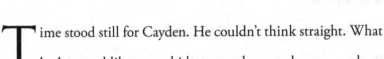

Time stood still for Cayden. He couldn't think straight. What had seemed like a good idea yesterday now became such an emotional roller-coaster ride. He was so confused.

Sister Mary Kathleen opened the door and motioned for him to come into the room. The first impression Cayden had was of a tiny woman propped up by pillows, her long black hair pulled back away from her face, which accentuated her high cheekbones. They were the same high cheekbones he himself had.

A small bronze hand reached toward him. He reached back, his much larger hand enveloping hers. He looked straight into her eyes and immediately saw himself—except her eyes were filled with sadness, and she looked like a small vulnerable child, not the mother of a twenty-two-year-old. Cayden's first instinct was to protect her as he would have protected any wounded creature.

"Hello, Cayden." Her voice was so soft and gentle that the hair on the back of his neck stood up. "Thank you for coming," Anna's heart was thundering in her ears, her stomach churning, and what little energy she had in her already weakened condition seemed to leave her. An awkward silence followed.

Sister Mary Kathleen stepped in. "Cayden, Anna would like to explain to you why she gave you up for adoption. Would you be okay with that?"

Cayden nodded his head yes, and for the first time, he spoke, "Yes, ma'am. I'm sorry. This is all happening so fast. It doesn't seem real."

Anna went backward in time—back to a happy child sitting in her warm Aleut home surrounded by her family members doting on her. The moment Cayden walked into the room, she saw both her mother and father in him. Handsome in a rugged sort of way and well-mannered, he stood taller than her father, but he had the same confident persona so prevalent in the chief of an Aleut village. She hadn't been prepared for the overwhelming motherly love she felt at seeing him. But she trusted it would be that love that would give her the courage to tell him the truth. She owed him that.

Cayden had pulled up a chair and was now sitting at the side of the bed, still holding one of Anna's hand. Anna blurted out, "You look like your grandfather, Cayden. My parents were pure-blooded

Aleut. That makes you half Aleut. Your grandfather and two uncles died in a drowning accident when I was fourteen years old. Your grandmother, Anuuk, died two and a half years later in one of the internment camps here in southeast Alaska. Do you have grandparents from your adoptive parents?"

"Yes," Cayden answered, "from both my mother and father." Cayden could see his biological mother flinch, so he quickly added, "I mean, Betty and Mike."

Anna immediately responded, "Cayden, it's okay to call them your mom and dad." Sister Mary Kathleen sat quietly in a corner of the room and nodded her head in agreement.

Weird, Cayden thought, *how the approval of both women helps take some of my anxiety away.*

He went on, "My parents, Mike and Betty, have their own logging company out at Echo Cove. After I graduated from high school, I went to work for my dad full-time. I guess it's a good place for me because I love nature—you know, the mountains, trees, and wild animals. I've lived in the same log cabin all my life out at Auke Bay."

At that moment one of the lay nurses briskly walked into the room, bent over, and whispered something in Sister Mary Kathleen's ear. She immediately stood up, apologized, and left the room. Sister

Mary Kathleen was grateful for the emergency. She had to get Cayden Jennings out of her head.

Mother and son were now alone. It wasn't uncomfortable, just different. Anna knew the moment had come. She sent a silent prayer up that he would be able to forgive her and then began, "When I was fifteen, I was kidnapped from my Atka village by two men in a fishing vessel." Anna swallowed hard. "I was on that vessel for about two weeks, and they raped me every day and every night. I only know their first names. One was Alex, and the other Jay. I never knew the name of the fishing vessel. Not that it matters. I've never seen them since the night they dropped me off at the small boat harbor dock here in Juneau."

"Anyway, I soon realized I was pregnant, but then I thought I'd had a miscarriage. I found out the night you were born that I'd miscarried your twin." She said another silent prayer. *Please, God. It would only hurt him to know I deliberately tried to get rid of him.*

"I was only fifteen years old, Cayden, and I had no way to support or take care of you. I thought if I gave you up for adoption, you'd have a better life, and I could forget all that happened on that boat. Maybe even return to my village where I'd been so happy. But then World War II happened. My village was burned to the ground. All the Aleut people were taken off their islands and put in internment camps here in southeast Alaska."

Anna hastily went on blocking her emotions in utter fear she would become hysterical. "I thought about you every single day, Cayden. All I had was the image of you as a newborn, and the image was burned into my brain. I had no control over it. It was like a ticker tape that would flash through my head, and I often felt as if a vise was clamping down on my heart, taking my breath away. You were my son, and regardless of how you were conceived, I loved you."

For a few moments, silence filled the room before Anna was able to ask, "Can you forgive me?" In Cayden's thoughts there was nothing to forgive, only a deep sorrow for the women who had given birth to him.

"There's nothing to forgive, Anna," Cayden firmly said.

Anna breathed a sigh of relief, and even though she really hadn't had anything to do with raising him, she felt proud as any mother would of this young man who was obviously good. "My Aleut name is Ahha, Cayden, and I would like it if that's what you called me."

"I have one more thing I think you should know. You have a half sister four years younger than you. I'd like to arrange for you to meet her—that is, if you want to." Anna lowered her eyes, afraid of what she might see in Cayden's face.

"Okay, Ahha." His smile filled the room, taking some of the tension out of it. Both mother and son began to relax

"In fact, I want to tell you all about your heritage because you have every reason to be proud of being Aleut. You have royal blood in your veins, Cayden, and I don't want the truth to die with me."

Anna's hand loosened its tight grip on Cayden's. She was struggling not to doze off in her weakened condition. She had just drained what little energy she had. Cayden sat with his mother for a few more moments like a sentinel guarding something precious.

Cayden had always known he was part Aleut just as he'd always known he had been adopted. It just had never seemed important. Sure, there had been those moments, especially in his teenage years, when he had felt that something was missing. That deep empty spot inside him remained a mystery. He had once talked about it to his mother, and she had told him that everyone felt the same way from time to time and that only God could fill it. Cayden didn't think of himself as religious, but he believed that there was a God and He was real. He followed the Catholic religion because that was how his parents raised him, but he had never gotten caught up in church doctrine or theology of any kind for that matter. Cayden felt the presence of God not necessarily in church but in the woods where the smell of pine dominated and the rustle of wildlife filled the air.

Then Anna revealed to him that he had been a twin. It was like a light went off in his head. All those times when from nowhere this strange feeling "of something missing" had overwhelmed him, and he had to physically shake the moment off time after time, accepting that it was a mystery he just didn't understand. Cayden knew his life had just changed forever. He was a twin. He had a half sister, and he was the son of an Aleut princess.

CHAPTER 15

Sven woke up in a cold sweat. Today was the day he was going to meet his daughter and see if she was willing to meet her mother. He'd seen her from a distance a few times, the last time a little more than a year ago. He found out she was a cheerleader for the Juneau-Douglas basketball team, and he'd gone to one of the games just to see her. He was careful though, and he kept his promise not to interfere in her life.

He'd called the adoptive parents and explained that her biological mother was dying and had requested to see her daughter. They'd agreed to meet him with their daughter for a late Saturday breakfast as long as Kimberly was agreeable. How was he going to explain to her why he had signed off on her adoption paperwork? "Well, it's like this, Kimberly. I wanted to be a fisherman more than I wanted you!" No, no, that wasn't true. He had wanted his daughter. It just hadn't been in his frame of reference to think he could provide any other way than fishing. For the second time in less than twenty-four hours, Sven went to his knees, praying for God to help him. How had he made such a mess out of his and Anna's life?

Kimberly Banks had always known she was adopted. She would graduate from high school in a month, and she would also turn eighteen years old. She was already enrolled in the University of Alaska in Fairbanks for the fall semester. She wanted to be a teacher, specifically a music teacher. She had two older sisters, one who worked as an Alaska Airlines stewardess and the other married with two children who only lived a couple of blocks away from her parents' home in Douglas.

Douglas Island is seventeen miles long and eight miles wide at its widest portion, and it's directly across the Gastineau Channel from downtown Juneau. Mount Jumbo (aka Mount Bradley) rises 3,337 feet above the town of Douglas and is part of the Tongass National Forest.

Gold was discovered in 1881, and by 1910, Douglas was the largest city in southeast Alaska because of the Treadwell Gold Mine, which produced $62 million in gold in 1917, but then the population declined. The Douglas Bridge was constructed in 1935, making transportation between Douglas and Juneau much easier. A fire in February 1937 took out six hundred homes of the seven hundred on the island, and Douglas became a bedroom community to Juneau. Within a couple of years the small Douglas High School would close and Juneau High School would become the Juneau-Douglas High School. It took a few years for the competitive spirit between Douglas youth and Juneau youth to dissipate. Some of that same competitiveness remained when Kimberly entered high school.

Today was the day Kimberly was going to meet her biological father and maybe even her mother. She had bounced in from school the day before to find both her parents sitting at the kitchen table. Both her parents worked for the state, and they were home early. Something was up.

They told her that her biological father had called and wanted to meet her because her mother was in St. Ann's Hospital, dying. Kimberly was stunned, not that he'd called but that they both lived in Juneau. "Have they always lived in Juneau?" she asked.

"Yes," both her parents answered at once.

Kimberly flashed a look of confusion. How could that be? How could she have not known? It wasn't like she'd spent a great deal of time thinking about her adoption. But she'd been curious and asked questions. In fact, she asked, "How come my skin is darker than my sister's?"

"Because your mother is Aleut," her mother answered.

"And my father?"

"I think he is Swedish."

"Is that why my eyes are blue?"

"Probably."

Over the years Kimberly had pretty much gotten the whole story. Her mother couldn't have any more children after Kimberly's two sister were born, and they had always wanted a big family. And one day out of the blue, a friend had asked her if she would be interested in adopting a three-month-old baby girl because the mother couldn't take care of her any longer. Her parents said yes and brought her home a day later, and six months later Kimberly was legally adopted. She was the baby of the family, and both her sisters and parents doted on her. Kimberly knew—but would never admit to it—that she was probably just a bit spoiled.

There were two restaurants in Douglas. There was Mike's Place, which was a high-end cocktail restaurant, but only Douglas folks as well as the Juneau population and tourists went there. If you were on one of the tour ships docked in Juneau, your tour wasn't complete without a shrimp dinner and cocktails from Mike's Place. The other restaurant was the Douglas Café, a local hangout for Douglas people that was famous for its breakfasts. It was the café where Sven was to meet Kimberly with her parents.

He got there early, and he was on his second cup of coffee when the three of them walked in together. Sven stood up as Kim's father, Brian, acknowledged him with a nod of his head. He had never seen his daughter so close up. He was a little startled at how much she looked like his father—the same blue eyes and ash blonde hair. Her hair was long falling to her shoulders with the tight curl on the ends so popular among young people. Her beauty took Sven's breath away. He stood there, feeling awkward.

It was Kimberly's mother, Elaine, who broke the silence. "Kim," she said gently, "this is your father, Sven Hasson."

Kimberly took a step forward and hugged her father. There were tears in his eyes. Her hair smelled like fresh apples and lemon. She looked directly into his eyes, and Sven saw the glassy tearing. He reached up and wiped at her eyes and whispered, "I've always loved you."

She sat with him in the booth, facing the parents she loved and respected across from her. Brian spoke, "Kimberly's mother, Elaine, and I want to thank you for the gift you gave us eighteen years ago. She has been nothing but a joy to our family." Kimberly smiled. She was so proud of her parents.

Kimberly was surprised at her own reaction at meeting her father. It felt natural to hug him. He lifted her chin and then gently wiped the beginning of her tears. She thought to herself, *Wow, I have two dads.*

The group ordered breakfast. Sven remarked at how much food this petite young lady could consume, and they'd all lovingly teased her about it. Halfway through the meal, Kimberly asked about her biological mother.

Sven had told them about Anna's illness and about the fact that she was dying and requesting to see Kimberly. He didn't want Kimberly to blame Anna for giving her up for adoption, so he took the responsibility on himself. "Kim, I want you to know your mother was frail after she had you. It was the beginning of fishing season, and I had to leave when you were only six weeks old." He explained that Ahha was her Aleut name before he continued, "Anna Ahha begged me not to leave, trying to tell me she didn't think she could take care of you without my help. I guess I just didn't really hear her, and well, it just didn't go well. So you were given to your parents. I hope you will forgive both of us. We only wanted what we thought would be best for you." Sven wasn't a big talker, and he thought it was the most he'd said at one time ... ever!

Kim looked at her parents, and they both nodded, giving her the go-ahead. They had talked it through the night before. "Sven," Kim began, "I've had a wonderful life. I have two sisters. I've lived in the same house in Douglas, and my parents are the best. I'm happy. And I'm happy to meet you, and I want to meet Anna. My folks have told me I'm part Aleut, and I really want to hear about it, find out about my birthright. My dad always says, 'It's all good, Kim. It's all good.' And that's how I feel."

Sven nodded his head in agreement, and they all decided that Kimberly would go with him to St. Ann's so she could meet her mother.

Sven used the pay phone right outside the café and called Sister Mary Kathleen to prepare Anna Ahha for meeting their daughter.

CHAPTER 16

S ister Mary Kathleen went straight to Anna's room after receiving the phone call from Sven. She was concerned for Anna because she was growing weaker each day, and the emotional energy from meeting both her son and daughter within twenty-four hours was taking its toll on her already weakened condition.

Anna's eyes were closed; however, she wasn't really sleeping, and the click-clack of Sister's wooden rosary beads alerted her.

"Good morning, Anna. Sven is on his way here with your daughter. Are you up to it?" Sister inquired.

"I'm so tired and excited at the same time," Anna answered. She was in a talkative mood. "What did you think of my son, Cayden? Isn't he wonderful?"

"Well … I only talked to him for a few minutes." Sister's voice trailed off, leaving a troublesome silence in the room.

Anna's penetrating dark eyes bored into Sister Mary Kathleen's green eyes. "What aren't you telling me? Is there something I should know about my son?" Anna rapidly fired the questions at sister.

Sister Mary Kathleen quickly gained her composure, and for the first time since she could remember, she lied. "No, nothing like that. I was just so focused on you and seeing you light up that I wasn't paying any attention to anything else." *God, forgive me*, she thought to herself. Sister Mary Kathleen couldn't even admit to herself the feelings that had arisen in her when meeting Cayden.

In less than twenty-four hours, Anna's world had changed. Both her children had come! *Thank You, God! Thank You. Thank You. Thank You.* "How do I look? Will you braid my hair for me? Can you prop me up with more pillows?"

Sister smiled, and while brushing and braiding Anna's hair, she said, "Do you see the mercy of God working for you, Anna?"

"I don't deserve it," Anna answered.

"None of us deserve it, Anna. That's why we have a Savior who died on a cross. No one has a monopoly on sin, Anna. Forgiveness is a gift, and like any gift, it needs to be received for it to work in our lives. Accepting His forgiveness, Anna, means you have to forgive yourself. Can you do that, Anna?"

"I don't know, Sister. I just don't know." Anna grew silent, overwhelmed with guilt and still not ready to let go of one last secret, the one sin she didn't think she could ever forgive herself for.

There was a knock on the open door, and when Anna looked up, there stood Sven with their daughter beside him. Sister Mary Kathleen quietly slipped out of the room without anyone noticing.

"Anna Ahha, this is our daughter, Kimberly Banks." Sven voice was shaky. Anna would have recognized her if she had run into her on the street. She looked like her father—round blue eyes with long dark eyelashes and soft, smooth skin that looked as if the sun had turned her a light golden brown. The only telltale signs of her Aleut heritage were her high cheekbones. The combination of Swedish and Aleut acted to make her appearance unusually beautiful.

"Kimberly, that's a pretty name," Anna said while thinking. "The first three months of your life, I called you Stephanie. Is your life good, Kimberly?"

Kimberly smiled a big happy smile. "It is. I graduate in just a few weeks. And I'm going to college in the fall. I want to be a music teacher." It all seemed surreal. She had so many feelings all going on at once that she couldn't think straight.

Anna reached out her hand and told Kimberly to sit down. Sven pulled a chair up next to the hospital bed and stood behind it with his hands-on Kimberly's shoulders.

The second Kimberly touched her mother's hand—so small and thin—a sadness came over her, and tears welled up in her eyes. When she looked up at her mother, Kimberly could see she was also furiously blinking, fighting back tears.

"Do you know you're half Aleut, Kimberly?" Anna asked.

"Yes, I've always known," Kimberly answered.

"How do you feel about it?"

"I've never given it much thought … until today. Sven told me on the way to the hospital that you were once an Aleut princess. Were you for real a princess?"

Anna had thought about this moment with her daughter, even fantasized about it, thinking they would fall into each other's arms without reservations. In reality, Anna was cautious, concerned with overwhelming her daughter, and she could see Kimberly was also holding her emotions back.

"Your grandfather, Kimberly, was chief of our village until he drowned in the sea, hunting whales, and that made me a princess."

"Why did you leave your village?" Kimberly asked.

"When I was fourteen years old and just a month shy of turning fifteen, I was kidnapped off the island I had been born and raised on, and I was brought to Juneau." Anna continued, "I was never able to return to my village because of World II. Kimberly, I gave you away because I loved you, and I wanted you to have a better life than I could offer you."

Kimberly had no idea how she felt or what to think. Being adopted and being part Aleut had never seemed that important to her ... until today. It was just too much to assimilate. She needed time, and she wanted to talk with her parents. She did not want to hurt these two people in any way, and she understood that there had been some kind of connection, something that bound them together.

Anna was wondering if it was time to tell Kimberly she had a half-brother. She looked at Sven, and he was shaking his head no. He still knew her so well that he could accurately guess what was on her mind. Anna thought, *All these years apart, and we still love each other as we did in the beginning. Oh, God, what have I done?*

It was Sven who spoke up. "How about I bring you back tomorrow, Kimberly, and give us all a breather. It's been an emotional day for all of us."

Anna was fighting not to close her eyes. She was so weak, so tired, and she nodded her head yes, almost in relief.

Much to Anna's surprise, Kimberly bent down and kissed her on her forehead, smiled, and whispered, "I'll see you tomorrow."

CHAPTER 17

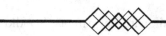

JC couldn't sleep. His shift as the short-order cook from five in the evening to about four in the morning, although busy, seemed to go on endlessly. Usually, he could get into his job, priding himself on his ability to quickly put out a good meal, even if half the people ordering weren't really hungry but rather were trying to sober up after a night of drinking. He still made the best hamburger in town.

He couldn't get Anna off his mind. No, he couldn't get Ahha out of his mind! The woman Anna had become a stranger to him. He'd accepted a long time back that he was doomed to always be in love with the Aleut princess Ahha. This Anna woman had hurt him so badly he had vowed to never get involved with a woman again. She'd asked him not to come after her, and he hadn't. As a matter of fact, it had been a little more than a year, as he remembered it, before he'd seen her after their little tryst. JC bitterly thought it had been almost fifteen years now, and he speculated that maybe Anna wanted to see him because they had grown up in the same village and had once cared deeply for each other.

It was early Sunday morning, and it was JC's one day off. He might as well get up and go see Anna in the hospital. He was definitely curious, even baffled by Anna's insistence to see him. Anna was dying, which was something JC really didn't want to think about. How had he become such an expert at pushing his feelings so far down inside of him that he now had a difficult time showing any kind of emotion? It was one of the reasons he didn't like to go to church anymore. It just brought to the surface too many painful memories, and since he never got off work before four on Sunday mornings, it was just easier to sleep until Sunday afternoon.

Maybe it was because Anna was dying, or maybe it was reading what had happened to his people to Sister Mary Kathleen. But the memories and the devastating pain that went with them came pouring into his consciousness. He went weak in the legs, and he sat down hard on the side of his hide-a-bed, allowing the feelings to wash over him.

The last year in his Atka village had not been a happy one, not just only for himself but all the hundred-plus villagers. It was as if with the disappearance of their Aleut princess, the very spirit of the whole tribe had disappeared with her.

It had been JC's father who had taken over as the leader of the village when Anuuk's husband and her two sons had drowned. Anuuk grief had lasted most of the winter. JC's father led the rest of the villagers to assist by bringing Anuuk and her daughter, Ahha, food each day, and he kept them in oil and wood for warmth throughout the harsh winter weather. Looking back on it now, JC realized now that was that winter he'd fallen in love with the Aleut princess. Ahha was barely fourteen years old then and was developing into a beautiful young woman. At nineteen years old, JC was easily mesmerized by her dark brown eyes, and she stirred in him feelings he had never before experienced.

Spring had come early that year, and with it, Anuuk's grief seemed to lessen. Both she and her daughter were out among the villagers more, and Anuuk was once again leading other women of the village in some of the old ways of the Aleut people.

And then the unthinkable happened. The Aleut princess disappeared. And Anuuk would go into a downhill spiral she would never recuperate from.

To make matters worse, the winter following the Aleut princess's disappearance was the hardest winter JC had ever seen in his nineteen years of life. Food was scarce, and there were days when most of the villagers went hungry. They had to kill most of the foxes for food. Their furs had subsidized them for the past few years. Fewer ships with supplies to trade docked in the harbor. Rumors of war dominated any conversations between the outside people and the Aleuts.

Because of foreign diseases, harsh treatment, and the disruption to their traditional society, the once proud Aleut race had gone from approximately twenty-five thousand Aleuts to about two thousand by World War II. As small as their population was, they believed in their country and considered themselves Americans.

Then on a windy winter day, one small fishing vessel with a small amount of food to trade docked and brought the news that Pearl Harbor had been bombed by the Japanese and that the United State was at war. There was talk among the Aleuts and soldiers stationed on various island that Japan would invade America via the Aleutian chain of islands. It left the Aleutian people restless and fearful of their future. JC now sat remembering the nights he along with the various elders of the village sat around a warm stove, speculating, debating, and sometimes downright fighting about what was going to happen if the Japanese invaded their islands. They usually concluded that the United States was too powerful, that the Aleuts would be protected, and that the invasion would never happen. For the next six months, there was a buildup of soldiers on all the island, which only succeeded in building the fear that lived inside JC all that winter and early spring.

Sure enough, six months later on a June morning, the Japanese touched down on American soil, taking hold of the remote islands Attu and Kiska. Taking Attu, the Japanese assailed an entire village. They held the Alaskan villagers for two months and eventually corralled all of the survivors into a freighter bound for Japan, including a six-year-old boy. He would end up one of the only twenty-five survivors who would return to a homeland torn apart by occupation and forced internments.

It all came flooding back to JC as if it had happened yesterday. On June 12, 1942, one of JC's friends spotted a Japanese scout plane flying over their village, and everyone in the village was sent to their fish camp some three miles away. JC remembered it well. Everyone was in a panic, grabbing what few personal items they could carry. He went to Anuuk and helped her put a few cherished personal items in a homemade leather bag. She was in shock, moving like a robot, and JC held her hand, guiding her along the slow march to the camp. They returned to their village later that night to find it consumed in flames. As a part of their "scorched earth" policy, American troops felt it was necessary to burn the Aleuts' homes rather than allow the Japanese to occupy them.

They were ushered aboard the *USAT Dlelarof.* Women were wailing, confused and frightened. JC could feel that same rage from that night so long ago welling up. It started in his feet, and like a hot fire, it traveled up his body until finally, he was sobbing so hard that his stomach was wrenching. He had pushed it down so far inside of him for so long. It left him physically weak. Shaking his head back and forth, he began to understand how he'd stayed so emotionally detached for so many years. Except for the Aleut princess Ahha the one thing he had never been unable to get out of his head. It was his Hercules heel, his weakness, and now Ahha was dying.

CHAPTER 18

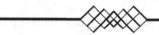

I t was only a four block walk, all uphill, from JC's efficiency apartment to St. Ann Hospital. He felt a little better after a long shower, but he still needed to clear his head, so he welcomed the walk. It was a cloudy day with a fine misty rain coming down. The rain didn't bother him. He was used to it, having lived with it all his life. People born and raised in Juneau didn't let the rain bother them. It rained 234 days out of the year. Newcomers often found it claustrophobic with both the rain and the high surrounding mountain encompassing the area.

Entering Anna's hospital room, JC's heart skipped a beat. She looked so vulnerable like a small child who had been abused and didn't know how to find the help she needed. JC bent down, brushed her hair away, kissed her forehead, and simply said, "Ahha."

Anna was emotionally drained from meeting both her son and daughter in the last twenty-four hours, and it took every ounce to strength she had to reach over and squeeze JCs' hand. She whispered in a hoarse voice, "Thank you for coming, John Charlie." Anna had always called him by his full name just as he had always called her by her Aleut name. It was indicative of the childhood bond that was still so strong between them.

Anna asked, "I've always wondered, John Charlie. Why didn't you return to Atka after the war. I mean, your parents returned, right?"

Confused, JC thought, *Was this what she wanted to know—why I never returned to Atka?*

For the first time in his life, JC admitted to another person the burden of guilt he'd carried the last few years. "Well, my mother died in the internment camps shortly after your mother did. At first, it was because I thought I could help my father best by keeping my job and sending him money. But then my father died within two years after he returned to Atka. I guess I behaved like a coward because I couldn't bear to see in person the sadness and devastation of our people."

"But I thought the Aleuts were given money from the government to rebuild their villages!" Anna exclaimed.

"Ahha," JC stated, "the amount they received worked out to only twelve dollars per Aleut. It is true that some of the soldiers helped build the village back after the war, but nothing has ever been the same since the war. The Aleut way that we knew as children, Ahha, is gone forever.

Something welled up in Ahha, the Aleut princess, an unrelenting passion she hadn't felt since the moment she had been taken off her Island. "But John Charlie, we need to fight for our people. We need to let the world know what happened to the Aleut people and who we really are. It's time the Aleut people stand up and be counted! Anna's feelings were so intense that for the moment all she felt was the deeply buried love for her people.

"I know, Ahha. I know," JC replied.

"It's too late for me, John Charlie, but not for you. Promise me, John Charlie! Promise me that you'll do whatever you have to do so our people are recognized for their courage and all they lost for their American patriotism." Ahha's penetrating dark eyes stared, piercing into his very soul. The Aleut princess was back, at least for the moment.

"I promise, Ahha. I promise!" JC said, looking her straight in the eyes. "Is that why you wanted to see me?" Then half-jokingly, he said, "To give me your royal command?"

Anna hesitated, biting at her bottom lip, and her eyes filled with tears before blurting out, "You have a daughter! Well … we have a daughter."

John Charlie couldn't process what this strange women Anna had just said to him. It was as if his ears heard the words, but the rest of his body left the room. He heard himself say, or at least he recognized it as his voice say, "What in the hell are you talking about!"

Anna had never heard JC curse, not once, not ever. She hadn't meant to blurt it out like she had. She'd prepared this little speech, slowly revealing the truth to him. She knew he would be hurt, even angry, and she'd thought she was prepared for his reaction. The pain and shock that flooded his face filled her with guilt, shame, and uncertainty.

Speaking slowly, Anna began to justify her actions. "You remember those few days I spent with you, John Charlie?

"Yes." He choked on his answer.

"I left, John Charlie, because you are like a brother to me, and that's how I love you. It wasn't fair to let you believe I loved you any differently than I always had. And I knew I would probably always be in love with Sven. You know we have never gotten divorced?" Heavy silence filled the room, and by the look on John Charlie's face, Anna could see he couldn't or wouldn't answer her, so she continued.

"When I dicovered I might be pregnant, I knew it was your child. I thought about telling you. I even prayed about it. Because

I'd already had a son and a daughter that I'd given away, I knew it would be too hard for me to keep your baby. Besides I'm not a good enough person to be a mother. I thought you'd never know, and so you'd never be hurt, but … well—"

JC jumped up from the chair and yelled, "But what, Anna? You gave my child away. You know I'd have taken her, loved her, cared for her. You knew, Anna. I know you did. Why? Why are you telling me fifteen years later?"

"John Charlie, I'm so sorry. I held her for a few minutes right after she was born. I loved her then, and I love her now. She looked like an Aleut baby, and she had your eyes. I just believed she deserved a better life than either you or I could give her. I had planned to never tell you, but I'm now dying. I know, John Charlie, that telling you is the right thing to do. I have to face my mistakes, my sins. All I can do is beg for your forgiveness."

JC stared hard at Anna. "Forgive you? I don't know if that's possible, Anna." He no longer saw Ahha, the Aleut princess. He saw Anna Hasson, the alcoholic who had given his child away. For the first time, JC now understood how Sven must have felt when she had given their daughter away.

"Do you have any idea where she might be, Anna?" JC asked, his anger coming through each word.

"No, it was a closed adoption. There's a sealed letter I wrote. It's with her adoption papers, and it identifies both of us. If she chooses to come looking for us after she turns eighteen years old, all the information is there for her to find us. Well ... to find you. I won't be here.

"How could she have been adopted without my consent, Anna?" JC demanded.

"Because I put down 'father unknown' on the birth certificate," Anna confessed.

JC couldn't stand to look at Anna any longer, and he turned on his heels and practically ran out of the room, almost knocking down Sven standing in the doorway. He slid past him without a word.

CHAPTER 19

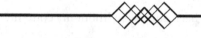

J C didn't notice it was still raining. He was in such emotional turmoil that he paid no attention to his surroundings. Hands in pockets, head down, all he saw was the wet gray cement sidewalk. JC thought, *Just like my life—wet gray cement.* How long had he been frozen in this time warp? Since the day he'd watched his village burn to the ground? All those pent-up emotions colliding with each other caused him to go weak in the knees. He sent up a silent prayer, *God help me.*

One block down the steep hill from St. Ann's Hospital was the Russian Orthodox church Saint Nicholes. It had the distinction of being the oldest, continual used Orthodox structure in southeast Alaska and was just letting out from its Sunday worship.

By 1880, Juneau was robust frontier. First came the prospector and the gold mines. Then came the solon keepers and their associates, all closely followed by the missionaries wagging their fingers.

St. Nicholes was built in 1893–94 and financed by the Orthodox Missionary Society. It was approved by his imperial majesty Tsar Alexander and established through the efforts and initiative of local Tlingit leaders. The story is told of the Tlingit leaders experiencing a common reoccurring dream. In their dream a short, white-bearded elderly man encouraged them to become Christian. When these leaders saw an icon of St. Nicholes, the wonder-worker, they all recognized him as the man in their dreams. Three days later these same leaders were baptized, and following their example, some seven hundred Tlinget came forward to embrace the orthodox faith.

Father Lavern was standing just outside the church doors, and like a magnet, JC was drawn toward him. Father Lavern recognized the man slowly walking toward him, but he'd forgotten his name. "Can I help you, my son?"

"I think God just led me to you," JC said in a voice he barely recognized.

Father Lavern could see the man was troubled. "Well, who am I to question God's leading. I'm sorry. What is your name again?"

"John Charlie, but most everyone calls me JC."

Father Lavern suddenly recognized him. He was a shy young man who seldom attended church because he worked on Sundays?

He remembered thinking he was personable but shy, an extremely closed person, and one not to display much emotion.

"That's right. I remember now. Would you like to step inside the church?"

JC nodded in reply, remembering it had been more than a year since he had stepped foot in any church. On top of everything else, now he felt guilty and thought he had to explain his poor church attendance.

"You see, Father, I work every Saturday night until four o'clock Sunday morning, and usually, I sleep until noon or so."

Father Lavern smiled. He was used to people trying to explain why they weren't in church every Sunday. "Well, I think that's between you and God, John Charlie. Tell me what else is on your mind. You look like you could use a friend."

"I just found out I have a fifteen-year-old daughter I never even knew existed." JC choked on his words. He felt his face growing hot. But with anger? Embarrassment? Shame? He wanted to put his fist though a wall, something that would hurt so bad physically he wouldn't feel the hurt inside of him.

"How did you find this out, John Charlie?" Father Lavern spoke with kindness, gently laying a hand on his shoulder.

"Her mother," JC answered. "She's dying in the hospital. I guess you could call it a deathbed confession. We were never married. She was from my village. Maybe you know her? Anna Hasson?" His bitterness spilled out in every word.

Father Lavern had to think for a minute. Anna Hasson? Yes, yes, he knew who she was. A tiny little thing of the Aleut race. She had trouble with hooch. He'd prayed with her several times over the years.

"Wasn't she married to someone named Sven?" Father Lavern asked.

"Yes." JC answered, and for the next hour, he told Father Lavern the story from the time they grew up in Atka to the present. He finished with explaining her Aleut name, Ahha, and how she'd been considered an Aleut princess.

Father Lavern felt deep sadness. He was well aware of the suffering the Aleut race had endured and were still enduring as well as the political fight to bring justice to these people. His immediate concern was for JC. "Can you forgive her, JC?" Father finally asked. And then went on before JC could answer. "You know, forgiveness is more about you than the person you're trying to forgive. As long as a person carries unforgiveness inside of them, it will control their life. Do you remember the Lord's Prayer? Forgive us our trespasses as we forgive those who trespass against us. That means, John Charlie, God forgives us as we forgive others."

JC was shaking his head back and forth, back and forth. "I can't. I just can't. Not now. I need some time to think." In that moment he had an epiphany. He became consciously aware that he'd never forgiven the American soldiers who had burnt his village or the American military who had put his people in the internment camps, where both Anna's and his mother and so many others from their village had died. Worse yet, he understood for the first time he had never forgiven God had been blaming Him for all of it, his whole miserable life.

"I'm not good at forgiveness, Father. I haven't forgiven anyone in my life, not even God." It was a clear and concise statement coming from the depth of John Charlie's soul.

Father Lavern nodded in understanding. "You, JC, and thousands of others, probably millions. We all want to believe we're in control of our lives and the lives of those we love, but we're not. It's an illusion. So when things go wrong, when we get hurt or those we care about get hurt, if we can't rationalize something or don't have someone to blame for it, we end up blaming God, and He becomes the enemy in our minds, souls, and spirits. And that, too, is an illusion, JC, for our God is a God of love."

JC knew Father Lavern was speaking the truth, or least he knew that was what he had been taught as a child growing up in the Russian Orthodox church. He needed some time. He felt like he was on a roller coaster, up and down, around and around, all those emotions he'd buried for so many years now surfacing.

"Father, could I come back and talk with you in couple of days? I just need some time," JC said.

"Certainly, but here. I want to give you this, and I'm just asking you to open it up and read it." With that, Father Lavern reached into the slot in the pew in front of them and handed him a well-worn small Bible.

CHAPTER 20

S ven was a little startled when JC slithered passed him in the doorway. He hadn't said a word, but his face was red hot with anger. Sven looked over at Anna Ahha. The head of the hospital bed was up, and she sat, silently crying.

"What's going on, Anna Ahha?" he asked as he approached the bed. She lifted her hand in the stop position that said, "Give me a minute." Sven sat down by her, took her closest hand in both of his, and waited.

Meanwhile sister was in the delivery room assisting in the birth of a baby. It was Sister Mary Kathleen's happiest moments. Sister Mary Kathleen was seventeen the first time she had seen the birth of a baby. A registered nurse showed her how to bathe and clean a baby immediately after birth. Holding and bathing a newborn, stirred feelings in her she had never before experienced. The miracle of birth had left her in awe and all those nurturing, motherly instincts rose to the surface. She flashbacked to her eight-year-old self and caring for her newborn baby brother, Patrick. Throughout the years that remained one of the highlights of her life. It also remained a conflict of emotions, a strange yearning to give birth to her own child while at the same time dedicating her life to God as a nun.

In the delivery room, Sister Mary Kathleen had just assisted in the delivery of her 212th birth. She kept count over the years, and each brought a smile to her face. The joy she felt with each birth was always negated by the powerful yearning to have her own child. *Mia culpa mia culpa. Mia maxim culpa.*

When Sister Mary Kathleen stepped out of the delivery room, her DON (director of nursing) was waiting for her. She informed Sister that there had been a slight ruckus in Anna Hasson's room and that Anna was requesting to see her.

Entering Anna's room, Sister Mary Kathleen could feel the tension. It was like a rubber band that had been stretched to its limit and was about to break. Sven's head was bowed, and he was squeezing one of Anna's hands so hard that his knuckles were ghostly white. Anna was sobbing.

"What happened?" Sister Mary Kathleen asked while going to the sink, wetting a washcloth, and soothing Anna by softly wiping her tears away.

"I'm not good enough. I've never been good enough," Anna matter-of-factly stated.

Seven could see the look of confusion on Sister Mary Kathleen's face, and shrugging his shoulders, he asked, "What are you talking about, Anna Ahha?"

"I'm not worthy of being a mother. My children deserved so much better them me. That's why I gave them away." Anna hesitated and added, "All three of them."

Sven immediately understood. So many incidents that had not made sense to him at the time fell into place like pieces of a puzzle—the many times JC had avoided him or acted distant and uncomfortable around him; the many time Anna had also avoided him, even cursing at him, telling him to leave her alone; JC running out of the room just a short while ago, obviously upset and angry. Sven looked Anna straight in the eyes and asked, "When, Anna?

Anna stared almost defiantly at Sven, avoiding looking at Sister, and whispered, "A little more than two years after you left Sven, I stayed with JC for about a week. I left because I still loved you, and I knew it wasn't fair to JC to stay with him. I got pregnant, and I kept it a secret from everyone. I had another little girl nine months later. JC didn't know he had a daughter until this morning. That's why he left here so angry." Anna gulped in a breath and went on.

"I've never deserved to have children, and I certainly never deserved to be a mother. I knew my children would have a better life without me in it. Now … well, now I don't have long to live, but I think my children have the right to know who they are and to have pride in their Aleut heritage. I'm sorry. I know how self-centered and selfish I've been, never considering how you or JC might feel about being fathers."

Sven thought about JC. He knew exactly how he must have felt. At least he had known he had had a daughter and had been able to watch her grow up from a distance. He made a resolution to himself to find and talk to JC as soon as possible. Sven blamed himself for the mess all their lives were in. If only he had given up fishing. If he'd just stayed with Anna like she had begged him to when their daughter was born. If, if, if. All their lives would have been so different. "Anna Ahha, it's not all your fault. I'm as much to blame as you are. I'm so sorry, so very, very sorry."

Anna began to cry again, and looking at Sister Mary Kathleen, she said, "Please, Sister, can you help us? We've made such a mess out of our lives?" Anna laid her head back on her pillows, physically, mentally, and spiritually exhausted, and she closed her stinging eyes.

Looking at the two broken human beings in front of her, Sister Mary Kathleen felt totally inadequate. Their sadness filled the room like a black cloud, and she couldn't remember ever feeling so sad herself except maybe when her mother had died. What on earth was she to say to a woman who only had days to live and the man who loved her and had left her? He had been bitter, angry, and unforgiving, and he hated himself for it.

Sister Mary Kathleen began slowly speaking. "Everyone feels unworthy and not good enough. It's a part of being a human being. Because the truth is we are all imperfect, and it's that very humanness that God loves. John 3:16-17 "For God so loved the world that he gave his only son, that whoever believes in him shall not perish but have eternal life. For God did not send his Son into the world to condemn the world, but to save the world through him.)

"Do you believe in eternal life, Sven and Anna?"

Sven answered first, "I hope there's eternal life, Sister."

Anna was quiet for a minute. "I've never thought much about it until the last few days," Anna said. "I think God has given me a second chance because He let me meet two of my children, and they both have had the kind of life I dreamed for them. Since I've been in the hospital. Yes, I believe in eternal life."

Sister Mary Kathleen could see how physically exhausted Anna was, and she was becoming weaker by the day. All the emotional upheaval was taking its toll on her. Sister Mary Kathleen was about to suggest that Anna get some rest before she saw any more visitors, and just at that moment, there was a light knock on the open hospital door. Cayden Jennings walked into the room.

Much to Sister Mary Kathleen's dismay, her whole body began to quiver on the inside. Only her hands were visibly shaking, which she immediately hid in the folds of the wide, long sleeves of her nun's habit.

CHAPTER 21

C ayden was grateful for the thirty- to forty-minute drive from St. Ann's Hospital in downtown Juneau to his home in the Auke Bay area. He needed time to put his thoughts together. Never in all of his life had he ever experienced so many different emotions all at the same time. He had met his biological mother for the first time and found out that his conception was due to his mother being rapped many times over. He instantly felt a sadness come over him like a dense gray fog enveloping him. She was so tiny, covered in sterile white, her long black hair flaying out around her. Cayden had instinctively wanted to protect her. He wanted to take the despair he saw in her dark brown eyes away. He had been a twin and made it into the world, but his twin had not. Cayden was humbly grateful for his life, for his adoptive parents, and now for his biological mother.

Cayden's earliest memories were of his mother, Betty, and her innate knack for knowing just what he needed in moments of fearful restlessness that always seemed ready to consume him. For as long as he could remember, she would take his, hand and they would walk together, winter, summer, spring, or fall. They had made their own trails around the woods surrounding Auke Bay. He had learned and grown to even need the peace that came with the pristine nature of the woods. He smiled to himself. His mother had used nature to teach him, and he had learned.

He had learned of the devil's club with its benign-looking leaves and stems covered with sharp spines. Once he had slipped on the wet forest floor with it various mosses, lichens, and plants and grabbed one to hinder his fall. It had taken his mother most of the evening to pull out the thin, piney slivers from his hands. His mother had distracted him from the pain by teaching him of the devil's club medicinal purpose. She told him how it was often dubbed as aspirin by the Tlingits and used for coughs, colds, stomach ulcers, even tuberculosis and hypoglycemia. Later she made him write a paper about it.

He had learned of the Mendenhall Glacier fireweed, named for its ability to quickly regenerate and for its light purple bloom blanketing the meadows and signaling the end of summer. And he learned about the For-Get-Me-Nots, the Alaska state flower, which grows wild, their small blue flower signaling that summer is in full bloom. He also learned of the pussy willow with their soft gray fuzzy bud that grew as large as a man's thumb and the Alaska cotton with is golden fluffy ball that sways in the wind like golden clouds swimming across the fields. Cayden's mother had saved several of the Alaska cotton bouquets he picked, pressed them in the family Bible, arranged them on black velvet, framed them in a large frame, and hung the picture over their stone fireplace.

How many bouquets had he picked for his mother over the years? Their home had always been filled with them and with the love that went with them. Cayden was profoundly thankful for his adoptive mother. The warmth of her love flowed through him, and for the first time, he understood just how smart she was. She'd taken a baby with fetal alcohol syndrome and nurtured him into a whole and healthy man.

Thirty minutes into Cayden's drive home, he felt so grateful— grateful for his life, grateful for having the opportunity to meet his biological mother, but most of all, grateful for his adoptive parents.

Betty Jennings was waiting on the front porch for her son when he pulled up into the driveway in their Chevrolet truck. Betty had always disliked the army green color, but Mike and Cayden had outvoted her. She smiled to herself. Cayden was so much like his father that no one would ever guess Mike wasn't his biological father.

Cayden ambled up the four stairs to the front porch and gave his mother a snuggly hug, holding her longer than usual. Then he said in a husky voice, "Thank you, Mom, for all you've done for me. I love you." Betty had loved him from the first moment she'd held him in the hospital nursery, and she was confident their mother-son relationship was solid. Still, a warm glow spread through when she heard his words now.

"How did it go?" she asked.

"Mom, she's the saddest person I've ever seen. Her name is Anna, but she asked me to call her by her Aleut name, Ahha." Cayden proceeded to tell her the rest of her story, how she'd been stolen from her island and had been raped by two men, one of them being his biological father. He told her all of it and finished by telling her he had a half-sister he hoped to meet soon, hopefully before Ahha died.

Betty couldn't be prouder of her son. He had become a man of honor, and she was eternally grateful that he was in her life. "I'd like to meet her, Son, and thank her for the gift of your life. I'd like to write a note asking her for the honor of meeting her. Would you give it to her?"

"I'll take it to her, Mom. I'm going back tomorrow to see her. I want to stay in town and visit with her. I'm told she only has weeks to live. Will that be okay with Dad? I know he was counting on me to help him get the logging season started."

Betty replied, "I've already spoken with your dad, and we thought this might happen. So yes, we will support you in any decisions you make regarding your biological mother. Your dad is coming in tonight from the logging camp, and he and I will fly back out tomorrow. We'll keep the same schedule we always have and be on the two-way radio every night at six."

Cayden got a lump in his throat and choked out, "Thanks, Mom. I'm going to take one of my 'clear my head and heart' walks before Dad gets here."

Betty smiled. How old had he been—maybe four or five—when she had taught him how nature could ground a person?

It had taken him less than a half an hour to put the situation with his biological mother, Ahha, into perspective. He sighed. Meeting Sister Mary Kathleen was another matter. They had connected in a way he had never connected with any other living thing.

He remembered a story his mother had told him on one of their many walks. Betty had praised him, telling him how well he connected with all the living things in the woods. Cayden was only about eight years old and had asked her what it meant to connect with something. They sat down under the large pine and spruce trees on a soft cushion of pine needles. Some of the tops of the spruce trees were bare, a sign that there had been porcupine activity when the tree was young.

Betty began, "You know who my good friend Dottie is?" Cayden nodded. "Well, as you know, Dottie is one of my closest friends, and this happened a long time ago before you were even born. Dottie's mother got very sick and died. I really didn't know Dottie's mother very well, but I went to her funeral out of respect and love for my good friend. I don't remember all the things the minister said about Dottie's mother, with one exception. He said Hattie had loved butterflies and had pictures of them all over her house. So whenever you see a monarch butterfly, remember Hattie. That was more than thirty ago, Cayden, and to this day whenever I see a monarch butterfly, an image of Hattie's pops into my head. That's a connection, Son."

"Mom," he said now, "do you still think of Dottie's mother Hattie when you see a monarch butterfly?

"Well, yes, I do. What caused you to remember that?" Betty said with a quizzical look on her face.

Cayden stumbled over his answer because it was only partially the truth. It was a lie by omission, something both his parents had taught him. "A lie of any kind was a betrayal to others, to yourself, and to God."

"Well, I *connected* with my biological mother." He lowered his eyes, looking at his feet so as not to see his mother's piercing look, which still caused him to squirm even as a grown man.

Cayden shook his head, feeling a little crazy. Sister Mary Kathleen was a nun, and all he could see in his mind eyes was her beautiful face with her freckles and her emerald green eyes and her long chestnut brown eyelashes.

Betty Jennings knew there was something her son wasn't telling her, but she respected the space he needed. She only hoped it wasn't anything that would cause him grief.

CHAPTER 22

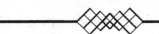

Something was wrong. He sensed it after only taking one hesitant step into his mother's hospital room. Sister Mary Kathleen stood on one side of his mother's bed and a man he didn't recognize and wasn't sure who he was stood on the other side. "Is it okay if I come in?" Cayden asked.

Sister Mary Kathleen turned to look at him. She had the strangest look on her face. Anna was tugging on the sleeve of her habit and said, "Let him come in. He might as well hear all of the truth."

Sister quickly turned back to face Anna and said, "Anna, you're very weak. Maybe you should get some rest, and we can all come back later."

"No, no, I want to get this over with. I want my son to know the truth!" Anna exclaimed.

Sven walked around the bed and held out his hand for Cayden to shake. "I'm Sven. I'm married to your mother, and I'm the father of one of your sisters." Cayden absently shook his hand, and at the same time, he remembered that his father had told him to always shake hands firmly because it was a sign of an honest man. His mind was scrambling to understand "one of his sisters."

Sister continued to hold Anna's hand, not taking her eyes off Anna. Cayden stood at the foot of the bed, gazing at his mother. He could tell she'd been crying. Her eyes were swollen and red. But she looked him straight in his eyes, their darkness penetrating, which left him feeling exposed in her presence. She spoke in a quiet but firm voice.

"You have two sisters, Cayden. One is Sven's daughter, who just turned eighteen. The other sister is younger, almost fifteen, and her father is a man I've known since I was a little girl. We grew up in the same village. This man didn't know she existed until today, and I don't think he's ever going to forgive me. I don't even know if I can forgive myself. I gave my three children away, and I've suffered for that every day of my life."

Cayden had so many questions, and he looked at the other two people in the room for some kind of guidance. He tried to get Sister Mary Kathleen's attention, but she quickly lowered her eyes. He looked at Sven and saw a man so consumed in his own sorrow that there wasn't any way he could reach out to another person. Cayden was on his own. The moment was strictly between him and his mother.

"I'd like to meet them, Ahha. Is that possible?" His tone was gentle as he waited patiently for her answer. Ahha never took her eyes off Cayden, her oldest child, her only son. She had to make it right.

Anna Ahha finally spoke, "Sven's and my daughter lives in Douglas, and she's graduating from Juneau-Douglas High School next month. She wants to meet you. I don't know where your second sister is. It was a closed adoption. You can write her a letter if you like and have social services put it in her file. You can make a request that you'd like to meet her. The file is open to her when she turns eighteen." Anna Ahha was too weak to go on. She lay her head back on one of the many pillows and closed her eyes.

The dark, heavy silence in the room seemed to consume all four people. It was Cayden who finally broke the silence.

"I have a thank-you letter with me from my adoptive mother. Could I read it to you, Ahha?" Anna Ahha kept her eyes shut but nodded.

Both Sven and Sister Mary Kathleen asked if they should leave. It was Anna Ahha who emphatically said, "No, please stay. No more secrets!"

Cayden began to read.

Dear Ahha,

Cayden tells me you prefer being called by your Aleut name, Ahha, so that is what I'll call you. He also tells me you are of royal blood and are also an Aleut princess. This does not surprise me, as I've always known that Cayden was and is an exceptional human being.

I pray you believe that "all things work together for good for those who love God," that there is a reason for everything, and that God's will for each of our lives is being played out in this process we call life.

There are no words sufficient enough to thank you for the life of our son, Cayden Michael Jennings. The gift of his life has not only blessed my husband and me, but the impact of his presence also changed both of us, making us better people. I know his presence in your life now will help to heal the grief you've carried inside of you all these years and bring you comfort as you see what an honorable man he has become. Yes, we nurtured him, but you, Ahha, gave him life. And no one can take that away from you.

I can't even imagine how terrified you must have been at such a young age to be kidnapped from the village where you were loved and honored and brought to a strange place, and then to find out you were pregnant. I am in awe of the courage you demonstrated in giving birth to Cayden and giving him a chance at life.

I am a nurse and work part-time at St. Ann's Hospital and had the honor of holding Cayden when he was less than twenty-four hours old. I was only told that his biological mother was Aleut, that his father was unknown, and that you were too young to care for him. My heart prayed that someday I would meet you and I would be able to thank you for his life in person.

If it is too painful for you to meet me, I will understand. Meanwhile, I will keep you in my daily prayers. To God be the glory.

Sincerely,
Betty Jennings

Anna Ahha had kept her eyes closed while Cayden was reading Betty's letter, and her hot, salty tears slid down the sides of her face, cleansing her as never before. Only Anna Ahha knew what a true miracle Cayden's birth had been. He'd been born both physically and mentally whole, and that only emphasized the miracle of his birth even more. For the first time in her painful life, Anna Ahha could see the hand of God in her life, and it was that her son was a *bigger* part of whatever God's plan was for all of their lives. The terror of Cayden's conception was still with her like a lump of coal in the pit of her stomach. Yes, she'd suffered, some of it not of her doing and some of it because of her own self-destructive behaviors and her addiction to hooch. But none of it mattered anymore. She opened her eyes and looked at her son. Even if she'd had the power, she knew she'd change nothing, for to change it in any way would change who Cayden was.

"I do want to meet both your parents, Cayden. Please let them know," Anna said.

Cayden was more than just embarrassed by his mother Betty's letter. He didn't really see himself all that wonderful. He wondered what his adoptive mother would think if she knew he was more than just a little attracted to a nun. He didn't need this complication in his life. He felt like he was somehow being disrespectful to her. He just had to shake it off.

Hesitantly, he said, "Well, my mother has always been biased when it came to me. Believe me when I tell you that I'm just an average guy. Perfectly imperfect, as I think all human beings are."

Anna Ahha smiled. It was the first-time Cayden had seen her smile. Her smile filled the room, and her answer made both Sister Mary Kathleen and Sven also smile.

"So not only are you a good person, but you're humble too! Now you have two mothers who think you're wonderful!" Anna was teasing him, and but half of her believed he really was perfect.

Cayden shuffled his feet and shrugged his shoulders, changing the subject. "So when can I meet my sister?"

Sister Mary Kathleen answered him. "Well, I think Anna needs some rest, and we're going to give her a blood transfusion this afternoon. How would it be if you all come back this evening?" She didn't look at Cayden but at Sven for his approval, and he nodded agreement.

Cayden wondered why Sister Mary Kathleen never directly looked at him. Did she suspect his attraction to her? Had he offended her in some way? He asked, "What time this evening?"

Sister simply said, "Seven." Then she proceeded to quickly leave the room without another word. She had to get out of there before everyone would see on her face she thought Cayden Jennings was one of the finest human beings she'd ever known.

CHAPTER 23

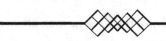

O utside the hospital Sven and Cayden stood talking for a few minutes. Sven assured Cayden that his sister was anxious to meet him and that she would be with him that evening. Both of them realized they had seen each other around several times, and in fact, Sven had one time brought the Blue Lady into Echo Cove Logging Camp during a storm. At the time Sven had suspected that Cayden possibly was Anna's son. Cayden, however, had no idea that Sven was the man who was married to his biological mother. At that point in time Cayden had given very little thought to knowing or meeting his biological mother. There was a natural curiosity, but his adopted mother filled all his needs so well that it just wasn't a priority. At the hospital, they had shaken hands and parted, both looking forward to the evening while at the same time concerned for Anna Ahha. They hoped the blood transfusion would give her the physical and emotional strength it would take to have two of her children together for the first time.

Sven was on mission. He was determined to find JC. He had no idea where he might be on a Sunday afternoon. He knew the bar and grill where JC worked was closed on Sundays, and as Sven suspected, it was the only day of the week he took off. Sven wondered if he'd ever taken a vacation. In Sven's opinion, JC was more of a workaholic than he was.

After arriving at JC's apartment, Sven knocked on the door for at least five minutes. JC was either not answering, or he wasn't home. Sven had no idea where he might go. Maybe he was just walking around the scenic downtown area of Juneau. Distracted by the traumatic events of the last few days, Sven descended the two-story cement stairwell slowly. He was physically weary and emotionally overwhelmed. The only thought going around and around in his head like a broken record was, *What a mess, the three of us have made out of our lives.* It felt like a ton of bricks was on his shoulders, and Sven blamed himself. If only he had given up fishing, their lives would have been so much different, so much better. He wanted—no, he needed—to find JC and tell him how sorry he was.

The bottom stairs exit door opened just as Sven was coming down the last flight of stairs. He hoped it was JC returning. The man entering the stairwell was familiar, but it wasn't JC. Sven recognized him. It was the owner of the two-story building and the bar and grill where JC worked.

Sven introduced himself and asked him if he would by any chance know where JC might be as he had something important to tell him. The owner was a well-known and highly respected Asian man around the Juneau area named Mr. Chang. Mr. Chang knew who Sven was and also knew he was an acquaintance of JC. "As a matter of fact," Mr. Chang replied, "I just lent him my car. He said he was going to take a drive out to the Shrine of St. Theresa." Sven thanked him and headed for his sister's home on Star Hill, where he kept his 1949 light blue Chevy truck, which was pretty beat up but still running.

The Shrine of St. Theresa is twenty-two miles north of downtown Juneau or "out the road" as lifelong residents referred to anything past the Juneau-Douglas High School on the Glacier Highway, which was a two-lane highway that ended only another few miles past the shrine at Eagle River. Talk of a new highway that would extend as far as Echo Cove (where Cayden's father's logging operation was) had been circulating for years, but no one seemed to know when construction might even start because of budgeting issues in the newly founded state.

Sven had been to the Shrine many times. It was one of his mother's favorite places, and in the summertime they sometimes attended Mass there. The shrine is located in the Tongass National Forest, where in 1945 a special act of the US Congress secured the sale of 46.61 acres from the government to the Catholic bishop of Alaska.

The Shrine of St. Theresa is named after St. Theresa of Lisieux, the patron saint of Alaska. Known for her "little way" in her autobiography, *The Story of a Soul*, she wrote that what really mattered in life was not our great deeds but our great love.

The crossway like a small bridge to the actual shrine island where the churchsets was built out of beach stone, was actually built as early as 1934. The island was completely surrounded by the ocean waters only when the tide was high. A two-story-high marble crucifix stands to the left on a small hill outside the heavy wooden doors to the entrance of the stone church. The twelve stations of the cross circumvent the Columbarium niches, and large pine trees create a green canopy over the spiritual holy place.

Sven hadn't been out to the shrine in years. He remembered the last time, the only time he had taken Anna Ahha. She was pregnant with their child, and they had a happy, wonderful day together. He could still see her tiny frame as if it were yesterday, her standing below the marble crucifix, looking up at the intricate carved face of Christ in absolute awe. If only he could have captured that moment, held onto it, and made it a part of their lives. Instead all he had now was a memory that brought him to his knees. He had let the possibility slip through his fingers. *Stupid. Just plain stupid*, he thought to himself.

It was a Sunday afternoon, and there were several cars parked in the small parking spot and several small groups of people strolling around the property. Instinctively, Sven headed for the stone church. When he opened the door, he spotted JC sitting alone in one of the front pews. He slid in next to him, not saying a word. JC acknowledged his presence by a quick nod of his head. These were the two men who loved the Aleut princess but had lost her to her addiction. They sat in silence, watching the red glow from the many lit candles. So many prayer, so many needs, so much pain, the lights slowing burning with the hope that a merciful, forgiving God would see them.

It was JC who got up first. He walked toward the votive candles in their scarlet red containers, pulled some change out of his pocket, deposited into the donations box, and lit a candle. Sven followed suit a few minutes later. Sven spoke first, "For Anna Ahha, so that she will have peace."

JC husky voice whispered back, "For Ahha, so that she will have peace and that I find my daughter."

JC looked Sven in the eyes and said, "I thought you might be here to slug me. I guess you know now why I've been so distant with you these last fifteen years. I've loved her since she was a little girl. You know, Sven, she was truly our village's princess. Wherever she went, she brought a sense of meaning and joy to the Aleut people. After she was taken, it was as though the very spirit of our people was gone. And then World War II happened, and none of us were ever the same again. I've been able all these years to bury my feelings. I suppose I'm basically a coward, sticking my head in the sand like an ostrich and taking the path of least resistance. She only spent five days with me, Sven, and for those five days, I hoped we could recapture the spirit and freedom we had once had when we lived in the village. But then she was gone, and I just went back into my shell. Now I find out I have a daughter by her, and I can't see her or even find out where she is." JC swallowed hard, fighting back his anger and fear. "Not that I deserve anything better." His voice trailed off.

"I'm sorry, JC. Really sorry." Sven's voice was firm as he went on. "If I hadn't been so selfish, so self-centered, I would have given up fishing, and all our lives would have been different. If only I'd stayed with Anna Ahha and helped her raise our daughter. Do you know she begged me to stay and not go out fishing? And all I did was tell her to grow up and quit acting like a child. When I came in a couple of months later, she'd given our daughter away, and I ended up signing the adoption papers because I didn't think I could take care of her. I was so angry and hurt. I thought that I could never, that I would never forgive her. Now she's dying, and I've wasted all those years."

JC was shaking his head in amazement. Why was Sven apologizing to him? He had never understood until today Sven's anger when Anna Ahha had given their daughter away. JC had even judged him as too hard on Anna Ahha, even cruel. He had known Anna Ahha's love for Sven and consciously pushed it deep down into that dark place in his soul where he had tried to hide from anything and everything he found painful.

Out loud, he said, "Sven, you don't owe me any apologies. I should apologize to you. I've been able all these years to keep my real feelings buried. I guess the worse lies we tell are the lies we tell ourselves. Finding out today I, too, have a daughter, one whom I may never see or know, has shattered all the delusions I've lived with since the day I watched my village burn." JC bowed his head, barely able to control the tears threatening to consume him and take away any control he might have. Aleut men didn't cry. It was a sign of the worse kind weakness, the inability to protect their family and village.

Sven spoke quietly. "JC, I've sinned in thought, word, and deed, and those sins have brought us to this place today."

"What do you mean in thought?" JC asked. I was always told that *thought* was simply temptation, and as long as a person didn't act on it—well, temptation in itself isn't a sin.

"I know that, JC. I'm talking about the kind of thoughts that control you, like—well, like the thoughts of anger I entertained all these years for Anna Ahha." It was a confession of sorts for Sven to admit to someone else all the negative feelings he'd been carrying around for the past seventeen years.

JC responded, "Well, at least you had feelings. Because what I've just realized today is that by burying the feelings that brought me pain and sadness, I also lost the happy and good feelings. It's pretty sad Sven when your biggest source of joy is making a good hamburger for someone. You chose to be angry. I chose to feel nothing at all."

Both men sat in silence, watching the votive candles they had just lit burn. In their own ways, each was feeling the pain that came with letting the light back into their spirits.

CHAPTER 24

S ister Mary Kathleen, her arms full from carrying a box filled with Anna Hasson's medical records, kicked the bottom of her office door closed behind her. After she put the box on her desk, she sat down, a little out of breath from carrying the heavy file from the storage area in the basement of the hospital. She'd realized with the events of the last two days how little she actually knew about Anna Hasson. She wished Anna's records were already on microfilm; however, it was an ongoing project, and the clerks working on the project had only gotten as far as the letter *E*.

Microfilming had actually been around since the late 1800s but was treated like a novelty until in 1928 when Eastman Kodak bought the first practical use of commercial microfilming from a New York City banker George McCarthy. He held a patent on his check-o-graph machine designed to make permanent film copies of all bank records.

It wasn't until World War II when the military used microfilming extensively for espionage and regular military mail that the value of it became common knowledge. The war brought the threat of destruction to the records of civilization. This threat added to the urgency for microfilming of all important records. St. Ann's Hospital was a small hospital in comparison to the large metropolitan hospitals around the country, so it was one of the last to implement the program.

Besides, Sister Mary Kathleen thought to herself, a new and bigger hospital was in the makings, and St. Ann's would soon go into the Alaska history books.

Sister Mary Kathleen went to the first files some twenty-two years later. Some of it was handwritten and fading, but she knew instantly it was the birth of Anna's son, Cayden. She immediately noted she was only two years older than Cayden. The handwritten note by the nurse on duty at the time stated Anna had been brought into the hospital already in hard labor. In the nurse's judgment, she was hysterical, and there was the heavy smell of alcohol on her breath. The staff had barely enough time to prep her for delivery, and she gave birth to a six-pound-eight-ounce perfect baby boy within forty minutes of her arrival at the emergency entrance. Anna had asked to be "put out" because she did not want to see the baby. It had also been documented that Anna had two separate placentas, which indicated she had miscarried a twin. There was an added note at the end of the summary that read, "See Baby Boy, unknown name, with date of birth, on file for more information."

Tears sprang to Sister Mary Kathleen's eyes. *Oh, Cayden*, she thought, *I pray you never know the way you came into this world.* She tried to shake the sad feelings off, forcing herself to focus on her patient, Anna.

She sat reading the file for more than an hour. She knew that the liver was the largest internal organ in the body and that it was very powerful. It not only protected all the tissues from damage by filtering out toxins from the bloodstream, but it could also repair its own damaged tissue if caught in time. It was all there in Anna's file. The symptoms were in chronological order and not diagnosed correctly until it was too late.

A few years after Cayden's birth, she had arrived at the hospital with her husband, Sven Hasson, and given birth to a healthy baby girl. She had been the typical newborn baby mother. It was even on record that she had been shown how to nurse the child, which she was considering.

One year later she'd arrived at the emergency room intoxicated and complaining of stomach pain. The nurse described the abdominal swelling as "a potbelly." The doctor on duty suspected possible ascites, where liver malfunction led to an imbalance of proteins and other fluids would build up. He suggested further testing, but Anna would have no part of it. She left the hospital the next morning against medical advice.

The year after that, Anna showed up in the emergency room in labor and gave birth to a baby girl. It was recorded she held the baby the day after her birth, but on the birth certificate, she asserted that the father was unknown and gave the baby up for adoption through social services. She'd had an excessive amount of bruising, which she claimed came from falling. Sister Mary Kathleen realized that had her liver disease been caught at that time, Anna would possibly not be dying now. She now knew that Anna's self-destructive behavior had started when she had been kidnapped and raped. Sister Mary Kathleen's heart ached for Cayden, and she wondered how he seemed to handle the truth of his conception in such a mature manner. "Dear God," she prayed silently, "please help me." Why was this man touching something so deep inside her, something that she had never known was there? Then she had another thought, one that frightened her so badly she could feel the bile rising up in her throat. What if it wasn't God? What if it was something evil? Sister Mary Kathleen knew there was no such thing as a red-hooded devil with a pitchfork. She'd seen enough life to know evil was real, but not like that.

Sister continued to read the rest of Anna Hasson's medical records. She had shown up at the hospital emergency room at least once a year, usually intoxicated and always with legitimate complaints ranging from sudden weight loss to nausea to abdominal pain in her upper right abdomen, sometime described by Anna as throbbing pain like a toothache and sometimes as stabbing pain that came and went but doubled her over.

The last five years were shown in typed records as documented by Sister Mary Kathleen herself. The first time Sister had seen Anna, the drunk woman was carried in by a man who never identified himself and just left her in the emergency hallway, vomiting. Sister found her there, reeking of alcohol, and she managed to talk her into being admitted. At that time Anna had stayed in the hospital for three days and had finally been diagnosed with cirrhosis of the liver. Sister Mary Kathleen had spent many hours with her those three days, talking to her about God and quitting drinking, encouraging her to live a healthier lifestyle, and she told Anna how the liver was the only organ that could heal itself. In the early morning on the fourth day, Sister entered her room only to find that once again Anna had left without medical approval. She tried to find her, but the address Anna had given was that of her cousin Linda's. And it turned out, the phone number she'd given them had been disconnected.

It was a few more years before Sister Mary Kathleen saw Anna. Again, she showed up in the emergency room late at night and intoxicated. That time she had jaundice, which was caused by an inability to eliminate waste from the body, causing a pigment called bilirubin to build up in the bloodstream and to turn skin and eyes yellowish. That time Anna had stayed in the hospital for almost a week. Sister Mary Kathleen had spent many hours with her that week and warned her that if she didn't quit drinking and start eating healthily, she was going die. Anna had been a little more open about beliefs in God. She'd even mentioned then that she'd had a son that she'd given up for adoption. She had even given Sister a phone number she could call and leave a message. Sister Mary Kathleen had called and left messages for Anna to call her several times after she left the hospital, but Anna never returned the calls.

Now Anna was dying. The blood transfusion would help clean the excess waste in her bloodstream, but it was only a temporary fix.

Sister Mary Kathleen put the files in order and back in the box. She sat quietly at her desk, her eyes closed. She had always been a strong person physically, mentally, and spirituality. Her faith had always sustained her. But on this late Sunday afternoon, she was bone-weary and confused. She drifted into that twilight place of half asleep and half awake, when she heard her father's voice as clear as if he was standing in the room next to her. "Desiree Ellen Lajour, what are you thinking?"

CHAPTER 25

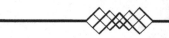

As the administrator of St. Ann's Hospital, it was Sister Mary Kathleen's responsibility to maintain a viable blood bank that was available at all times. Although a national blood bank had been founded a few years earlier in 1956, because of Juneau's isolation from the continental United States, it was necessary to rely on local donations with a list of individual who could and would give blood at a moment's notice, not only in an emergency but specifically for the rarer types of blood. In Anna's case, she was a universal O blood type, and there was more than enough in cold storage to meet Anna's needs. Sister knew it wouldn't save Anna's life, but it would keep her more comfortable during the few weeks she had to live. Sister knew the history of blood transfusions and wondered how many of millions of lives had been saved because of the technology.

Blood transfusions had been around since 1628 when the physician William Harvey discovered circulation of the blood.

It wasn't until 1665, however, when the first recorded successful transfusion occurred in England. Physician Richard Lower kept a dog alive by transfusion of blood from other dogs.

Skip a couple of hundred years, and in 1818, British obstetrician James Blundell performed the first successful transfusion of human blood to a patient for treatment of postpartum hemorrhage. Then in 1901, Karl Landsteiner and Austrian physicians discovered the three human blood groups, and by 1907, Reuben O'Herberg performed the first blood transfusion using blood type and cross-matching.

Anna was anemic, and she had many of the symptoms for internal bleeding—fatigue. elevated heartbeat, headaches, dizziness, leg cramps, anxiety, and numbness in her hands and feet.

It takes about four hours to finish a transfusion for a pint of blood. Sister Mary Kathleen pulled her small pocket watch out of the folds of her long white skirt. She must have dozed off because it had been more than four hours. She quickly stood up and put her hand on the desk to steady herself. She told herself she would soon—maybe tonight—get some badly needed sleep. She rationalized hearing her father's voice as a delusion. She figured it was nothing more than the result of skipping a meal in her busy day and being overly tired.

Anna felt better than she had in months. She lifted the small tray open on her oblong hospital table and dared to look at herself in the small mirror imbedded into the top lid of the tray. At least the yellow tinge to her skin was gone, and her bronze skin had a slight glow to it. In little more than an hour, she was going to have two of her children in the same room. She wanted to look her best, and taking her hairbrush out of the drawer next to her bed, she began brushing her black hair in long, even strokes. Anna began going over in her head what she wanted—no, what she needed—to say to her children. Her spirit was filled with love and hope.

Anna heard the clicking of Sister Mary Kathleen's long wooden rosary beads as she entered the room and spoke first. "You know what I wish, Sister? I wish I could live long enough to meet my youngest daughter. I feel so good. Do you think that might be possible?" And she smiled one of her rare smiles that enveloped her face and lit up the room.

Sister Mary Kathleen had seen it many times before—a person whose death was imminent and experiencing those few hours or sometime even days when they felt physically better because of some medical treatment. It was common at those times for individuals to go into denial, and they would be filled with hope that maybe they'd been given a reprieve. She understood that facing your own immortality was always difficult and left a person with many what-ifs. What if there was no such thing as eternal life? What if a person just simply stopped existing and there no longer was any kind of aware consciousness? What if there was eternal life and there really was a place called hell and one might go there because of the faithless life he or she'd lived?

Sister Mary Kathleen faith was unwavering in her belief that through Jesus Christ, she would live eternity in heaven and that faith indeed took the sting out of death. How many times had she witnessed to dying nonbelievers? She would say to them, "Well, if I'm a believer in Jesus Christ and I'm wrong, it isn't going to matter because I won't know any difference. I will have ceased to exist, and I will still have lived a life filled with hope, faith, and love. But if I'm right and you're wrong and there really is eternal life, where do you think you will spend eternity?" She would then quote Hebrews 11:6, which says, "And without faith it is impossible to please God, because anyone who comes to him must believe that he exists and that he rewards those who earnestly seek him."

Walking slowly towards Anna's room Sister Mary Kathleen secretly wished she could turn her mind off. Why did she always have to over think everything? On entering the room she gently took the hairbrush out of her hands, and began brushing Anna's hair for her. She sent up a quick silent prayer, "Fill me with Your Holy

Spirit and help me say the right words." The last thing Sister Mary Kathleen wanted to do was take away the life and hope she now saw in Anna's eyes, but she didn't want to give her false hope either.

Sister was silent for so long that Anna gave her a quizzical look and asked, "Why are you so quiet?"

"I was just thinking, Anna, about how to answer your question. I want you to understand that the blood transfusion is only a temporary fix like putting a Band-Aid on a wound. It's wonderful to see you feeling and looking so good, and I suggest you take this time to just enjoy the evening and be grateful for the time you're going to have with your children." Sister Mary Kathleen wanted to distract Anna from focusing on her death, so she added, "You know, Anna, you've never really told me about your parents or about your early childhood before you were kidnapped."

Anna didn't really answer, and after a brief pause, she asked Sister if she would braid her hair, stating she wanted to look her best before her children saw her. Sister began french braiding Anna's hair into one large braid, pulling her black hair strand by strand up toward the crown of her head. The braiding style emphasized Anna's high cheekbones, which had a slight rosy color as a direct result of the blood transfusion.

"So tell me, Anna, about your family, your mother and father. Tell me how it was for you before you were kidnapped."

Anna smiled as she began talking about her childhood. "My mother's name was Anuuk, and my father's name was Aalux. I had two brothers, Chuuyugis and Tixlax. My brothers were much older than me. Both of them had wives by the time I was twelve years old. My mother had me when she was more than forty years old, and she always said I was a miracle from God. She was very wise, and all the younger women in the village came to her for advice. And she taught them many skills, such as basket weaving.

"My father was the bravest man in the village and one of the oldest. All the villagers looked up to him, and they all said he was good to look at, meaning he was handsome. I always felt safe, secure, cared for, and special because I was the only daughter of the Chief Aalux. We were never cold, not even in the winter, and I never remember being hungry. We always had enough meat to eat, Snowshoe Rabbits, caribou, seals, sea lions, and fish.

"We went to the Russian Orthodox church every Sunday. My mother was very religious and taught me about God and Jesus Christ. It was a good life. I was happy. Then everything changed in the early summer when I was fourteen years old. My father and two brothers went out whale hunting with most of the other men of the village. They drowned and never came back. My mother changed that winter. She lay in bed for days at a time. It's the Aleut way to give away much of the deceased's things, and seeing all my father and brother's belongings, most of which they had made … well, it seemed like I cried all the time that winter. Then spring came, and my mom seemed better. We went berry picking, and she began weaving baskets again. Then I was kidnapped." Anna's voice trailed off.

Sister Mary Kathleen finished up the long braid, bringing it around to cascade down her left shoulder. The french braiding on both sides crowned her head, giving Anna a regal look. Gazing at Anna, Sister could see how truly beautiful the Aleut princess was. In spite of her alcoholism for so many years and giving up three children for adoption, there was a sweet innocence about her, and her persona was one of intelligence. What came out of Sister's mouth next even surprised her. "You know, Anna, if you hadn't been kidnapped and come to live in Juneau, there would be no Cayden … or Kimberly. Would you want to change that?"

The stunned look on Anna's face told Sister Mary Kathleen she'd have to wait for her answer. It had happened to Sister Mary Kathleen before—something coming out of her mouth that she had thought about first. She had learned that those kind of spontaneous statements or questions came straight from the Holy Spirit because it always touched the soul of the person she was speaking to. It had begun when she was in her early teens, and for a long time, she'd kept it to herself. Eventually, she talked to a priest about it in the confessional. He told her to gage its truth by the way the other person reacted. Eventually, Sister Mary Kathleen spoke with others who encountered the same kind of phenomenon in their lives, if only to validate that she wasn't alone or worse yet, delusional. With time and experience, Sister Mary Kathleen came to understand that in those moments it was paramount she completely trusted God because divine intervention was a humbling experience.

Anna's thoughts stumbled one over the other with all the what-ifs in her life, and no matter what direction her thoughts went in, it all came down to one question. Would she choose to live it all over again if only to give birth to her three children no matter who their fathers were? It was in that moment that Anna Hasson's life changed. She was no longer a victim.

She looked up at Sister Mary Kathleen, and in a trembling voice, she answered, "Yes, I would go back through it all again just to give birth to the same three children." She was as free as she'd once been as a child, and the joy she felt consumed her.

CHAPTER 26

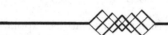

Cayden was standing in the doorway, listening to the last few minutes of the conversation between Sister Mary Kathleen and Anna Ahha. He stood in the door frame, the left palm of his hand up against the frame, balancing his slightly leaning body, and he had a sheepish grin on his face.

It was Anna who spotted him. "Cayden," she called out. He'd arrived a few minutes early for the appointed time and hadn't wanted to interrupt his mother and Sister Mary Kathleen. He'd heard Sister Mary Kathleen's question, and he was instantly intrigued about what Ahha's answer would be. He'd stood there in the door frame, waiting quietly to hear his mother's answer, and when he heard it, a warm flush started in his feet and went straight to his heart and validated his very being. The horror of his conception was no longer an issue in the scheme of his life, and in a split second, it became inconsequential.

Sister Mary Kathleen turned quickly as she and Cayden came face-to-face, their eyes locking. Cayden's admiration for the nun was evident. He tried to hide any other thoughts, including how beautiful he thought she was, nun's habit or not. Sister Mary Kathleen lowered her eyes, and in a shaky voice, she said, "How nice to see you, Cayden. I was just leaving." And with that, she scooted out around him, almost running down the hospital hall.

Cayden came over to his mother's bedside, took Ahha's hand, bent down, and kissed her on the forehead. His mother looked radiant, so much better than the first time he'd seen her. She patted the side of her bed, signaling him to sit down. Her eyes followed his every move, which made him feel a little self-conscious. "I'm sorry, Cayden. I just can't help wondering how I had such a handsome son. Is it okay if I call you son?"

Cayden nodded.

Anna Ahha had noticed how quickly Sister Mary Kathleen had left the room, and she casually said, "Sister seems a little skittish around you. Have you noticed that?"

Cayden had noticed, but for some strange reason, he felt protective of Sister Mary Kathleen, so he shrugged his shoulders and answered, "Not really."

Anna was about to say something more, but just then Sven

walked into the room with Kimberly, who exclaimed, "Cayden!" Cayden was shaking his head back and forth. He knew Kimberly. He'd ridden with her just a year earlier down the mountain from the cabin ski area in Ola-the-Cat when she'd broken her ankle while skiing.

"Kimberly Banks!" He looked at his mother, the Aleut princess. "This is my sister?"

Both Sven and Anna answered in unison, "Yes!" Cayden walked around the foot of the hospital bed and reached out his arms, and Kimberly went straight into them. Both Kimberly and Cayden were half-laughing and half-crying. "Well, well," Cayden said, "Little Kimberly Banks is my sister."

Both Anna and Sven were grinning from ear to ear. It turned out that the brother and sister knew each other, and they were about to spend the next half hour hearing about the details. It quickly became clear they were both avid skiers, and it was their love for the sport that had brought them together.

When Cayden was twelve years old, his parents bought him skies for Christmas, and for the next two years during the skiing season, they had taken him every Sunday afternoon up to what locals called "Second Cabin," which was a ski area developed in the 1930s in one of the many meadows on Mt. Jumbo. By the time

Cayden was fourteen and a freshman in high school, he loved the sport, and he was one of the better skiers for his age group too. He joined the high school ski club, becoming one of its most active members. Cayden spent every Saturday and Sunday, all four of his high school years up at Third Cabin during the ski season from early November to late April.

The Dan Moller Cabin—or as the locals call it "Third Cabin"—is located three miles up the Dan Moller Trail, which is known as the Douglas Ski Bowl. The cabin had a loft that can easily sleep twelve. The actual trail begins in west Juneau on Douglas Island and ends at Third Cabin with a 2,200-foot vertical drop. The actual elevation is two thousand feet. The cabin was actually built by the Forrest Service and given in 1935 to the Juneau Ski Club with exclusive use for skiers. The Juneau Ski Club was formed from the Juneau Hiking Club, and with many avid skiers in the Juneau-Douglas area, the club thrived because of voluntarism and financial donations.

Shortly after World War II, a prominent member of the ski club located a thousand feet ski rope just outside the town of Seward, and because it was considered army surplus, he was able to buy it for fifty dollars. In addition to the rope, the assemblage included an old Dodge truck engine and wooden pulley. A tow shack was built by members of the ski club, and the tow rope was up and running in the Douglas Ski Bowl, only a few hundred feet from Third Cabin.

Interestingly, Kim had also received skis for Christmas when she was in the seventh grade. Her father was a skier, and he began taking her with him on Saturdays up to Third Cabin. They had to be at the beginning of the ski trail by six in the morning if they were going to catch the first ride of the day on the orange snowcat, nicknamed Ola and manned by various members from the Juneau Ski Club. Six could ride in the cabin and another ten to fifteen on the orange iron trailer the snowcat pulled. Kim kept close to her father the first few times she'd taken the three-mile ride up the mountain. It was always a winter wonderland ride. The brows of the evergreen trees hung low with the fresh white snow glistening in the sunlight. The smell of the pines combined with the new snow cleansed the lungs, making one happy just to be alive.

More than once on those early morning rides, Ola had been unable to make it up a small but steep hill nicknamed "killer hill." If there had been a heavy snowfall the night before, the riders had to get off and walk up the hill while the adult skiers and some of the high school skiers helped dig out the snow. Cayden was always in that group, and by the end of that first ski season, Kim knew his first name. More than once when the tow rope broke down (an occurrence that happened once or twice a month) and many of the skiers would go down to the cabin to eat their bag lunches, Kim would sit on one of the several wooden benches with other skiers her age. Cayden would usually come in the heavy wooden door, stomp the snow off his ski boots, and announce, "Tows up." A couple of her girlfriends would become giddy on more than one occasion, giggling in a whisper to one another, "I have such a crush on him. He's so good-looking." Kim thought he was drop-dead handsome too, but she was a bit more realistic and would remind them. "Yeah, but he's in high school. I doubt if he even notices us lowly seventh-graders."

By the time Kim was a freshman in high school, she'd become a relatively good skier herself, so she joined the high school ski club with dreams of making the ski team by the time she was a junior. Cayden was a senior and president of the high school ski club. They weren't close friends, but they were skiing friends. When they ran into each other in the hallways at school, they always spoke.

After Cayden had graduated from high school, he became an active member in the Juneau Ski Club, got his first-aid certification, and joined the active ski patrol. There were always two people on duty every weekend, and Cayden was on duty every other weekend. In Kim's junior year, her skill as a skier had progressed to the point where she was confident she would finally make the five-member high school ski team. It was a wet and snowy day, freezing the ski hill with icy ruts, and one hour before the competitive Solomon race was to begin, Kim's left ski got caught in one of the icy ruts. She fell, tumbling down the hill several feet. She was stunned and a little disorientated, but Cayden was kneeling next to her within seconds. "Okay, Kim, take it easy. Just let me check you over." Her right foot was twisted in an odd position, and when Cayden touched it, the pain shot straight up her leg clear into her hip. She started crying not from the pain but because she wasn't able to compete in the race. Cayden stayed with her all the way down the trail in Ola and to the hospital. He called her parents and only left after they had arrived. Kim had broken her right ankle and was in a cast for eight weeks.

Cayden had never given it much thought, but he'd always had a soft spot in his heart for Kim. Now he knew why. And Kim had secretly admired Cayden since she was in the seventh grade.

They spent about a half hour reminiscing. They laughed at themselves and with each other because now all their many different encounters were now seen and felt through the eyes and ears of a brother and sister who genuinely loved each other.

CHAPTER 27

It was like an awakening from a dark nightmare. Anna hadn't felt such a sense of well-being and contentment that she hadn't experienced since before she had been kidnapped from her village. It was the same feeling she'd always had walking the rocky shores of her village, collecting seashells.

Sven was holding Anna's hand the while Cayden and Kim were talking. He squeezed her hand and winked at her several times, indicating his approval of something one of the siblings had said. Anna would squeeze his hand and wink back in agreement. It was such a joy for both Sven and Anna Ahha as all the heartache of the past began to slowly melt away.

Cayden asked Kim, "So Sven is your father?" Kim nodded, but it was Sven who answered him. "Yes, I have the distinct honor of being her biological dad."

Kim was curious. Who was Cayden's father? But she didn't ask.

Maybe she'd ask Cayden sometime when they were alone together. There was so much about her mother and father she didn't know, and the fact that she was adopted hadn't really been important to her … until now! Now Kim needed to know. She had just turned eighteen and was just beginning to find her identity and place in the world. She had either read it or someone had once told her, "Much of who we are comes from where we've been. Choices made in the past will always influence are choices in the future.

Cayden was standing behind Kim with his hands on her shoulders, and her father was sitting in a chair on the other side of Anna's hospital bed. Kim looking at both her mother and father and realized she and Cayden had been so engrossed with each other that they had almost forgotten about Sven and Anna's presence. Embarrassed, she apologized. "Sorry. We didn't mean to ignore you two."

It started with a wide smile on Anna's face, and then when she saw the grin on Sven's face, she giggled. Within seconds all four were laughing—deep belly laughs that filled the room with pure joy, the kind of joy that came from the heart, mind, and spirit being in perfect harmony.

In between little spurts of laughter, Anna could barely get the words out. "I'd like to tell you two a story. A story from my mother, your grandmother, Anuuk. A story that I heard hundreds of times as a child not only from my mother but from all the people chanting in my village on many a winter night around the warmth of a large bonfire. Cayden and Kim nodded in agreement.

"Long ago the ancients of our people lived in a land that we are now separated from by the sea. In those days it was only a small distance by the sea separating the two lands, and in the winter the sea between the two lands would become frozen enough that the ancients could walk on it. Many of them came across and stayed on the land we live in. As time went on, the distance between the two lands became too big for our people to cross, and so we became forever separated. We became many in number (history estimates twenty-five to thirty thousand) before the outsiders came to our land.

"The ancients believed the spirits of humans, animals, and natural entities required placation. This was done by the shamans who also cured the sick, foretold the future, and brought success in hunting and warfare.

"We did not call ourselves Aleut. We called ourselves Unangan, which came from our word *Una*, which means people of the sea. It was the outsiders who gave us the name of Aleut because of the name of the islands we lived on.

"It was the harshest of weather, but the ancients knew how to create and protect warmth. They wore parkas that extended below the knees. The women wore the skins of seals or sea otters. They also had bird skin parkas, and the feathers would be turned in or out, depending on the weather. When the ancient men hunted on the water, they wore waterproof parkas made from seal or sea lion guts or the entrails of bears, walruses, or whales.

"The ancients held many ceremonies, mostly in the winter. They sang, chanted, danced, drummed, and wore their specially made masks. The more gifts that were bestowed on an individual, the higher their rank in their village. They carved in wood, ivory, and bone and made birds, animals, and even boats and masks. They were expert storytellers, a trait that was passed on from generation to generation, and women were expert basket weavers.

"The ancients showed their accomplishments as well as what they believed in by displaying body art they believed would please the spirits. By piercing their noses, mouths, and ears, they believed they would stop evil entities called *khoughkh* from entering their bodies. Piercings like nose pins were common in both men and women and performed a few days after birth. The ornament was made of various materials, a piece of bark or bone or an eagle's feather shaft. Adult women decorated the nose pins by hanging pieces of amber and coral from string on it. The precious objects dangled down to their chins. Tattooing for women began when they reached maturity at about the age of twenty. Men traditionally received their first tattoo after killing their first animal as a rite of passage. They would sew or prick different designs on the chin, the side of the face, or under the nose.

"The ancients believed that death stemmed from both natural and supernatural causes, and many believed that the spirits of deceased individual continued to *live*.

"Then the outsiders arrived, and they often enslaved our people, forcing them to work for them, often killing the men and using the women for their own comforts. Some of them even married and had children with them. They brought with them many of the white man's diseases, and countless numbers of our people died. Most of our customs disappeared as our people were converted to their religion, Russian Orthodox. Our numbers became less and less until we numbered only a few.

"We tell the story as often as we can so those of us who are left will always remember that we were once a great nation and that we will always be proud to be Aleut."

Anna looked at her son and daughter and said, "I want you to be proud of where you came from, and I hope that someday when you have children, you will tell them this same story. I will see that it is written down for you both. Would you like that?" Both Cayden and Kimberly said yes in unison.

"Meanwhile, there is still a political fight going on for a monetary restitution to the Aleut people. You both will qualify for that should it ever happen. The rule is you must have at least one-eighth Aleut blood to qualify for any restitution. You both are half Aleut: Sven will see you both get the paperwork you need to prove your heritage." Anna looked at Sven nodding yes in response.

Cayden was the first to speak. "I don't know if I really deserve money for being half Aleut. But I promise you that I will pursue for the sake of the Aleut race the progress of the restitution for them." Anna looked at her son. She was so proud, so grateful for the kind of man he had grown up to be.

Almost choking on her words, she replied, "You deserve it, Cayden, because your biological family has suffered greatly, and it is their blood in your veins." Then she added, "You asked me if I would see and talk to your adopted mother. The answer is yes. Please let her know. You too, Kimberly, I'd like to meet your mother as well."

Kimberly was feeling a little overwhelmed by all that was happening to her, meeting her father, finding out she had a brother and then realizing it was someone she knew and liked and respected, hearing the story of her heritage and feeling sad that the people she was a part of had suffered for so many years. It made her angry, more than angry. It was the first time in her eighteen years that she realized just how unfair the world could be. She looked at her biological mother and quietly said that she would let her mother, Elaine, know she could meet Anna.

Anna was watching her daughter closely. She was so beautiful, but she sensed she was emotionally overwhelmed. Anna wanted to tell her that she had another sister, but she was nervous. She wondered if she should wait. But what if Cayden told her? Anna looked first at Kim and then at Sven. There was a questioning look in her eyes, and for once she and Sven were on the same page. He barely nodded his head no, and Anna knew it just wasn't time yet.

It had been a long day for Anna Hasson, and even though she was feeling better than she had in months, she could feel her energy slipping away. It was Sven who suggested that maybe it was time for all of them to leave, assuring Anna they would all be back the next evening.

After they left, Anna lay her head back on her pillows and thought that it had been a perfect evening. Well, almost perfect. Would JC ever forgive her? It was as though a piece of her was still in limbo. She fell asleep, dreaming she was back in her village and everyone was there, her mother, father, brothers, Sven, JC, and her three children. In her dream she saw the face of her second daughter. Undeniably, she had the face of a young Aleut girl, and she was smiling.

CHAPTER 28

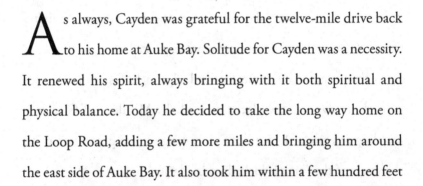

As always, Cayden was grateful for the twelve-mile drive back to his home at Auke Bay. Solitude for Cayden was a necessity. It renewed his spirit, always bringing with it both spiritual and physical balance. Today he decided to take the long way home on the Loop Road, adding a few more miles and bringing him around the east side of Auke Bay. It also took him within a few hundred feet to the face of Mendenhall Glacier.

The lake itself covered more than 177 acres and had a depth of 113 feet. It was an anadromous system supporting coho, sockeye, pink, and chum salmon as well as cutthroat and rainbow trout. The lake and its surrounding area was considered part of the Tongass National Forest, the largest national forest in the United States. Its seventeen million acres are remote enough to serve as the home of many endangered species and rare flora and fauna. Baked salmon was a delicacy appreciated by both Alaskans and visiting tourists.

The clouds were low over Mendenhall Valley with drizzling rain off and on. Cayden paid no attention to it. He was used to it. Like most in the Juneau population, drizzling rain didn't stop any outdoor event or work for that matter. Cayden always carried a thin hooded windbreaker that also doubled as a raincoat in the truck, and he slipped it on as he stepped out of the truck.

He was always awed by the massiveness of the glacier, which was more than miles long. Glaciers were considered almost like living things. Glaciers form over many years as packed snow accumulates faster than it melts. When its forward edge melts faster than the ice behind, it advances the glacier as a whole. Mendenhall Glacier is receding at a rate of 1.75 miles a year. A significant percentage of all the water of the earth is locked up in glaciers.

Cayden had heard the many rumors going around Juneau for the past several years that the powers that be were going to build a building, probably right on the spot where he was standing. The tourist trade was becoming more and more important to the economics of Juneau. They brought busloads of tourists out to the glacier, and they would wander around, taking pictures of themselves against the backdrop of the glacier. A building with the glacier's availability and written geography and history, snacks, restrooms, and a large viewing window would bring in more money to the Juneau coffers. Cayden was grateful that he was the only person within sight right now. He stood there in reverence, seeing God's hand as far as his eyes could see. In his mind only God could have created such beauty—the whole of the glacier area in complete harmony with nature, everything in its place and a place for everything.

A few feet from where Cayden stood, two willow ptarmigans, the Alaska state bird, were moving around in the bush. He immediately knew there had to be a nest of four to fourteen eggs nearby because the male was the only grouse in the world that was involved with parental care. The male and female remained together throughout the whole breeding period. The glacier's open tundra provided the perfect breeding ground with its mosses, herbs, and shrubs. Cayden observed they were in the process of changing into their summer coat of rusty brown after they had been pure white during the winter months. He enjoyed listening to their hoarse chirping for a short time before turning his thoughts back to the events of the day.

Little Kimberly Banks was his half-sister. It was unbelievable! He'd always been drawn to her ever since he had seen her up the ski trail when she was still only in seventh grade. Now he understood why. Maybe it was true that blood ran thicker than water. Yet his strongest bonds were with his adopted parents, Betty and Mike. He'd just met his biological mother, and his strongest feeling for her was one of protection combined with a sadness for all she had suffered. He came to the conclusion that there were many facets to love. There was no measuring it. You either loved someone or something, or you didn't. He loved hot chocolate with marshmallows. He did not love coffee, but he tolerated it. He loved humanity, yet he did not love people who hurt other people.

Then there was Sister Mary Kathleen. Cayden had never been big on the girlfriend-boyfriend thing. He dated very little in high school. He'd gone to a couple of proms, and once in a while, he attended some of the sock hops. But it was always with girls who were his skiing buddies. There were girls he thought were pretty, Kim being one of them, but that was as far as his thinking or his feelings had gone. Now something different was happening, something he couldn't rationalize to himself. He not only thought Sister Mary Kathleen was pretty, but he felt she was incredibly beautiful—her face, the way she moved, the way she lowered her eyes in prayer, the way her green eyes sparkled when she looked a person straight in the face, the way her voice sounded almost like a melody yet strong, firm, and intelligent too. In the seventh and eighth grade, Cayden had been taught by St. Ann's nuns, and he'd loved them just like he loved most people. He also understood that they were *married* to God. Why was he being tempted? Tempted to what? Cayden thought to himself, *This is crazy*, and then he recited a stanza in the Lord's Prayer, "And lead us not into temptation, but deliver us from evil." He sent a quick prayer up, trusting that God would help him get past these feelings he was having for a nun.

Getting back into the truck, Cayden took his windbreaker off and shook off its dampness. It was another fifteen minutes before he arrived in the family home driveway. He chuckled to himself when he saw the smoke bellowing out of the large stone chimney. His dad was home. Too many times to count in Cayden's lifetime, he'd come home to find his parents sitting each in their own chair in front of the fireplace, his father reading the local newspaper and his mother with a book in her hands, reading. It was a familiar sight that warmed his heart.

They both looked up as he entered the room. Cayden's father got up out of the chair to give him a quick hug. He'd been out at the logging camp getting ready for the logging season the past two weeks.

"I hear you've had quite the time for the last few days," Cayden's father stated.

"Well ... yes, I guess it has been," Cayden answered.

"Do you remember the young girl I escorted to the hospital

with a broken ankle a couple years back?" Cayden asked his parents. Before they could answer, he exclaimed, "Well, she's my half-sister!"

The look of surprise on both his parents' faces matched his own stunned feelings when he'd found out. His father was the first to speak. "Isn't she the same young lady who won a trophy for fastest record time for a woman during the ski tournament this year in Solomon? Kim something, right?"

"Yes," replied Cayden, "one and the same, Kimberly Banks." Both his parents sat back down in their chairs, while he sat down on the fireplace hearth, warming his back, which was damp from his glacier stroll.

Betty looked directly at her husband, "Mike, I think we know her parents. Remember when we went up the ski trail to watch the races? We spoke with them. They were pointing out their daughter Kim to us. After the races we rode down from Third Cabin in Ola's cab with Kim's mother. Her name is Elaine if I recall. Her husband is also skier. I can't remember his name."

Cayden said, "His name is Brian. He's an active member of the ski club, but I think he travels for his job because he's only up at the ski trail a couple of times a month."

Betty and Mike had never seen their son so animated, so excited. "This is important to you, isn't it, Son?" Mike asked.

"Mom and Dad, I don't have just one sister but two!" Cayden exclaimed. "My second sister is now about fifteen years old. Kim doesn't know that yet, but Sven is going to tell her and try to arrange a meeting with my second sister's father. He lives somewhere here in the Juneau area. Ahha told me it was a man she'd known since she was a child, someone who had lived in the same village where she was born and raised.

"All I know, Mom and Dad, is finding out I have two sisters and hearing how much the Aleut race has suffered has given me a compelling desire to somehow change all the sadness surrounding the Aleut princess into something good. You both have always taught me that God is merciful, that He can take something bad, even evil, and turn it into something good. I've come to believe in the last couple of days that He is going to use me in some way to accomplish justice for the Aleut race. And I think that somehow God is going to use my two sisters. There is one scripture that keeps playing over and over again in my head. Philippians 1:6 says, 'Being confident of this, that he who began a good work in you will carry it on to completion until the day of Jesus Christ.'"

Betty and Mike looked at each other. From the first day they had brought Cayden home at only a week old, they'd known that

God had a plan for his life, that somehow they would be a part of that plan.

Choking on her words, Betty said, "We are so proud and at the same time humbled at the man you've become, Cayden." Betty couldn't go on, her emotions taking control.

Cayden looked at the two people who had raised him and said, "No son could have asked for better parents."

CHAPTER 29

S ven was on a mission. When they left the Aleut princess's hospital room, he lingered at the door, signaling Cayden to come back toward him. Kim stopped to wait for her brother. Sven quickly whispered in Cayden's ear, "Don't mention anything about her sister to Kim, I'll take care of it." Cayden acknowledged by nodding his head and hurried back to his sister's side.

Laughing, Kim asked, "What was that all about?"

Cayden draped his arm over her shoulder and answered, "It seems your father wants me to look after you." Then on a more serious note, he added, "You do know that I will always look after you now that I found out I'm your big brother."

Kim teared up and answered, "Yeah, I know."

Sven walked back into the room and assured Anna Ahha that he had personally talked with JC and that their friend would be okay after a little time had passed. Sven also asked her if it was okay for him to tell Kim about her sister. Anna Ahha was more than relieved. She hated confrontations. They made her sick to her stomach, and she avoided them at all costs, even to her own determent. Sven bent down and kissed her. She reached up and caressed his cheek, the love between them as strong as it had always been.

Sven dropped Kim off at her home and drove straight to JC's apartment. He knew he wasn't giving JC much time to process his newfound fatherhood. He also knew there wasn't much time left. It wasn't a matter of weeks but a matter of days, The Aleut princess was dying, and her death was eminent.

JC opened the door on Sven's first knock, and his annoyance was obvious. "I thought you were going to give me a little time to think all of this over," he said, grumbling.

"I'm sorry, JC, but I don't think we have much time. Anna Ahha is failing fast. Every day she gets weaker. It would mean a lot to me and to Anna Ahha if my daughter, Kim, and her son, Cayden, could meet you and have some kind of connection to their sister, your daughter," Sven implored.

Sven wilted under JC's silent angry stare. They stood in the middle of JC's small apartment, neither man flinching. One filled with guilt, and the other filled with anger. These two men loved the Aleut princess, and their lives had been forever changed because of their love for her. Sven spoke first, "Please, JC, before she dies!" His voiced was so filled with emotion it sounded shaky.

JC lowered his eyes and motioned for Sven to sit down in the opposite chair across from him. "What do you want me to do, Sven?"

Sven swallowed hard, "I want you to agree to meet Cayden and Kimberly."

JC put his head in his hands, trying to hide the raw emotion that filled him. "Why, Sven? What good will it do?"

"If you could just see the love between this brother and sister, maybe it will give you hope for the future of your daughter. You know, Anna Ahha held her when she was first born. She told me she looked Aleut with lots of dark black hair and a round face. In Anna Ahha's defense, she believed with her whole heart your daughter would have a better life than she or you could give her."

"What do you think, Sven?" JC asked.

"I don't know, JC. I know that Cayden and Kimberly have both had good lives. I know that on finding out they were brother and sister, they were instantly bonded. And as much as I hate to admit it, my daughter probably has had a better life, and her finding out about her mother and me just seems to have filled her life with even more love. But then I've always been able to keep my eyes on her from a distance."

JC was silent for a few minutes before he looked directly at Sven and said, "Okay, Sven. I'll meet them.

"How about late tomorrow after Kim gets out of school?" JC nodded in agreement. Sven got up, shook JC's hand, and then pulled him toward him in a bear hug. "You won't regret it, my friend." JC prayed he was right.

Sven had one more stop to make—Linda Kolvalski's. They had long ago moved out of the army-owned Quonset hut and into a home up on Basin Road. Basin Road led to the Perseverance Trail, which led either up to the top of Mt. Juneau, about a five-mile hike, or up to the old Perseverance Gold Mine, a part of the Alaska Juneau Gold Mining Company from the 1800s.

Linda opened the door on Sven's first knock. Sven was a little startled. He hadn't seen Linda in a few years. She had put on some weight. Her dull salt-and-pepper hair was pulled back in a loose ponytail. Her baggy faded blue T-shirt knotted on the side only drew attention to her widening waistline, and her sad eyes just added to her general disheveled look. She wasn't really surprised to see him. "So how's Anna?" It had been Linda who had started calling her Anna when she'd first arrived in Juneau.

Sven came straight to the point. "She dying, Linda. It's only a matter of days, not weeks."

Linda sat down on one of the chairs at the kitchen table, which was covered with half-eaten bowls of cereal and empty milk glasses. Then she motioned for Sven to take a seat. "Do you know how many times I thought she was dying, Sven? More times than I can remember. I gave up on her a long time ago. I've got enough of my own problems to deal with." She gave Sven a defiant look.

"You know, Linda, I've never really known how you and Anna Ahha are related. I know she wants to see you she told me you were really the only family she had left."

Linda gave Sven a sad, dog-eyed look. "Her great-grandmother and my great-grandmother were half-sisters. Same mother, different fathers. Did you know I'm not Aleut, even though I've always claimed I was. That was simpler than explaining the truth. I'm Alatiig or Suqpiaq as we like to call ourselves. It means 'true people.'"

"Really?" Sven asked. "Is there any difference?"

"A long time ago—I'm not sure when—my people split off from the Aleut race, going farther southeast to Kodiak Island and the Prince William Sound area. They developed many different customs and even their own language. My mother was orphaned at eight years old and somehow ended up at the Minifield Home Orphanage here in Juneau. I didn't talk about it much because my mother never really wanted me, and I don't know who my father is.

I just know he was not the man she was married to for a few years. My mother died of cancer when I was twenty-two. Just before she died, she apologized to me for the way she had treated me all my life, and I was grateful. But I have never been able to feel the love of a daughter for her mother."

Sven sat back in his chair and honestly looked at Linda for the first time. He saw a depressed, unhappy person, which saddened him. "Linda, I'm so sorry. I've always been so focused on Anna Ahha. I never thought about how you might feel or even thanked you for all you've done for Anna over the years."

"I've pretty much failed at everything I've ever done." Linda quietly replied. "When Anna landed in Juneau, I thought that I could do something good for someone else and that it would make me feel better about myself. But I really didn't help her at all. Did you know I was the one who introduced her to hooch?"

"Linda, the way Anna Ahha has lived her life isn't your fault," Sven firmly stated.

"Nor is it yours, Sven!" Linda exclaimed, and they both sat in silence, contemplating all the years they had loved her and also blamed the Aleut princess for their unhappiness.

With a new awareness about herself, Linda spoke first. "I've used Anna's unhappiness all these years as an excuse for my own unhappiness."

Sven thought about his words carefully. "You know, Linda, I think Anna Ahha has always had that magnetism about her, that special something that pulls people in. And once a person is caught up emotionally with her, it never leaves, and it easily becomes a controlling factor in their lives. It's called charisma, and it can impact our lives both positively or negatively."

Linda nodded in agreement and told Sven she would go and make peace with Anna in the next couple of days. She just needed a day or two to get her relationship with the Aleut princess straight in her head.

Before he left, Sven gave Linda a bear hug, assuring her he'd keep in touch. Getting into his truck, he was almost giddy with relief. He had finally let go of the heavy burden that came with a heart filled with unforgiveness.

CHAPTER 30

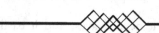

JC woke up with a start. One second he was sound asleep, and
the next second he was wide awake. For a brief second a person
is in a twilight zone, you know who you are, and you feel safe if you
wake up in familiar settings. It is that brief minute when the reality
of your life is kept at bay. JC awoke in the same hide-a-bed and in
the same room he'd slept in for almost twenty years. The apartment
was immaculate and well maintained. Every two years he gave the
rooms a fresh coat of beige paint. The room was twelve by fifteen feet
with a small alcove for his kitchen where only a coffeepot and toaster
sat on the small counter. Off to the left of him were two closed
doors, one a bathroom and the other a hall-like closet. Between the
doors there was floor-to-ceiling shelves filled with books and various
Alaskan keepsakes. His favorite was a cribbage board carved from
the tusks of a walrus.

Then the reality of his life and the past couple of days came flooding into his mind and heart. He gasped for breath, the emotional pain consuming him. He felt so many emotions after finding out he was a father and had been for some fifteen years, but he also had a newfound consciousness of the heartbreaking suffering of his people. He'd stuck his head in the sand, living only in the here and now, blocking from his heart all the sadness that came with the real truth about his people.

The small ragged Bible the priest from St. Nicolas had given him lay on the small kitchen table in front of the only two side-by-side single windows in his apartment. JC slowly walked to it and picked it up. For the first time in his life, he wanted to *hear* from God. He let the pages fall open, and one scripture passage popped out at him. "Not that I have already obtained all this, or have already been made perfect, but I press on to take hold of that for which Christ Jesus took hold of me. Brothers, I do not consider myself yet to have taken hold of it. But one thing I do: Forgetting what is behind and straining toward what is ahead, I press on toward the goal to win the prize for which God has called me heavenward in Christ Jesus" (Philippians 3:12–14).

JC sat in the kitchen chair. He had two goals. One was to somehow meet his daughter, and second, he would do whatever it took to bring justice and a better life to the Aleut people. The first step was meeting Ahha's other two children today at four o'clock.

Sven picked up Kimberly from school as planned. He had an hour with her before they were to meet JC and Cayden. He'd spent all day going over and over in his head how he was going to tell Kimberly about her other sister, and now seeing her come out of the building, his mind went blank. He watched her come out the double doors, surrounded by girlfriends, laughing and obviously happy. Sven choked up. His daughter was a happy person with a happy life. That was important to him, maybe even the most important thing. Kim bounced into the car, smiling, telling him that they had been measured for their graduation gowns today. Her excitement about graduating in two weeks was contagious. The last thing he wanted to do was put a damper on her obvious excitement. He silently prayed that God would give him the right words.

They sat down in the small café. Sven ordered a cup of coffee, and Kim ordered a Coke. Kim could see the serious look on his face and questioned, "Is something wrong? Is Ahha okay?"

"Yes, she's the same, but I do have something important I need to tell you. How do you feel about all of this? I mean, meeting Anna Ahha, Cayden, and me in the last couple of days?"

Kimberly voice was filled with warmth, "It's makes me feel

happy. It's like my heart has expanded over these past couple of days because I'm loved by so many people. It's hard to explain. I just know I love all of you, my mom and dad, two sisters, now a brother, and both my biological mom and dad." Kimberly smiled at her father Sven, and reaching across the table, she patted his hand.

Sven looked her in the eyes and said, "Is there room in that big heart of yours for one more?"

Kimberly cocked her head to one side and questioned, "One more?"

"Yes, Kim, one more." The man you're about to meet is the father of Anna Ahha's second daughter, a daughter who is about three years younger than you. His name is John Charlie, but everyone calls him JC. He grew up in the same village Anna Ahha grew up in, and he has always loved her. Your mother was kidnapped from the village and brought to Juneau the year before World War II broke out, and that was when she gave birth to Cayden. JC came to Juneau a year later when all the villagers were taken off the island and brought to camps here in southeast Alaska." Sven paused. He could see the look of confusion on Kim's face.

"Is she here? I mean, can I meet her?" Kim responded.

"I'm afraid not, Kim. Like you and Cayden, she was adopted. It was a closed adoption. She's fifteen years old now, and only she has the right when she turns eighteen to have her adoption papers opened. None of us, including JC, knew of her existence until a couple of days ago." Sven stopped. He could see the look of bewilderment all over her face, and he watched as her eyes filled with tears and slowly streamed down her cheeks.

"Kim, I'm so sorry. I'd hoped this wouldn't hurt you!" Sven exclaimed.

Kim whispered, "No, no, it isn't that. It's just that I think my mother has had one of the saddest lives I've ever heard of."

Sven could see the high level of maturity his eighteen-year-old daughter had, and he thought about what a fine job Kim's adopted parents had done. He conceded to himself that Anna Ahha had probably done the best thing for their daughter by adopting her out. He took Kim's hands in his and said, "Kim, you have such an old soul. I couldn't be more proud of you. We all have the opportunity now to bring your mother happiness in these last few days of her life." Kim nodded in agreement.

Cayden was the first to arrive. He could see that Kim had been crying and was immediately concerned. "You okay?" he asked as he gave her a big hug.

Kim gave one of her huge smiles, nodded, and said. "Can you believe it? There are three of us."

Right at that moment JC came through the café doors. Sven motioned for him to come over to the booth they were sitting in, and then Sven introduced him to both Cayden and Kim.

For the first few minutes, JC felt totally uncomfortable, but as he watched the brother and sister banter back and forth as if they'd been raised together, it gave him hope that his daughter would someday be able to join them.

CHAPTER 31

Betty Jensen never made any decisions involving relationships without praying about them first, so she was praying about making a phone call to Elaine Banks, Cayden's newfound sister's mother.

She was a young woman in her first job as a certified licensed practical nurse (LPN) when she'd learned the tough life lesson that some people acted and reacted based on some hidden agenda. Betty had always been forthright and open and accepted people at face value, so the incident was imprinted in her mind, and she remembered it like it only happened yesterday.

Betty was only three months into her job at St. Ann's Hospital, and she was assisting in her second delivery. Her role was to keep the delivery room sterile and to assist with the aftercare of the newborn's birth. It was a normal delivery of a perfect seven-pound baby boy. The mother was a young white local girl whose family was wealthy and well-known in Juneau. She had just graduated from high school a few months before as had her husband, who was Tlingit Indian. Half the girls in highs school had a crush on him. He was handsome and intelligent, and he was voted most popular senior in his senior year along with most valuable basketball player.

In the early fifties mixed marriages were still not accepted in most social circles in Juneau. It was an unwritten law that any dating between a Caucasian and Indian was a big no-no. Most of the younger generation didn't agree with that unwritten rule and often helped certain couples keep their *secret*.

Both sets of grandparents were waiting in the waiting room after the baby's delivery. They appeared not only friendly with each other but equally excited about their new grandson. It was late morning the next day when the mother of the girl appeared at the nursery and asked several questions about her new grandson. Betty had been on duty and graciously answered her questions, thinking only she was just being a bit overprotective of her grandson.

Later that afternoon Betty had gone to the young lady's room to bring her baby to her for a feeding. She found her curled up in a fetal position and uncontrollably sobbing. Her parents had informed her that they were going to do everything in their power to gain custody of their grandchild so that their grandchild would have the

LORETTA SANFORD CUELLAR

proper upbringing and not be embarrassed or humiliated by who his father was. They had also told her that she and her husband were no longer welcome in their home and that they would give them enough money to move out of the state if they did not fight the custody petition. Betty was horrified. How could someone pretend to be so accepting, even loving, when all along their attentions were so harmful? Betty asked the young lady what she was going to do, and through sobs but with a firmness filled with anger, she said, "Over my dead body they will ever get my son!"

A few months later, Betty heard that the couple had moved away from Juneau with their son. She smiled and thought. *Good for them.* But after that incident Betty always entered a possible relationship with caution and always with prayer. Over the years Betty had learned to listen for and hear that still, small voice that was a quickening of her spirit and warned her something was not quite right. She acquired her own personal gage to measure if it really was the Holy Spirit guiding her or just her own personal humanness. If she prayed about the decision she was thinking about making and it left her without affecting her daily thinking, she would not act on it. But if the decision kept coming up over and over again in her thinking after prayer, she would then act on it, believing it was from the Holy Spirit. Betty had her own safety net. Even if she did get it

240

wrong, her faith taught her God in His infinite power would turn it around for the good of all concerned.

After praying in the early morning whether or not to call Kimberly's adopted parents, she thought, *Call her parents*, and it nagged at her all day as she went through all her chores and assisted her husband with getting all the necessary items together for the summer at the logging camp. Finally, she spoke it out loud, "I've been praying, Mike, about calling Kimberly's parents and setting up a meeting with them. What do you think?"

Mike immediately stopped loading the back of the pickup truck and answered, "I've been thinking the same thing. Yes, let's do it!"

That was absolute confirmation for Betty, and she went immediately in the house and called Elaine and Brian Banks. A woman answered the phone. "Hello. This is Betty Jennings. Is this Elaine Banks?" Betty asked.

The enthusiasm in Elaine's voice reassured Betty that she was on the right track. "It seems our children are siblings. Kim is thrilled. She's always expressed a desire to have a brother, and the fact that it's Cayden, someone she's has always admired … well, it's like frosting on the cake."

"I know," Betty replied. "Cayden feels the same way. I was wondering, Elaine, if you and your husband had time to meet for coffee with my husband, Mike, and me. We're thinking about the possibility of meeting Anna Hasson. Cayden has spoken to her about it. She's not only agreed to see us, but Cayden said she wanted to thank us. Frankly, the way my husband and I feel, we're the ones who should be thanking her!"

"We feel the same way," Elaine replied.

The two women set a time to meet early in the morning and to visit with Anna as soon as possible since Mike was on a time line and needed to get out to the logging camp soon.

Betty made one more phone call to Sister Mary Kathleen because Cayden had shared her involvement with Anna. It was apparent to Betty when he shared the information about Sister Mary Kathleen that this was a woman Cayden highly respected, even trusted. Betty had thought at the time she must be an exceptional person because Cayden had never showed such respect and trust for anyone so quickly.

Unable to immediately reach Sister Mary Kathleen, she had left a message to call her back, and she was surprised when Sister returned the call within a half hour. Betty explained to her what they and the Banks were intending to do. Sister assured her that meeting would benefit Anna emotionally and spiritually.

After hanging up, Sister Mary Kathleen found her hands shaking. "Oh, God," she prayed, "Please help me!"

CHAPTER 32

Sister Mary Kathleen found a pastel pink lacey bed jacket that some patient at the hospital had left. She took it into Anna and helped her put it on. The color complemented her bronze complexion. Anna once again asked Sister to braid her hair. Sister braided a french braid down both sides of Anna's head, pulling them together at the nape of her neck, allowing the rest of her long hair to hang freely down her back. The head of the hospital bed was cranked up to the complete sitting position. "You indeed look like an Aleut princess, Anna." Sister complimented her and then asked, "Are you ready for this?"

"I am," Anna quietly replied. "I'm so proud of both Cayden and Kimberly. What fine people they both are. And I know I have their parents to thank for that. Don't you think they are exceptional?" The quizzical look on Anna's face told Sister Mary Kathleen that Anna needed all the reassurance she could get.

"Yes, I do, Anna. You are truly blessed," Sister firmly said, quietly thinking, *if you only knew how exceptional I think your son is, you'd probably be shocked.*

As usual, it was a cloudy and rainy day in Juneau, and after sharing coffee, doughnuts, and their positive feelings about their children's biological mother, they decided to drive together in one car to St. Ann's Hospital. They knew that parking in the downtown Juneau area was always a problem. The streets were narrow, and most of the houses leading up the hill to the hospital didn't have driveways, so families had to park their cars on the already narrow street. The Jennings and Banks used the small Catholic church parking lot, so they were only a block uphill from the front entrance of the hospital. Being longtime Juneau residents, they paid no mind to the rain, automatically pulling the hoods of their raincoats up over their heads.

Entering Anna's room, all four people could see this tiny person almost lost in the hospital bed. She looked like a living doll, a beautiful living Indian doll. Both Cayden and Kim had told their respective parents that their mother was an Aleut princess. There was no doubt in any of their minds upon seeing her that she indeed was just that.

After introducing themselves, Anna said in a sweet but firm

voice, "I wanted to thank all of you for raising and loving my son and daughter. They are both exceptional people, and I know it's because you've all been good parents." Tears began to fill Anna's eyes and silently roll down her cheeks as she continued, "For so many years, the pain of their births haunted me, and I felt such bitterness and even hatred, not for them but for the circumstances of my life that took me from my village and from the people who loved me and whom I loved. From the Indian village where I was honored as an Aleut princess."

Elaine reached out and took her petite hand in hers. "But Anna, if you hadn't come to Juneau, there never would have been a Kimberly, and there are no words I can say to you to express my thankfulness for that!"

Betty and Mike both noticed how much Cayden looked like his mother. The resemblance took Betty's breath away. Betty stood at the head of the bed and couldn't help but reach out and softy touch Anna's cheek. Anna had raised her hand and patted Betty's hand. "The same goes for Mike and me, Anna. Cayden has been our whole life, and he's never done anything that hasn't made us proud to be his parents. I have thanked God every day for his life." Betty kept choking on her words, overwhelmed by all the emotions she was experiencing.

All three women were silently crying. The eyes of both men in the room were downcast as they fought back their own tears, embarrassed by all the emotions. Anna finally spoke. "After Cayden was born, I still had some hope that I could go back to my village and live the life I had always believed I would live." The bitterness in Anna's voice was noticeable as she continued, "But then World War II broke out. My village was burned to the ground by American soldiers, and everyone in my village was taken to an internment camp not far from Juneau. My people were not told their destination and were placed in housing where space was so inadequate that it was impossible to separate the sick from the healthy. The people from my village were taken to a defunct herring factory on Killisnoo. Some of the wooden buildings were so rotten that people actually fell through the floor. There was only one outhouse, and the drinking water was the color of tea. There were as many as twelve people living in poorly insulated spaces partitioned by only blankets. Food was so scarce that young children would chew on their thumbs to ward off hunger pangs. Rats and mice scurried across the floor, and the odor of human excretion and waste was so pungent that it was stomach-wrenching. Children were found naked and actually covered with excrete. My people suffered for almost three years. They had come from treeless islands against their will, and they were taken to a rainy slice of dense, damp forest wedged between mountains and ocean. My mother, Annuk, died of pneumonia in the second year. There wasn't anyone or even a village for me to return to. I've hated the government since then. Yes, the government said they did it to protect my people, but the truth is that many white folks had a racist attitude toward the Aleuts. They thought we were all dumb drunks. And worse than that, no one wanted to talk about it ... *ever*." Anna stopped talking but not before everyone in the room had heard and recognized the deep-seeded rage that seemed to consume her.

Brian then said, "Anna, we know your people have suffered and suffered almost to the point of genocide, but the fact the Aleut race survived after World War II shows the Aleut race has immeasurable resilience and courage. World War II brought suffering to many. American Japanese were also sent to internment camps. Within days of the Pearl Harbor attack, a little more than a hundred Japanese were arrested here in Alaska. One Japanese family that owned a restaurant here in Juneau was sent to an internment camp in Idaho. I'm a bit of a history buff, Anna, and I'd like to tell you another side of the story. Would you mind?"

Anna glared at Brian, but then slowly, her face softened. "Mr. Bank, I know I'm dying, and I'm told that I must forgive others if I'm to be forgiven. God knows I've done plenty of things that need to be forgiven. So maybe you can help me forgive a government who forgot about the Aleuts. Worse than that, the government treated us like we were animals. Twenty percent of more than eight hundred Aleuts who were taken from their villages died, and when they were finally returned, they found their villages looted by American soldiers. And my village had been burned to the ground."

Brian spoke softly but with confidence. "The Pearl Harbor attack on December 7, 1941, took America by complete surprise."

Brian stopped and made eye contact with Anna and then said, "I just realized you must have been about seven months pregnant with Cayden. Is that right?"

"Yes," Anna answered, "I'm ashamed to say that I was so immersed in my own problems and so filled with fear that I paid little attention to what was happening in the world. I even paid little attention to World War II, except for how it affected my people, and I've carried that resentment and hate with me all these years." Anna let Brian know it was okay to continue by nodding her head.

He continued. "The attack on Pearl Harbor destroyed twenty American naval vessels, including eight enormous battleships, and more than three hundred planes. More than 2,500 soldiers and sailors died, and more than a thousand were wounded. It was the Japanese plan to destroy the Pacific fleet. However, by what some believe to be divine intervention, all the aircraft carriers were away from the base at the time. By May 1942, Japan had swallowed up Southeast Asia and the islands of the South Pacific. She had crushed all Allied strength in the western ocean. Then that Japan turned its biggest guns on Midway and toward the Aleutian Islands."

"The Aleutian Islands are the most brutal thousand miles in the Pacific Ocean, and for fifteen months from 1942 to 1943, it was one of the toughest campaigns of World War II. In the winter there was only four hours of daylight, and temperatures dropped to forty degrees below zero. Everything froze. Even the coal to fuel the stoves had to be thawed before use. No general or admiral was as powerful as the weather. In the thousand-mile-long battleground between Dutch Harbor and Attu, the weather dictated that both sides would spend most of the war searching for each other, usually without success. It seems the only people who knew how to live in the weather of the Aleutian Chain were your people, Anna, the Aleut people. About five hundred thousand men took part—Americans, Canadians, Russians, and Japanese. It cost scores of ships, hundreds of airplanes, and at least ten thousand lives. It was the only campaign of World War II fought in the United States, and when it was over, people often referred to as 'The Forgotten War' or 'The Thousand-Mile War.'

"The Aleutian Islands lay only 650 miles from Paramushiro in the Japanese Kuriles, and a Japanese beachhead on the Alaskan mainland would have threatened the entire United States and Canada. Six months after Pearl Harbor in June of 1942, Japan seized the remote and sparsely inhabited islands of Attu and Kiska."

Noting the distorted look on Anna's face, Brian hesitated for a moment. Anna looked at Brian with one of her "peer into the soul" looks. It unnerved Brian.

"I know many people suffered because of the war. But why did my people, the Aleut people, get treated like animals? I just don't understand!" Anna exclaimed.

Brian softened his voice. "I know, Anna. I'm trying to explain it to you. It was like—well, it was like your small race got lost in the shuffle. It wasn't intentional. There was so much political chaos at the time that sometimes the right hand didn't know what the left hand was doing. Did you know that your island, Atka, was so strategic that the American soldiers who burned your village were ordered to by the US government? The government really thought they were protecting your people by extracting them off the islands. It was a military decision made quickly and with little preparation, and your people suffered. There's no justification for it, Anna, only the cold hard truth. War is hell, and innocent people die and suffer." Brian looked Anna straight in the eye and added, "But we go on trying to move forward, Anna, and young people like Cayden and Kimberly will learn from our generation's mistakes and march into the future with much more knowledge and wisdom than our generation had. It wasn't because no one cared about the Aleut race, Anna. It was because no one knew. There was only a vague perception that Alaskan people were all Eskimos who lived in igloos and ate nothing but fish."

In all their thirty-six years of marriage, Elaine Banks had never heard her husband so emotionally open except in the privacy of their bedroom. She was astounded at the passion he displayed for the Aleut race. She wondered, *is it because our daughter is part Aleut, or is it because of the mysterious charisma Anna Hasson had been gifted with?*

Anna Ahha's deep brown eyes circled the room as she made direct eye contact with the four people surrounding her hospital bed—Betty, Michael, Brian, and Elaine.

"In her sweet, soft, but firm voice, she spoke, "I know now that it will be my children who will bring the story of the Aleut people to the rest of the world. I am humbled before God and His angels that He has allowed me to understand my preordained destiny before I die." When she stopped speaking, there was a slight glow that surrounded the Aleut princess's face, and Betty, Michael, Brian, and Elaine were intrigued by the mysticism of this Aleut princess.

CHAPTER 33

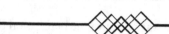

J uneau is the only state capital that boarders another country, and
its population eventually outgrew the small St. Ann's Hospital.
The city bought some property to build a new and bigger hospital,
and construction was to begin in spring of the following year. It was
unclear at what point the Sisters of St. Ann would be returned to the
Mother House in Victoria, Canada. Sister Mary Kathleen was aware
that her time in Juneau was growing short. However, she often had
to work double duty both as a nurse and as the administrator of the
hospital, and now in the late evening of the day and within the last
twenty-four hours, she'd only had four hours of restless sleep.

In the early afternoon, the small emergency room had more
than its usual run-of-the-mill patients—a child who'd spiked a fever
in the middle of the night, an intoxicated person found passed out
and lying on the ground in the cold weather, or the various small
accidents that happened in everyday living.

A fishing vessel moored in the small boat harbor had exploded and caught fire. The two people aboard had been burned with second- and third-degree burns. They were alive and would be transferred to a hospital in Seattle on the first flight out of Juneau in the morning, but Sister Mary Kathleen had called off-duty staff in to care for them through the night.

A four-year-old child had been severely bitten on the leg by a dog, requiring more than thirty stitches. In spite of the new laws for pet control, the dog problem in Juneau was still out of control, and more than half of the pets were still free to run. One could not walk down any of the sidewalks in Juneau without watching out for the many piles of dog feces.

A young woman had gone into premature labor at only twenty-three weeks. The survival rate for fetuses that old was less than 1 percent, and then only if the mother was fortunate enough to be near a modern hospital that had the very latest in technology. Little St. Ann's Hospital was just beginning to catch up with the rest of the world as was the city of Juneau. The baby was born alive but only lived for two hours. The young parents were devastated, and Sister Mary Kathleen took the time to pray and counsel them in their grief.

Juneau was still isolated from the lower forty-eight states without roads leading in or out. Canned black and white television had only been available in the last few years. Alaska was still a diamond in the rough, still considered "the last frontier." People born and raised in Juneau knew nothing different. They were set in their ways, and they fought change of any kind, especially if those changes were suggested by someone from the lower forty-eight. The old-timers were confident in their experiences and knowledge of the mountains, their many trails, and the wildlife that roamed and lived in them. Sure enough, almost every spring someone would find a body after the winter snow melted. Some lone person arriving in Juneau in the summer and hiking one of the many trails would get lost or fall and die in the brutal weather. The old-timers would shake their heads and put up more signs on the trails warning lone hikers of the dangers. They did not readily except *outsiders* but only trusted them after they had proven themselves. So although the population had grown from the original hundred in 1881 and was now almost twelve thousand and growing, the progress being made in the lower forty-eight was slow to come to Juneau.

Sister Mary Kathleen had been in Juneau for a little more than five years. She thought she'd earned the respect and trust of the Juneau residents, but sometimes she sensed one of the older "good ole boys" thought she was a female that was far too young to hold such a position as hospital administrator. She wasn't so sure at times that they were wrong.

Today she was physical weary and overwhelmed, and she briefly wished she was back on Swan Lake, listening to the mating call of the loons. One more stop before going to her sleeping room.

A small night-light attached to the head of Anna's bed cast a ray of dim light that surrounded her head. She looked like a small china doll with her black hair spread out and encircling her head against the white pillow. Sister Mary Kathleen called out her name in a whisper.

Anna opened her eyes and smiled. "I knew you'd come as soon as you could," Anna whispered back at her. Sister Mary Kathleen immediately noticed a change in Anna's voice, a softness that hadn't been there before. Her whole persona had changed. There was a euphoric, peaceful joy that enveloped Anna.

"What exactly does it mean, Sister, to give God the glory?" Anna asked.

"Well," Sister Mary Kathleen said, searching for an understandable answer. "Glory means to rejoice proudly, to exult. To give God the glory testifies to one's actual condition being divinely prearranged by a power far beyond our control. In other words, God lets us see, if just for moment, His hand in our lives and shows that we are not only where we were born to be but who we were born to be."

Anna was silent for a few moments before she said, "Than to God be the Glory for the birth of my three children … and my life!"

Sister Mary Kathleen had witnessed many miracles in her lifetime, but the miracle of one seeing for the first time his or her life through the eyes of God was the most profound of all in her opinion. It was a mystery! How was it that in one moment of time a person saw the world through one paradigm but then saw the world through a completely new paradigm in the next moment? Through the power of God behind the transformation of the individual, the old paradigm was swiped over, leaving a completely new perspective. It was like checking your balance on your credit card, and instead of being zero, it showed an unlimited number of funds.

As much as Sister Mary Kathleen curiosity was aroused, she was also exhausted. Besides, Anna was obviously groggy, her eyes blinking rapidly in an effort to stay awake.

Lifting Anna's hair back from her forehead, Sister spoke softly, "We will talk tomorrow, Anna. Both of us need to sleep." Half-smiling, Anna closed her heavy eyelids.

CHAPTER 34

The room where Sister Mary Kathleen slept was little more than a cubicle. It was nine by twelve feet, and it was immaculate, stark, and impersonal. In one corner sat a small twin bed made up in white hospital bedding. A pinewood nightstand with a small lamp sat next to the bed. A small black book with edges worn thin from use sat next to the lamp. The gold letters imprinted on the book read *The Way of the Cross*. It was Sister Mary Kathleen's daily habit to read one of the fourteen stations the last thing in the evening, and while falling asleep, she would meditate on whatever station she had just read. She'd read the stations for so many years that she now knew most of the prayers by heart. The small black book also held "The Seven Sorrows" or "The Via Matris," a devotion to the mother of sorrows, Mary, the mother of Christ. Sister Mary Kathleen had a love for the mother of Christ, but she was very cautious not to worship her and always kept Christ first in her thoughts and prayers.

A small closet and chest of drawers held all her worldly belongings. Over the head of her bed, there was a framed picture of the Sacred Heart of Jesus, symbolic of Christ's physical heart as the representation of His divine love for humanity. One black-and-white picture sat on top of the dresser. It was a photo taken at her brother Gabriel's graduation from high school, with her father, Miss Elsie, her three siblings, and her three step-siblings. In the corner of the picture, a small wallet-sized picture of a three-month-old baby girl was stuck in the frame. It was her niece by her brother and his new wife, Abby. They had named the child after her mother, Patricia, and they referred to her as Patty.

Sister Mary Kathleen hadn't seen her family in more than six years, but she prayed for them daily and thought of them often, especially when she saw other families together. She missed the safety and comfort that came from being a part of a close-knit family. More than that, she missed the emotional intimacy that came with sharing everyday ups and downs with people you loved.

There were no mirrors in the room. As a matter of fact, there were no mirrors anywhere in the hospital except the small mirror in the lid of the roll-away table that was basically used for the patient's food tray. The small square lid could be opened for the convenience of the patient. Men used it to shave themselves, and women used it for their makeup and hair.

It had been quite the controversy a few years back. The roll-away table tray with the opening lid was expensive, twice as expensive as the trays without the opening lid. Because of the charitable focus of the hospital, the hospital often ran overbudget, and there was seldom enough money to buy expensive extras. The St. Ann's Hospital guild had come to the rescue and held several fundraisers to pay for them.

The "no mirror" rule was meant to emphasize the fact that vanity was one of the many human traits that could take a person's focus away from God. It amused Sister Mary Kathleen as vanity had never been problematic in her life. Maybe it was because she had so much responsibility at a young age, but she suspected it was more about her curly and thick head of auburn hair, which always made her look like she been in some kind windstorm. When she was wearing a nun's habit, no matter how tight she had pulled her hair back away from her face, there were always wisps of red curly hair encircling her face. She'd given her hair little thought in the last few years, keeping it cut short and covered with the bonnet headpiece and veil that flowed down to the center of her back. Her demeanor was one of humility.

The nursing nun's habit was always spotless, and it was always a challenge to keep clean throughout the workday. Ingenious as she was, Sister Mary Kathleen had designed a white apron they could wear over the actual habits. The upper part of the apron was pinned to the habit at both the right and left shoulder. Sister Mary Kathleen went through at least three aprons a day and only had to put on a freshly starched habit every three days.

Sister Mary Kathleen cherished her Roman Catholic upbringing. It had led her to God and given her an unwavering faith in the divine. She had plenty of weaknesses, the biggest being that she would overthink things. It was her nature to overanalysis every question that arose, whether it came from someone else or it was just a question that popped up in her own head. The Roman Catholic church doctrine on indulgence was one of them.

With indulgences, a person could reduce the amount of punishment for sins by performing certain actions listed by the church. In the Middle Ages, the abuse of indulgences had become a serious problem, mainly through commercialization. Indulgences were targets from the beginning of the Protestant Reformation for Martin Luther and all other Protestant theologians. The church recognized it and curbed the excesses, but indulgences continued to play a role in church doctrine.

Sister was aware that the subject of indulgences within the church was changing, and she knew that reforms were coming soon and that the quantification of indulgences was soon to be changed. It couldn't happen soon enough in Sister Mary Kathleen's opinion. It was just plain wrong, taking away from the completed works of Jesus Christ on the cross. Her little black book, *The Way of the Cross*, listed the indulgences she could receive by doing the fourteen stations. She secretly disliked the indulgences. Her motivation was to fall asleep focused on one of the stations to reassure herself how much God through Jesus Christ loved her and the world.

Sister Mary Kathleen quickly read the ninth station, "Jesus Falls the Third Time." She considered how Jesus Christ, weak and exhausted, fell for the third time while the cruel executioners tried to make Him walk faster, though He hardly had the strength to move. She finally laid her weary body down under the covers, thinking she would be asleep the minute her head hit the pillow.

It wasn't the picture of Jesus falling for the third time that appeared in her mind. It was Cayden Jennings standing in the frame of the door in Anna's hospital room, leaning with one hand against the frame, one foot crossed in front of the other, and the most charming of smiles on his face.

"Oh, God," she whispered with tears filling her eyes, "what do you want from me?"

There was no answer, only the welcoming blackness of sleep.

CHAPTER 35

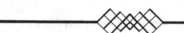

The day was clouded over. Deep gray clouds cast dark shadows over the downtown area of Juneau. The downtown area sat between two tall mountains, Mt. Juneau and Mt. Roberts, and residents referred to being there as "being socked in." The town itself was built on the tidal flats, the residential houses meandering up the foothills of both mountains. Folks who lived in Juneau either all or most of their lives paid no heed to it. They knew they could walk or drive less than two miles and see spots of blue where rays of golden sun fanned out and filled the random clearings with light.

JC couldn't care less about the weather. He had much more important things on his mind and in his heart. He hadn't slept well the last few days, and he was giddy from lack of sleep. All that had happened to him in the last two days was rolling around in his thoughts, tumbling over and over. He could in a matter of minutes become enraged, sad, confused, loving, hopeful, despairing, and filled with such emotional conflict he thought he might just be going a little crazy. JC had spent the last twenty years keeping his feelings buried, and now it was as if every feeling had surfaced. He had no idea how to cope with such raw emotions.

JC had spent the last two days writing and rewriting a letter to his daughter. He could still hear Anna's voice as he stomped out of her hospital room. "You can write her a letter and have it put in her adoption file." He wanted to read the letter to Anna, but first, he had to go see her in person and try to make peace with her.

Without thinking of the time, JC grabbed his yellow raincoat and marched out of his apartment. It took him ten minutes to walk the four blocks uphill to the hospital. The hospital staff was serving breakfast to the patients, and they were down the hall from Anna's room. He slipped quietly into her room.

Anna was sitting up, sipping some green juice. The look on her face said she didn't like its taste, but she was forcing herself to drink it. Her face was as colorless as JC had ever seen it. Her long black hair hung straight down her back and needed brushing. The faded green hospital grown only added to the feeling of gloom the gray day had brought. The fogginess filtered in threw the window and filled the room.

JC felt his heart crunch. He couldn't just throw away more than forty years of loving this woman. Besides, Ahha—always Ahha to him—looked extremely vulnerable, and the thought of her dying soon caused his heart to pound so hard he felt weak in the knees.

Ahha looked up at him, and their eyes met. "Sven said you'd come back! Are you still mad at me?"

"I don't know how I feel, Ahha. I'm so bewildered I can't think straight. I have so many emotions all going on at the same time. I think I'm losing my mind. That or I'm just plain stupid. I just don't understand why you waited so long to tell me we had a daughter. I just want to know why! Something, anything that will make sense to me. Why in the name of all that is holy? Why!" His voice was shaking, and he could hear his voice getting louder and louder, his feelings taking control of his words. John Charlie was desperate for an answer, an answer that would make some kind of sense to him and magically take away all of his mixed-up emotions. He sat next to her bed, his head in his hands, silently waiting.

Ahha stretched out her hand, taking one of John Charlie's hands in hers and gently squeezing it. She prayed she could give him some of the strength she had only found yesterday.

Before Ahha could bring herself to speak, the static electricity in the room made it feel like time was standing still. In a hoarse whisper, she slowly began to talk, thoughtfully forming each word.

"Let me just say I am so sorry I've hurt you. It wasn't my intention. My intentions were to protect all of us, you, me, and of course, our daughter. My mother used to say, 'The road to hell was paved with good intentions,' and I know that my life for the past twenty years has sure felt like a living hell. I wish I had a clear-cut answer for you, John Charlie. I'm afraid I don't. I can only share with you the feelings I had at the time of our daughter's birth ... and the feelings I have today.

"When I discovered, I was pregnant with our child, I thought it would be so unfair to you to let you think I felt anything more for you than I did. I have always loved you since I was a little girl in our village, but like a big brother. I still love you, John Charlie, and believe it or not, your friendship and love are something I cherish. That week I spent with you was wrong. It was wrong because I let you make love to me for all the wrong reasons. I just felt it was like the least I could do because of all you had done for me over the years. I know now I only hurt you even more by not being completely honest with you, and by the time I came to my senses, I was already pregnant with our child." By the look on JC's face, Ahha could see she was only succeeding in hurting him even more, so she stopped talking.

JC knew he had to hear the truth no matter how painful it

might be. The days of turning a blind eye were over. He had to own up to the role he played in all of it—his fantasy as a young man that someday he would marry Ahha, his enabling her drinking by always giving her money when she asked for it, his taking sides with her when she had given her and Sven's daughter up for adoption, excusing her actions because Sven was always out fishing. But worst of all, he'd known deep inside that Ahha didn't love him the way two people in love should, and he'd only yielded to his fantasy of making love to her, telling himself that if he loved her enough, she would come to love him in the way he had so wanted all his life.

"It wasn't all your fault, Ahha. I'm just as much responsible as you are. I knew in my heart that it was Sven you loved and that I was more like a brother to you. I just wish you could have come to me and told me you were pregnant with my child."

"I know that, John Charlie, but at the time it just seemed best for all three of us to not tell anyone and put her up for adoption. I knew I was in no position to raise her, and well, I didn't think you were either."

John Charlie quickly interrupted her, "I don't think you had the right to make that choice for me, Ahha. Not that you aren't probably right about giving her up for adoption. I just wish I could have seen her if only for a minute. And I wish you'd have trusted me enough to know I would have made a decision that was best for her well-being and life. It hurts that you didn't even acknowledge me as her father on her birth certificate."

"I'm really sorry, John Charlie. I know I didn't handle it well. I know I don't have long to live, and I know I'm going to die without knowing our daughter. But that's one of the reasons I told you. I believe with all my heart that wherever she is, she will someday find out where she really came from and who she really is because you, her father, will tell her." Ahha's tears stabbed at JC's heart, and his anger began to fade as his love for her took over. He remembered what Father Lavern had said to him just two days ago, "Love always wins, JC, and God is love."

JC changed the subject. It was his way of conceding that maybe— just maybe—Ahha had done the best thing for their daughter by giving her up for adoption. "Did you know I meant Cayden and Kimberly?" he asked.

"Yes," Ahha answered, "how did that go for you? Aren't they wonderful?"

"You have every reason to be proud Ahha. They're both wonderful young people. I asked them if they would like to write a note to our daughter, their half sister, and they both enthusiastically agreed. I hope you're okay with that." As always when he looked directly into Ahha's eyes, he was a little intimidated. Even when they were both young and living in their village, her direct gaze could always rattle him.

"I have no more secrets, John Charlie. Sister Mary Kathleen gave me a Bible to read, and for the first time in my life, I'm reading God's Word. I want to read to you what I just read before you got here. Do you mind?"

JC thought to himself how strange it was that within the last two days, he'd been encouraged to read the Bible by three different people, Father Lavern, Ahha, and even Sven. He nodded in response.

Anna Ahha opened the Bible that was lying on her stomach and read Mark 4:22 (NIV), which said, "For whatever is hidden is meant to be disclosed, and whatever is concealed is meant to be brought out into open."

John Charlie was stunned. For the first time in his life, he actually heard the Word of God instead of hearing only what seemed to be nothing more than gobbledygook. Why hadn't he heard it before?

Ahha could see John Charlie had really heard the scripture because she, too, had been blind to God's Word up until the previous two days. Was this another miracle? It was all a bit overwhelming to know that God loved her and that He loved her unconditionally.

What was it that Sister Mary Kathleen had called it? Ah, yes, she had called it agape love, love that never fails.

Anna Ahha said, "I think JC that you, Sven, and I have bottled our real feeling up, each of us filled with hidden secrets and living only pretend lives. Instead of confronting our issues, we ran away from our pain. I know now that there is only one way out of pain, and that's through it."

JC nodded in agreement and asked Ahha if she would like to hear the letter he had written to their daughter. And he added, "No more secrets Ahha. No more secrets!"

Ahha teared up but quietly whispered, "Yes."

Choking on the words as he began, JC read from the letter,

Dear Daughter,

I never knew you existed until three days ago, and you're already fifteen years old. Even though I just found out about you, I love you as if I've known you all these years. You might ask why or wonder how I could love someone I've never seen. I don't have much of an answer for that. I only know that the moment I found out I had a daughter, my heart changed, and my mind has been filled with thoughts of you.

Your mother tells me yours was a closed adoption; however, we can write you a letter and have it put in your file. When you turn eighteen, the file will be opened to you if you so choose. It will be my prayer for the next three years that you will want to know where you came from and you will want to meet your biological father.

You are Aleut. Your mother is an Aleut princess who was kidnapped from her village when she was fourteen years old. I am three-quarters Aleut. I once lived in the same village as your mother, and we both ended up in the capital of Alaska, Juneau. The village we were from was destroyed during World War II, so we couldn't return when the war ended. It is a long, sad story about what happened to our people, one I hope someday to share with you in person. But for now I just want you to know that you come from a proud and strong people, a people who has survived against all odds, a people who lived simply in a harsh climate, and a people who understood there was a living God and put their faith and trust in Him.

Your mother shared with me that on the day you were born, she held you in her arms, and you looked like a true Aleut baby with a chubby round face, dark eyes, and lots of black straight hair. You were what the Aleut people call a *papoose*, and your mother loved you so much she put you up for adoption because she wanted you to have a better life than either she or I could give you.

By the time you read this letter, your mother will no longer be alive. She is now dying and doesn't have much longer to live. It is one of the reasons she finally told me about you. She did not want to die without giving you the opportunity to know who you are, the daughter of an Aleut princess.

There is so much more to tell you, but I will wait and believe I will be able to talk to you in person someday. Just know you are loved by your biological parents as well as a half sister and a half brother, both of whom are writing their own letters to you.

May the true and living God watch over you and bring you home to us when you are ready. I have enclosed a phone number and address where I can always be reached.

All my love,

Your father, John Charlie

Ahha was sobbing, deep sobs that can take a person's breath away, sobs that spoke of deep pain at the loss of her daughter. JC choked up so much that he had to stop and take a deep breath before he was able to continue.

It was Ahha who spoke first. "As much as I yearn to see her, I know I never will, but you will. I just know you will. Promise me, John Charlie. Promise me you'll tell her how much I loved her."

JC picked up Ahha's Bible. It was still lying open on her stomach, and holding it in one hand, he swore on it. "I promise you, Ahha, that when I meet our daughter, I will tell her how much you loved her. I will tell her about the Aleut people, and I will see she meets her brother and sister."

As painful as it was for Anna, it was like a thousand pounds had been lifted off her shoulders. Why had it taken her so long to let go? All those pent-up emotions of the last twenty years were now coming to the surface. It was going to take a while to sort them out. She trusted she could do that before she died. She wanted to die free, free from her own self-destructive behaviors that had kept her in bondage for more than twenty years.

CHAPTER 36

S ven turned the key in the door of Anna's boarding room. He couldn't remember the last time he'd been in it—four, maybe five years. It had been midwinter. The Taku winds were blowing with seventy-mile-per-hour gusts of wind that blew off the surrounding mountaintops and with temperatures that often went below zero. (The locals had named the winter storm Taku.) The blowing flurries of snow swirling in large circles could cut into one's bare skin like miniature pieces of ice.

Sven wasn't a big drinker, but once in a while, he liked having a couple of beers in a bar where many of the locals hung out. As cold as it was, he needed to get out of his sister's house, where he had his own bedroom and often stayed in the winter. Besides, he liked being bundled up in his furry parka and walking in the snow wind and cold. He'd literally shaken the snow off, stomping his feet as he walked into the welcoming warmth of the bar. There she was. He hadn't set eyes on her for several months. She was sitting on a stool at the end of the bar, and she was drunk.

Anna Ahha saw Sven enter the bar and practically fell off her stool. Not because she'd sat in the same bar many nights, hoping against hope Sven would walk through the door, but because she'd had too much to drink. He walked straight to her, and she'd almost fallen, throwing her arms around his neck and loudly saying his name over and over again.

He'd untangled her from him and simply said, "You've had enough. I'm taking you home!" He'd bundled her up, and basically carrying her, he walked her the four blocks up to the shabby hotel she lived in. Anna had gone on and on about how much she loved him and how she knew he loved her as well. It ripped at his heart, and he'd come too close to staying with her that night. And if she hadn't been so drunk, he probably would have. He stayed away from the bars after that. It hurt too much watching her destroy herself, and he was still unable to forgive her for giving their daughter up for adoption.

In Anna Ahha's world, she held on to the hope that he'd eventually come back to her, and she handled her pain by drinking until she passed out day after day and year after year. She'd lived in limbo, getting through each day by dulling her pain with hooch or cheap whiskey or whatever she could get her hands on first.

Sven was sickened at the condition of the room, and he knew Anna Ahha wouldn't be coming back to it. So on another one of his missions, he took it upon himself to empty the room of all her meager possessions.

Stripping the bed of its bedding, he laid it out flat on the floor, using it like a container for the items worth salvaging to take them to the Salvation Army secondhand store. There wasn't much, just a few pots, pans, and dishes. He opened the small closet door. The closest was crammed full, half the clothes on wire hangers and the other half piled halfway up the closet wall in a haphazard manner. Most of the clothes looked like they had been bought at the Salvation Army, and he wondered to himself how many times the clothes could be recycled.

It wasn't until Sven had pulled out most of the clothes that he spotted the fox fur parka he'd brought Anna Ahha that first winter they were married and she was pregnant with their daughter. The memories came flooding in, filling Sven with melancholy. They had both been so happy that winter. During the day he would go down to the boat dock and putter around with various tasks on the Blue Lady. It was his habit then—as it still was—to keep his fishing vessel in pristine condition. He would head home in the late afternoon once it started getting dark around four in the afternoon, and Anna Ahha was always waiting for him. He'd thought she was more beautiful than ever with her baby belly and her long black hair falling loose around her face. They would eat whatever meal she'd fixed, and then they'd sit on the couch together with Anna Ahha snuggled up, her head on his shoulder, watching their small black-and-white TV. It was the happiest time in Sven's life, and he was certain it had been a happy time for Anna Ahha too.

The fox fur parka was well worn but in good condition. Sven could see where Anna Ahha had hand-sewn and patched up places in the lining, he'd forgotten how well she could sew. and always by hand. He put the parka in the pile "for things to keep." It was a small pile as most of her clothes were in poor condition or just downright stained and dirty. To Sven it looked like Anna Ahha had worn an outfit until it was filthy and then went to the Salvation Army second hand store and bought another outfit. How Anna Ahha had lived for the past eighteen years tugged at Sven's heart. Why in the name of all that was holy had he not stayed with her when she had begged him not to leave her alone with their daughter?

Shoved back in the corner of the closet was a wire hanger covered in brown grocery store bags. Sven brought it out and tore off the dusty paper bag covering. When he saw what it was, he felt like his heart was going to pound right out of his chest. It was the dress she'd been wearing the day she had been kidnapped from her village. It was in pristine conditions, and obviously, Anna Ahha had painstakingly repaired any damage that had been done to it. She had also kept it immaculately clean.

Anna Ahha had told him how the dress was made from the skin of many different birds, such as the common Rosefinch, Siberian Rubythroat, Bluethroat, Lanceolated warbler, and the totem bird for her mother, the Puffin, also known as the artic parrot. She had told him how it took more than a year to make a garment because the process of tanning the skin took at least ten months.

First, the bird skin was soaked in urine for at least a day in order to make it more pliable. The flesh was carefully scraped off the skin, using a very sharp convex blade. This could take several days, depending on how many skins needed to be scraped clean. Once the skin was clean of the birds' flesh, the small individual skins were hand sown together and curried on a large wooden frame and left in the frame until semidry. The skin was then scraped vigorously with a very blunt blade and alternatively rubbed around with a canoe paddle. The leather is then smoked, suspended over an open fire, and then rubbed with whale oil.

Anna Ahha had become extremely melancholy when telling Sven about the garment. It was the last garment she had that her mother had made, and in fact, Ahha had only been wearing it for less than three weeks before she was taken. It was also the garment she had worn the day they went to city hall to get married. Sven could still see her on that day in his mind's eye. She'd looked stunning, and they turned heads everywhere they went. He'd been so proud that day, so proud that the Aleut princess was his wife. He laid the garment carefully on the "keep" pile. *Oh, God*, Sven thought, *why did I let her go?*

It took a couple more hours just to sweep up and dispose of the dirt and junk. The only thing left to go through was the small chest of drawers. There were only three drawers, and they were difficult to open, sticking and pulling out crooked. The bottom drawer had literally fallen apart, and its contents fell out onto the floor. It looked like nothing more than a junk drawer. It contained clothes that were rags, some half-used makeup, half-used tape rolls, broken pencils, and crumbled-up paper. Sven went to scoop up the clothes when something dropped out onto the floor. It was a small handmade Aleut basket. Sven immediately recognized it. It was a basket made by Annuuk, and JC had brought it for Anna Ahha back from the internment camp where Annuuk had died. Anna had kept it in a small shelf when they had lived in the Channel apartment. Sven dropped the clothes in the "throw away" pile and picked up the basket taking the well-fitted lid off. The carved ivory puffin was still inside along with the wedding ring Sven had bought her, a gold band with three small diamonds imbedded in it. Sven couldn't remember the last time he'd seen the ring on her finger, but he instantly knew he would get on his hands and knees if he had to and put that ring back on her finger, which was where he believed it belonged.

In that moment Sven had an epiphany. He'd been such a coward that day so long ago. He'd just plain been afraid of that unknown. His own fear overrided his love for his wife and daughter. Anna Ahha had pleaded with him not to go out fishing. He'd be gone for five to six weeks, depending how well the fish were running. She tried to tell him that she barely knew how to take care of herself, let alone a six-week-old baby. They'd gone back and forth. Sven would try to tell her it was the only way he knew how to make a living for them. Anna would try to tell him she'd never lived on her own, and as much as she loved their daughter, she was often overwhelmed with the responsibility. She was always afraid she was going to do something wrong and hurt her child in some way. Sven didn't know about after-birth depression, and he thought Anna was being silly. In his mind she was the mother, and she'd instinctively know what to do. Around and around they went in one vicious circle, and when he'd finally left, he'd left her crying at the door and literally wringing her hands. He returned six weeks later, and his daughter was gone. Fear had ruled their lives.

There were two other small items in the basket—both in clear plastic and sealed with tape. One was a lock of light brown baby hair, and the other was a lock of dark black baby hair. Sven knew without question that one was from Kimberly and the other was from JC's daughter.

Sven sat down on the now stripped bed with his head in his hands. Closing his eyes, the memories and emotions he'd buried for the past seventeen years came flooding in as if they had happened yesterday—their first meeting and how they had talked until dawn; Anna's smile and laugh, so spontaneous and filled with life like a little girl's without a care in the world; how they had driven all over Juneau and "out the road" to the Mendenhall glacier, stopping in the many fields and picking bouquets of wildflower. Sven's head jerked up. He'd forgotten about Anna Ahha's love for the wildflowers of Alaska. He knew now exactly what he was going to do. He would take her the biggest bouquet of Alaska wildflowers along with the meager but loved items she so treasured.

It took Sven just little more than an hour to make the drive out and back to the many fields filled with various Alaska wildflowers. He drove straight to his mother and father's small home just across from the Juneau-Douglas high school on Glacier Avenue. If anyone could make a lovely bouquet out of the conglomeration of flowers he'd picked, it was his mother.

Sven's parents were always overjoyed to see him. They had stopped asking about Anna years before because it was too heart-wrenching to see the pain in their son's face whenever they did ask. Sven's sister had called them and told them Anna was dying and that Sven was now in touch with his daughter and that her name was Kimberly. When they saw Sven coming through the front door, they hoped he would tell them about Kimberly. After all, it was their granddaughter.

He held in both arms a massive amount flowers, yellow buttercups, white daisies, blue forget-me-nots, the golden balls of Alaska cotton, and the reddish-purple Alaska fireweed.

"Mom," he asked, "could you make a bouquet out of all these flowers for me? They're for Anna. I remembered today how much she loved wildflowers." Instead of seeing the look of pain she usually saw on her son's face when he spoke of Anna, she saw ... What was it she saw? It was love. She saw love. Something had happened. The love for his wife had conquered his fear.

"I think I might just have the right vase for so many flowers," his mother said with a twinkle in her eye.

"So, Son, will you tell your father and I about our granddaughter, Kimberly?"

Sven watched his mother's nimble hands create the most beautiful bouquet he had ever seen, with the purplish fireweed in the center surrounded by the fluffy golden ball of the Alaska cotton and a double row of the white daisies, creating a thick white circle between the fireweed and Alaska cotton to the bottom rows of blue forget-me-nots and yellow buttercups. While his mother was putting the bouquet together, he told her all about Kimberly, where she lived, how proud he was of the young lady she'd become, and what she looked. In fact, she looked much like her grandmother. His mother smiled when he told her Kimberly looked like her. Before leaving, he promised both his parents he would bring Kimberly by and introduce her.

It was early afternoon by the time Sven got to the hospital. He had quite the bundle in his arms—the large bouquet, the basket, and Anna Ahha's bird-skin dress and fox fur parka. Anna Ahha was sleeping when he entered the room. He put the bouquet and basket on her hospital table and rolled it to the end of her bed so that when she woke up, it would be the first thing she saw. The bouquet was so huge it took up the whole width of the hospital bed. He laid the dress and parka on the back of one of the chairs and sat down. Sven had been going full speed since early morning, and he was determined to wait for Anna Ahha to wake up; however, he found his eyes closing, and quickly, he dozed off.

CHAPTER 37

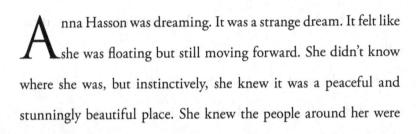

Anna Hasson was dreaming. It was a strange dream. It felt like she was floating but still moving forward. She didn't know where she was, but instinctively, she knew it was a peaceful and stunningly beautiful place. She knew the people around her were people who loved her. Even though she couldn't see any of their faces, she could see they were all dressed in the Aleut way. Most importantly, she wasn't sick, and all of her addictions had vanished.

Instead of going for her midday meal, Sister Mary Kathleen decided to check in on Anna. Entering the hospital room, she caught the pleasant fragrance of all the wildflowers sitting at the foot of Anna's bed. Sven was slouched down in a chair, sleeping. Anna automatically woke up at the sound of Sister Mary Kathleen's wooden rosary beads clacking against one another.

At first, Anna thought she was still dreaming because the first thing she saw when opening her eyes was the flowers. They seemed to fill the room. Turning her head toward the sound of the wooden beads, she saw Sister Mary Kathleen's smiling face. She smiled back. Sister nodded her head in a way that told Anna to look on the other side of her bed. Anna's heart skipped a beat when she saw the love of her life silently sleeping in a chair. It brought tears to her eyes because she immediately knew he had brought the flowers. He'd remembered!

Sister put her finger to her mouth, suggesting they keep their talk at a whisper.

Anna whispered, "I just had the strangest dream," and then she proceeded to tell Sister her dream. "I have no idea what it means. Do you?"

Sister Mary Kathleen knew she wasn't all that knowledgeable about dream interpretation, but she was sure of what this dream meant and believed she was supposed to tell Anna.

"Well," Sister started out slowly, deliberately picking her words. "They say that heaven is much like the place you described. They also say that it is a place where we feel totally loved. I mean the people who study these kinds of phenomena. I think, Anna, that your dream was from God, that He is telling you your time is soon. And when you get to heaven, you will be completely healed. You understand you won't have the same body you have now. Your body is nothing more than your earth suit. Remember, you are a spirit that lives in a body and has a soul."

Anna eyes were wide, "Do you really believe that God would talk to me in a dream? I mean, I haven't been faithful to Him, and I've done so many wrong things in my life. Besides, I have spent the last eighteen years mad—I mean, *really* mad—at God."

Sister couldn't help but smile. "Well, you had to believe there is a God if you were mad at Him. God talks to everyone, Anna, not necessarily in an audible voice but through His Word, through music, in dreams, through circumstances in your life that I call 'God incidences,' and sometimes through a living thing. People just aren't listening, or they don't believe, just like you, that God would ever talk to them. Or they just don't believe in a living God. God's Word says in Hebrews 11:6, 'Without faith it is impossible to please God because anyone who comes to Him must believe that He exists and that He rewards those who seek Him.' And Anna, if I know how sorry you are, don't you think God knows to?"

Anna voice was shaking as she said, "In just the last few days, I see everything so differently. It's hard to explain. It's like one day everything had a shadow surrounding it and appeared bleak and out of kilter. And the next day the shadow was gone, and there was nothing but love and light." Anna was focused on Sister when she spoke, so she didn't see that Sven had woken up and heard everything she was saying."

"Me too!" Sven chimed in. His voice startled Anna, and she looked at him in a way Sven hadn't seen for far too many years. Sven had never seen her look so serene. Her face almost glowed in spite of her illness, and she looked happy, happier than he'd ever seen her. Amazingly, he felt the same way.

Sister Mary Kathleen knew she was witnessing not one but two miracles. There was the miracle that happened when anyone came to salvation or as God's Word said, "You must become born again." It was a metamorphosis as a caterpillar turning into a butterfly. In the case of human beings, it was the heart and not the physical body that changed. She also knew there was no way of really explaining it because only those who experienced it truly understood it, and she also knew that much of the world thought born-again Christians were at the very least neurotics who couldn't come to grips with their own death. Some even thought they might also be psychotic, living their lives in some kind of surreal fantasy. No matter how many born-again Christians said they really hadn't lived until they had a relationship with Jesus Christ, the nonbeliever could not be convinced. It was much like a hamster going around and around on a wheel, headed nowhere, but their little legs would go faster and faster as they tried to reach the end. It was pointless, a complete waste of precious energy.

Sister Mary Kathleen excused herself. She knew she was definitely a third wheel at this point. She quietly closed the hospital door to Anna's room, giving Anna and Sven the privacy they needed.

Sven took Anna's hand into both of his, raising hers up to his lips, and lightly kissed it. "You know, Anna Ahha, how much I love you. I've loved you from the first moment I set eyes on you. I'm so very sorry! Sorry for being such a coward. I should have stayed with you when you begged me to. I was scared, Anna Ahha, just plain scared. Scared to try to make a living any other way than fishing. It's all I'd ever known since I was just a young boy going out with my dad in the summers to help him fish."

"I know," Anna Ahha said in soft voice. "I love you too. I always have. It's the reason I didn't stay with JC after I realized I was pregnant with his child. I just couldn't pretend to be someone I wasn't, and I, too, was scared. No, more than scared. I was terrified. It was like there was this big lump of heavy gray clay in the middle of my stomach that froze me in time. I couldn't move forward, and I couldn't move backward. And I could barely function, let alone take care of a newborn baby. I thought the only way for me to be a good mother was if you were physically present to help me with our daughter's care. You see the only times that heavy gray lump of clay would go away was when I was with you, or when I drank Hooch. That's what I've been doing for the past eighteen years, running, running away from the heavy gray lump of clay always there, controlling my life."

Sven kept kissing her hand over and over again. "Shhh, my love, it doesn't matter anymore. The only thing that matters is I'm here now and I will never again leave your side."

"No, no, let me finish!" Anna Ahha exclaimed. "Do you remember, Sven, when I tried to go out on the fishing boat with you? At that time I was terrified, and all those ugly memories when I was repeatedly raped came flooding back into my head as if they'd happened yesterday. I'd wake up in the middle of the night with the boat gently rocking back and forth and break out in a cold sweat and uncontrollable shaking. Then I got so sick every day, all day. Remember how we both thought I had seasickness only to find out a couple of week later that I was pregnant with our daughter? By that time the fishing season was over, we were together in our little apartment, and I want you to know that was the happiest time in my life. I didn't drink because I didn't need to drink. The heavy gray lump of clay in the pit of my stomach quit rearing its ugly head. Instead I had our baby growing inside me, and I was so sure you and I were going to be happy together the rest of our lives."

"It's not just your fault Sven, it's both of our faults. We both retreated into a cocoon, not living or dying but keeping our love buried because it hurt too much to feel anything. You can't pick or chose which feelings "e living dead. We were stuck because of fear—pure, unadulterated fear. Sister Mary Kathleen showed me a scripture passage about fear. Second Timothy1:7 says, 'For God did not give us a spirit of fear, but a spirit of power, of love and of self-discipline.'

"Sven, it's our love for each other and our love for our daughter that has overcome the fear we have lived in for so long. I don't know why we didn't see this sooner. I only know we both see the truth now and that God's hands are on us."

Sven nodded in agreement. Then he pulled from beneath his jacket the Aleut basket Anna Ahha had made so many years ago. It was the only thing she had from the years in her village. John Charlie had retrieved it from the internment camp after her mother had died.

"I went to your boarding room this morning and cleaned it out. Look what I found." Sven handed the basket to Anna.

Anna Ahha took it in her hands, caressing it as tears began to slowly roll down her cheeks. "Everything I love most in the world is represented in this basket," she said. Her voice was so low Sven had to strain to hear her.

She took the lid off, taking the items out one by one. She saw the black lock of hair. "This goes to John Charlie for the daughter I had with him. Do you have my Aleut dress, Sven?" He nodded his head yes and retrieved it from the chair he had thrown it on. "That, too, is to go to John Charlie, in the hope that he will connect with our daughter when she turns eighteen."

There was a lighter brown lock of hair. "This is for you, Sven, to give to our daughter, Kimberly. She's also to have my fox parka you bought me. Did you bring it?" Sven nodded his head yes and retrieved it as well. The bouquet had kept it from Anna's view.

Next, she brought out the ivory puffin bird, her mother's totem, carved by her mother when she had just been a young girl. "This is for my son, Cayden, along with the basket. I will make sure he knows it is his heirloom and his right as an Aleut man and my son."

The last item was her gold band with the three small diamonds. Anna Ahha handed it to Sven and whispered, "And this is for you, Sven. I pray you will always remember that in spite of all we've been through, I never stopped loving you."

Sven took the ring and put it on her left ring finger and said, "For better or worse, my Aleut princess. For better or worse."

Anna held her left hand up, touching it with her right hand, caressing the wedding band. She looked at Sven with sad eyes filled with love and whispered, "Until death do us part."

Sven stood, put his arms around her, and pulled her body close to him, her head resting on his chest. Their silence filled the room. They could feel only of God's love, agape love, unconditional love.

CHAPTER 38

After Sven left her house, Linda sat at her messy wooden kitchen table, staring into space. She really did love Anna. As a matter of fact, she was the one who had given Ahha the name Anna. Linda had thought people would accept her more easily if she used a more common name. She had to go see her. Anna was dying, and the guilt she felt overwhelmed her.

Slowly, she looked around the room. The whole kitchen badly needed a deep clean and a new coat of paint. When had she lost interest in the way her home looked? She used to pride herself on her good housekeeping skills. When had she lost any motivation to get up and move and to do anything other than lay on her couch and watch TV or read?

Linda and Willie had stopped fighting every single day over money, over everything—dirty laundry, dirty dishes, dirty floors, and clutter spread out all over every corner of the house. It was a challenge to find just about anything, including clean clothes and towels.

At least when they were fighting, there was some assurance that they still cared about life, about each other, and about their two sons. But now they barely spoke to each other. It was as if neither one of them really gave a damn about life. They were stuck at surviving and preserving security, unable to love and be loved. Neither could feel any self-esteem. Linda had read somewhere about self-actualization and realizing one's full potential in order to achieve self-fulfillment and personal growth.

But Linda had never been able to get past the heavy burden of guilt she carried on her shoulders, and every year the load seemed to get heavier, starting way back when she was just a young girl. She didn't know who her biological father was, and she had had two stepfathers, neither of which stuck around for any length of time. Both of them were mean buggers. Her bitter, angry mother had pretty much raised Linda by herself and had blamed Linda for her own miserable life. It wasn't until Linda's mother was diagnosed with lung cancer that they finally had a halfway decent mother-daughter relationship. Her mother had finally opened up to her about her heritage, her bloodline, and Linda found out she was more Alutiiq than Aleut. She'd never taken the time to tell Anna how they were related. She had just known by a statement her mother had made many years before that somehow there was a blood connection between her and Anna Ahha.

When Linda's mother died, which was only six months ago, Linda was at her bedside, and she walked away from her mother's deathbed, taking with her all the sad regrets of their lives together.

With the heavy and consuming guilt Linda carried about her relationship with her mother, one would think there wasn't any room left in her heart for anymore guilt. However, Linda also felt she hadn't been a good wife, mother, or even friend. After all, she had started both her husband, Willie, and Anna on hooch. On many nights the three of them would sit in the small living area of the Quonset hut, drinking while her young sons slept. It had seemed so harmless at the time.

It had been somewhat of a miracle, maybe even divine providence, the day Ahha was brought to the Quonset hut where Linda and Willie lived. It was a normal Juneau cloudy day with a constant drizzle of rain coming down. In the early morning, a well-known Tlingit native had been at the small boat dock, delivering diesel to several of the fishing boats. He'd spotted Ahha sitting on one of big logs separating the small parking lot from the road. She was drenched, and her long black hair hung down in clumps around her swollen red eyes. Her native garment looked dirty and coming apart around some of its many seams. She looked lost and scared.

Teylynn approached her and asked her if she was okay. Ahha had looked up at him and said, "Where am I?"

Teylynn answered, "At the small boat harbor."

"No, I mean what town am I in?" Ahha asked in her broken English.

Teylynn didn't quite know how to take her. She looked young, too young to be sitting alone on a rainy day. He hadn't seen her around Juneau, and the natives of Juneau were a tight-knit group, protecting one another no matter what their status was in the community. He asked her, "How long have you been here? Where are you from?"

Ahha lowered her eyes and head in shame. "I just got here. Two men took me from my village on Atka Island. I'm Aleut." She started sobbing uncontrollably.

Teylynn knew that something traumatic had happened to this beautiful young girl. He knew who Linda was, and he had heard somewhere in the close-knit native culture of Juneau that Linda was Aleut.

Teylynn knelt down on one knee in front of Ahha and said, "Come with me. I think I know where I can take you so you'll be safe."

Ahha had glanced at him, and as frightened as she was, she nodded in agreement. After all, she had no other choice. Here, freedom of choice had been taken from her the moment she had been kidnapped. She couldn't sit on this log in the parking lot of the small boat harbor in Juneau for the rest of her life!

Linda took her in without question, and she lived with her and Willie until she married Sven.

Then Linda snapped out of her daydream. Or was it more like a nightmare? Willie was in the bedroom, sleeping. He still worked evenings at the post office as the night janitor, and for all the years they had been together, he slept days. Linda didn't know what exactly had shaken her to her core, but she jumped up off the chair and began cleaning her kitchen. It took her three hours, and when Willie got up, he looked around the kitchen, and all he said was, "I'll be damned. What tripped your trigger?"

Linda answered, "Anna's dying. I mean, she's really dying this time. Sven was here, and he told me."

Willie stopped what he was doing and looked at his wife He knew in spite of the many fights his wife and Anna had had, she loved her like a daughter. "Are you going to go see her?" he asked.

"Yes," she answered, "tomorrow morning first thing."

CHAPTER 39

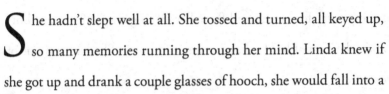

She hadn't slept well at all. She tossed and turned, all keyed up, so many memories running through her mind. Linda knew if she got up and drank a couple glasses of hooch, she would fall into a fretful sleep. She resisted the temptation. She wanted to have a clear mind when she went to see Anna.

It had been awhile since Linda had paid any attention to what she was wearing and how she might look to others. She looked in the full-length mirror, which was usually hidden under a hook filled with clothes in back of her bedroom door. Linda could see just how much the years had aged her. Her dark brown hair had once been a golden chestnut, but now it was a dull brown that she usually just pulled back into a scraggly ponytail. She spent an hour washing and conditioning it, giving it at least some shine and working it into a french twist.

She wasn't a big woman, only five foot three, and she was about thirty pounds overweight. With clothes that fit right, she didn't look too bad. She had one pair of blue jeans that fit well and a long pullover red sweater that complemented her light brown complexion. Standing in front of the full-length mirror, she thought, *I do clean up well.* Linda promised herself she would clean herself up every day from now on. She had to shake off the depression she'd been in since before her mother died. She could do it. Linda knew she had to quit feeling sorry for herself and force herself to get up off her lazy butt and take care of her husband, sons, and home. She had run out of excuses.

Linda walked the three blocks downhill from her house to the hospital, reciting to herself what she wanted to say to Anna. Entering Anna's hospital room, Linda was shocked by how fragile Anna looked, her dark eyes sunken and high cheekbones sharp with almost translucent skin covering the bones. She was ashamed of the way she had treated Anna the last time she'd seen her. "I'm sorry, Anna," she said. "I was just mad and scared."

Anna actually winked at her and said, "That's okay, I was mad at myself and scared too. I'm so happy you're here. I was worried that I might not ever see you again. Do you know I've met my son and one of my daughters?"

"Yeah, I know. Sven came to see me and told me. What do mean one of your daughters?"

"Sit down, Linda. I have one more secret to tell you." And Anna proceeded to tell her all about the daughter she'd had with JC.

Linda eyes grew wide. She wasn't completely shocked by it, just surprised. She was surprised because so much had passed without them seeing each other that Anna could have a baby without her knowing it. Her first feeling was one of guilt. Why did she always take everything into herself? How had it come to be that she felt responsible for the sadness in not only her life but in the lives of all the people she loved too?

"My God, Anna. I'm so sorry!" Linda exclaimed. "I should have been there for you."

"Linda, you were there for me. You took me into your home without question when I was like a wounded little bird. You loved me like a sister and put up with all my craziness. No one could have done any better than you, and in case you don't know, I couldn't love you more if you were my real sister." Anna's voice was firm and strong, stronger than one would imagine for a woman who only had days to live.

Linda shook the guilty feelings away and changed the subject. "You know my mom died a little more than six months ago.

Remember how we would go months on end without talking to each other?"

Anna nodded.

Linda continued. "Well, during the last few months of my mother's life, we actually began to like each other, just a little. She said she was sorry for the way she had treated me, and told me in great length about my heritage and where I came from."

That triggered Anna Ahha's curiosity. After all, she had just come to truly appreciate her own Aleut heritage, so she signaled for Linda to go on.

Linda began, "First of all, my mother explained to me how you and I are related. Your great-grandmother and my great-grandmother were half-sisters. We had different great-grandmothers. Mine was Alutiiq, and yours was Aleut. We had the same great-grandfather, an Aleut. When you and I were born, I only had one-eighth Aleut in me, I'm mostly Alutiiq. My mom was so secretive about where she come from that I grew up only knowing that she'd been orphaned at about the age of seven and that she was part Aleut. I just assumed I was Aleut.

"The Alutiiq people are a southern coastal people of the native peoples of Alaska. Their language is called Sugstune, which is one of the Eskimo languages. Alutiiq people are often confused with Aleut people who live farther southwest, including along the Aleutian Islands.

"My mother was born on Kodiak Island, which the Alutiiq natives have inhabited for more than seven thousand years. In the language of the Alutiiq people, *kadiak* means island. Sometime back in the late 1700s, the Awauq Massacre or the 'Wounded Knee of Alaska' occurred. The Russian fur traders attacked. Between 2,500 and three thousand Alutiiq people were slaughtered, and more than a thousand people were captured. More than four hundred of them were held as hostages. There were no Russian casualties, and the Alutiiq people were completely enslaved by the Russian traders. This treatment didn't end until about 1818 with a change in the management of the Russian American company.

"Then Russia sold Alaska to the United States in 1867, and Kodiak became a commercial fishing center, a tradition that continues today. When World War II broke out, the town of Kodiak was turned into a fortress with new roads, an airport, and Fort Abercrombie. Many of the Alutiiq men joined the military and fought in the war.

"When my mother was just a toddler, her father was killed by an Alaskan grizzly bear. She told me Alaska grizzly bears were the world's largest bears. Adult males exceeded a thousand pounds. Then a couple of years later, her mother died of some kind of infection. My mother was never really told why her mother died. There were two other orphaned Alutiiq children besides my mother, and all three of them were brought to the Minifield Home here in Juneau. My mother never knew why, and she was very bitter and angry all of her life, feeling that her people had abandoned her. It was one of the reasons she claimed to be more Aleut than Alutiiq.

"I've never known who my father was because my mother refused to talk about it until a couple of days before she died. She finally told me she wasn't sure who he was. When she was young, she was promiscuous. She was always just looking for someone to love her. When she told me, that was one of the few times I saw my mother cry. She then told me she now realized that I was the only person who truly loved her and she could never receive it because she always felt she wasn't good enough for anyone to love her, not even her daughter. It was so sad, Anna. She went through her whole life feeling so unworthy of love that she sabotaged herself whenever anyone tried to show her love. I remember once when I was like eight or nine years old, making her this card for Mother's Day, and when I gave it to her, all she did was criticize my drawing. I was so embarrassed and hurt."

Linda started crying, the salty tears rolling down her blotchy cheeks. "You know, Anna, those words 'I love you' keep rolling around in my head over and over again. It's driving me crazy!"

Anna reached for Linda's hand. "I love you too, Linda, and I know Willie loves you … and your sons. Don't make the same mistake your mom made. Let us love you as you love us."

"When did you get so wise, Anna?" Linda asked.

"Well, I don't know how wise I am, but I've see everything so differently in the last few days. I mean, I knew I was probably dying when I was admitted, and I thought I'd die alone. I felt like no one cared enough about me. Worse yet, I felt just like your mom, that I didn't deserve anyone's love because I'd done so many horrible things. But Sister Mary Kathleen helped me, and I stopped being so mad at God and asked Him to help me. It's changed everything, Linda. I have Sven and JC, you, and two of the children I gave away. Oh, Linda, I want you to meet them. They are such wonderful people."

In all the years she'd known Anna, Linda had never heard her speak so many words at one time. Not only that, but there was something different about her a steady calmness, and even though she was dying, she looked … happy!

CHAPTER 40

I t was a cloudless day with a blue sky in Juneau after a week of rain, and graduation day for the seventy-two seniors of Juneau-Douglas High School had finally come.

The past week had gone too fast for Kim. The senior class had their senior sneak day on Monday, and the class ended up out at the Eagle River Scout Camp, a two-mile hike from the end of the road. The Senior Brothers, which consisted of twelve of the most popular males in the senior class, had sneaked a few cases of beer out to the camp and hid them in the surrounding forest. It had begun to rain in the early afternoon, which put a damper on the whole day, and most of the class had hiked the two miles back to the road early and went home. Kim was one of them.

Kim didn't have a reputation for being a party girl, but she'd gone to a couple of beer parties in her senior year just because she didn't want her classmates thinking that she was a geek. One of the parties had been at the skaters cabin, built which was built on the edge of the lake in stone and accessible to the public. The lake had formed as the result of runoff water from the Mendenhall Glacier. She'd had a couple of beers and was having a good time, reciting by heart the two poems "The Cremation of Sam McGee" and "The Quitter" by the Alaska poet Robert Service when someone yelled out, "Cops!"

Everyone scattered, hiding in the surrounding woods. Kim thought her heart was going to pound out of her chest. If her folks found out, she'd be in big trouble. The cops had picked up a couple of the die-hard partygoers, and after an hour or so, they left. The teenagers left crammed into the couple of cars still parked on a side road and drove back into town. The teenagers' nervous laughter and false bravado filled the car as they drove around the Loop Road, which took them into the Auke Bay area. Kim promised herself, "Never again." It just wasn't worth the risk.

With the only exception of senior sneak day and with her newfound brother, Cayden, Kim visited her mother, the Aleut princess, every afternoon for the past week. Her biological father, Sven, usually came into the room shortly after she and Cayden would arrive. The four of them were talking incessantly, catching up on all the lost years. Occasionally, Anna Ahha would drift off to sleep for five or ten minutes, and then upon waking, she would say, "Oh, I must have drifted off." The three of them would smile, even giggle and then continue talking as if there had been no interruption. It seemed to Kim that every day her mother was shrinking. She looked like a small china doll with her black hair always braided in two loose breads and cascading down her shoulders. She wore a handmade, beaded headband like a crown. In one of their many conversations, Kim and Cayden found out their mother had made it herself and beaded it in many Aleut symbols, including a fish and a puffin bird.

Kim just turned eighteen, and she had her whole life ahead of her. Within the last six weeks, her life had dramatically changed. The list of changes in her life was long, and her dominating feeling was one of apprehensiveness. After graduation from high school, she would no longer be a high school student. She would be thrust into the world of adulthood. Attending college in the fall was a bit of a buffer; however, she would now be responsible for her own personal needs, meals that had always been provided, personal items such as shampoo, soap, and deodorant, and now she was going to have bills, bills addressed to her for payment.

Kimberly now had a brother, a brother she loved and had bonded with in a short six-week period, a brother she loved every bit as much as her two older sisters. And those sisters had been in her life since her earliest childhood memories. One of Kim's first memories—she must have been about three years old—was Christmas shopping with both her sisters. She didn't remember where or why their parents weren't with them. She only remembered sitting in a restaurant, sipping a thick chocolate milk shake through a straw. Mostly, she remembered her feelings at the time. The three of them were laughing about something, and Kim only remembered feeling happy, loved, and safe.

Kimberly now knew she had two sets of parents—her adoptive parents and her biological parents. She loved all four of them without restrictions or questions. She had talked about it with her adoptive mother. As a matter of fact, Kim had always openly talked with her mother, Elaine, about everything and anything. There had been a time in her sophomore and junior year of high school when she was trying to figure out her own separate and unique identity. Then Kim hadn't been quite so open with her mother, but it was like her mother understood. She didn't press her for answers that Kim didn't have. However, she talked with her two older sisters about how somethings—like sex, for example—were embarrassing for her to talk about. They had both told her the same thing. "Mom's always been sensitive about our feelings and given us the space we needed to grow up."

Kim had always had a vague awareness about being part Aleut. Meeting her biological mother and hearing the stories connected to her heritage had given her a sense of pride in being Aleut. With that pride had come a determination to aggressively pursue justice for the Aleut race.

"You know how much I love you and Dad, right? Kim asked, starting the conversation.

"Of course we do," her mother answered, and then looking at her daughter long and hard, she added, "It's okay for you to love your biological parents, my daughter." Kim breathed a sigh of relief. She'd been worried about hurting her adoptive parents.

"It's hard for me to put into words the way I feel about my biological parents. I know I love them, but it doesn't feel the same as my love for you and Dad. It's so confusing," Kim muttered to herself.

Kim and her mother were washing dishes. Her mother was washing, and Kim was drying and putting the dishes away. She'd grown up with her mother's philosophy of "everything in its place and a place for everything." Elaine gently took the dish towel out of Kim's hand and guided her to the small red and white breakfast nook with the built-in table and benches. She held both of Kim's hands in hers and said, "You're learning one of life's lessons, Daughter. Serious talks always ended with her mother calling her, "Daughter," and she and her two sisters always knew to pay close attention then because whatever their mother was about to say was important.

"Life is a journey, Kimberly, and whenever we get to a crossway in the road, we get to choose which direction to go in. To walk in love is the highest walk available. Basically, the more we love, the more we learn how to love. Love isn't just a feeling. It's a commitment to the other's well-being. It's like our heart or our spirit grows significantly larger to include more and more people. You love to ski, Kim, and you love both your fathers. That's because you have a great capacity to love. It's a gift, Daughter. Use it wisely. Let me forewarn you, Daughter. There will be those who won't receive your love. Some will use it to manipulate you to meet their own needs, and there will even be the few who might even betray you. Still, it's important for you to *choose* love. When it's all been said and its' all been done, you will know beyond a shadow of a doubt the most important thing in your life—the people you have loved and those who have loved you. Do you understand, Daughter?" Elaine had kept her eyes glued on her daughter's eyes the whole time she was speaking. "And one more thing, Kim. Love isn't love until you give it away."

Kim nodded and asked, "How did you become so wise, Mom?"

"Because life taught me, Kim, as it is already teaching you. Now young lady, you need to go and visit your other mother. I understand she wants to see you in your graduating cap and grown."

It would be the first time Kim visited Anna without her brother, Cayden. She was looking forward to one-on-one time with her Aleut mother.

A half hour later, Kim was in the hallway just outside Anna's hospital room. She put on her cap and grown and tiptoed into the room. Anna was focused on the huge bouquet, which now had some flowers that had wilted and turned brown, so she didn't see Kim when she first entered. Kim cleared her throat, and Anna looked up. "Oh, Kim," she exclaimed, "You are so beautiful!"

"Thank you," Kim answered and then continued, "I wish you could be there tonight.

Anna smiled at her daughter and said, "I wish I could be there too, Kimberly. You know, your dad, Sven, will be there. So will Cayden and JC." Anna quickly went on while she was still feeling brave. "Before I meant you, I wished I hadn't given you away. But now after seeing what a fine young lady you are, I know I did the right thing. I could never have given you the wonderful life you have had. I hope you understand."

"I do understand, Ahha. My mom, Elaine, and I were just talking about that earlier this morning. She said love was about putting another person's well-being before yourself."

Anna Ahha teared up. It had taken her forty years to learn that lesson, and her daughter knew it at age eighteen. "So are you excited about going to college? You're going to the University of Alaska in Fairbanks, right?" Anna inquired.

"Yes, one of my girlfriends is going too, so I'll at least know one person," replied Kim.

"Well, it gets mighty cold in Fairbanks. Now that's where your Aleut blood might kick in." Anna was only half-joking, so she continued talking. "See that closet door over there. Go open it. There's something I want to give you, something that will keep you warm when you're running between buildings for different classes. Something your father, Sven, gave me the winter you were born. I've kept it in perfect condition."

Kim opened the closet door and saw the most stunning fox parka she'd ever seen. "This is for me? It's so beautiful. Are you sure?" Kim's excitement at the gift was evident, and she took the coat she was wearing off to try the parka on. It was a perfect fit!

For the first time in her life, Anna Ahha's spirit swelled with a kind of joy she had never experienced. It was the rare feeling that came only with motherhood, where all the motherly emotions came together in one grand finale. The Aleut princess felt like a genuine mom.

CHAPTER 41

As the seventy-two seniors lined up in the hall of Juneau-Douglas High School, one boy and one girl marching together, the excitement was palpable like little surges of electricity. Some of the girls were already crying, but Kim was not. However, she did feel her insides shaking as the "Pomp and Circumstances" music began. Seventy-two young people were marching into the future and into that great unknown called life.

Kim was almost at the head of the line her last name being Banks, and students were loosely lined up alphabetically. As she marched into the bright lights of the gym, she immediately spotted her mom, dad and two sisters. Next to them was her father Sven, her brother Cayden, and JC. JC the father of her half-sister that she could only hope to meet someday.

The last six weeks had matured Kimberly beyond her young eighteen years. It wasn't only that she was graduating, it was the reality she was the daughter of an Aleut Princess and she was half Aleut. A race of people who by World War II had come close to experiencing genocide. Kim had at least a partial plan for her future, she would become a music teacher. She would not only teach the "the beauty music can bring into a life, she would also teach the history of music including the history of Aleut music.

Aleut music has two types of storytelling, The Qulirat tells of traditional legends handed down through generations within a certain family and often had a supernatural element. The other storytelling was Qaemeit, a personal and historical narrative that can be attributed to an individual author, even though he or she may have been forgotten. Anna told Kim just that morning that JC had authored a historical story about her family, including the story of the Aleut princess's disappearance from the village. Kim made a mental note to get that story from JC.

These narratives were usually danced out to the rhythm of drums made from the dried skins of different animals. The participants dressed up in all their symbolic dresses during the long winters in the Aleutian Island. They chanted the stories repeatedly until all of the people in all of the villages knew them by heart. Kim knew her future included advocating for her Aleut people. Cayden had told her there was a movement to provide compensation to the Aleut people for all they had suffered at the hands of the white man. Kim put that on her to-do list. She would find out who *they* were before leaving for college in the fall.

Cayden was sitting in an aisle seat and could have reached out and touched Kim as she marched by him. He didn't. Instead he just winked at her, and he could tell she was struggling to hold the tears back. He was distracted from the graduation ceremony because he was berating himself for acting without thinking earlier. That was a big mistake.

For the first time in a week, Cayden arrived at the hospital to visit Anna without Kim by his side. He knew she had visited Anna earlier, which left her afternoon free to get ready for her big night.

The main doors of the hospital opened up to a foyer, which led directly to a reception area filled with windows. There was also a hallway that led to an open staircase and elevator to the second floor. Just before reaching the staircase, there was a door that was always closed. Cayden had noticed it before and not paid any attention to it. For reasons beyond Cayden's understanding, today he read the small sign printed on the door, "Hospital Administrator, Sister Mary Kathleen."

Without thinking, Cayden had spontaneously reacted and knocked on the door. Sister Mary Kathleen had always had an open-door policy to her office and called out, "Come in." Cayden opened the door and stepped in.

It was a small narrow office. It almost felt as if it had been squeezed in between two solid walls. There was one small window behind the desk without curtains and with only a closed blind that shut out whatever light might be coming from the outside.

Seeing Cayden, Sister Mary Kathleen immediately stood up behind her desk. She was visibly shaking when she asked, "Cayden, how can I help you?"

Cayden's thoughts were so jumbled. They were coming at him millions of soft, fuzzy dandelion seeds on the wind, which made it difficult to come up with a coherent sentence. Silently, just for a brief second or two, Cayden and Sister Mary Kathleen made eye contact. Then Sister quickly lowered her eyes and started at some unseen object. Cayden finally said, "I was wondering if you could tell me how much longer my mother has to live?" He immediately thought, *Well, that was a stupid question, Cayden.*

"Well, like I've told you before, Cayden, it's impossible to predict the time and date of anyone's death. It's an event in all of our lives that only God knows." *Lordy,* she thought, *I sound like I'm chiding him.*

Cayden caught her tone of voice, but he felt he deserved it

because he had asked such a ridiculous question. He tried to justify it, hoping he didn't sound like a complete jackass. "Well, what I mean is if you can give me proximity. Days? Weeks? I'm only asking because I'm trying to make the right decision here."

"My parents need me out at our logging camp. It's not only the beginning of the season, but this is the last summer for us. My dad is retiring, and my folks want to do some traveling, so we will be closing the business out at the end of the summer. And I know my biological mother would like for me to be here for whatever time she has left. It's an emotional conflict for me." Again, Cayden repeated, "I just want to do the right thing."

In spite of her own emotional conflict, Sister Mary Kathleen raised her eyes to look directly at Cayden. She thought he was such a man of honor, a man to be respected. His wrinkled brow told her how hard he was concentrating. She wanted to ease the conflict he was feeling. She wished she could take away everything and anything that caused him pain, and her insight told her she was part of the substantial pressure he was under.

"I believe it's a matter of days for your mother, Cayden," she said. "Perhaps if you look at it differently. You have years to spend with your parents and only days with your mother. I think time gives you the answer you're looking for, Cayden." Sister Mary Kathleen couldn't maintain eye contact any longer. Her heart was beating out of her chest, and she couldn't stop shaking inside and out. *Oh, God*, she silently prayed. *Help me to be strong and to remember it's You I can't and won't let down.*

Cayden could see his presence in her office had unnerved her. He could see she was shaken. Her voice sounded strange, soft, even haunting like a piece of classical music, and yet there was distance to it.

He thanked her for her input and turned on his heels to leave. He grabbed the doorknob and firmly said, "I want you to know, Sister, I would never do anything to hurt you. I care enough about you to only want what is in your best interest, and we both know that for you it's serving God." When he opened the door, he heard her whisper, "Thank you, Cayden. That's a two-way street."

Cayden snapped out of his trancelike state when he heard Kimberly's name called out to come forward and accept a small musical scholarship she had won. Cayden was grateful—grateful that he now had a relationship with one of his sisters, grateful he'd had the opportunity to meet his mother before she died. Where had these strong feelings for a nun come from? He had no idea. There was no way he could ever tell anyone about them. He'd fallen in love with a nun, and he was both humiliated an embarrassed by it.

A part of him believed in some way it showed a lack of respect and honor on his part, and around and around his thoughts went in a vicious circle, causing him more anxiety than he'd ever experienced in his life. *Stop it, Cayden,* he said to himself. *Stop it right now.* And for the rest of the graduation ceremony, he was able to focus on his sister, Kimberly.

CHAPTER 42

Sister Mary Kathleen sat down in her chair and stared at the closed door. "Oh, God," she prayed, "what is happening to me?" She'd always been so sure of herself, always known what choices to make, always been at peace and filled with joy, even when her mother had died. Slowly, she picked the receiver of the phone up and dialed the long-distance operator to connect her to the Sisters of St. Ann's mother house in Vancouver. She asked to speak with the mother superior, Sister Mary Assumpta, but she had to leave a message for the mother superior to call her as soon as possible. Sister left her office and went directly to the hospital chapel, lit a candle, and knelt in prayer. Never in her life had she been tempted to put a man before her service to God, and physically, she felt nauseous, which caused her hands to shake even more.

Sister Mary Kathleen waited until after prayer time in the evening before she went to check on Anna. Anna wasn't sleeping well. The doctor had added another pain medication plus one to relax her so she would sleep. The doctor's note on her chart relayed the message, "Hydrate as much as possible, Keep comfortable. Has stopped eating."

She had sat with many dying patients, some with families and some all alone. The first time she'd watched a young woman die giving birth to a healthy baby boy, it had taken her back in time, back to her mother's death and the birth of her brother, Patrick, who was now in college majoring in agriculture. In that moment of time, she had missed her mother so much she had felt a deep physical desire to reach out and touch her mother just one more time. Grief like the wind came and went as it pleased, and all a person could do was flow with it. Trying to fight it or run from it just made it worse.

Sister Mary Kathleen could see death in Anna's face, and she thought to herself, *It won't be long now.* The medication had made Anna giddy and talkative. Some of Anna's words were a little slurred, but she didn't seem to notice. "Sister, I hoped you come this evening. Did you know that my daughter ... my daughter is graduating from high school this evening? She came wearing her graduation cap and grown. I was able to give a graduation present, my fox fur parka."

Sister Mary Kathleen was nodding at the dramatic change in Anna in only two weeks. Even though Anna was dying, she was animated and full of contagious joy. Sister just smiled and squeezed Anna's hand and said, "To God be the glory, Anna."

Anna facial expressions changed. Frowning, she continued, "Sister I can't thank you enough for being my friend when everyone else had given up on me. I know I'm dying. I can feel the energy leaving my body. It's important to me that you are with me when I die. I don't think I'll be that afraid if I can feel your presence. Thanks to you, I know my family, the people I love most, will be here. Promise me, Sister. Promise me!

"Oh, Anna, thank you for the honor of asking me. I'll try, but I can't promise you."

Sister Mary Kathleen had been warned not to get too emotionally involved with her patients. She'd been warned by the nun whom she was now awaiting a phone call from. What had she said? It had been several years now. It happened just before she left for St. Ann's hospital in Juneau. Mother superior's words flashed Sister Mary Kathleen's mind. She could see each word and read it as it quickly as it appeared. "Sister Mary Kathleen, you have a great capacity to give love. Your empathy for others is a God-given gift. But there's danger in that. It's paramount that you keep your emotional distance. You're going to see many tragic people in unspeakable physical, mental, and spiritual pain—lost people, lost souls. It will break your heart a thousand times over. More importantly, it has the potential of breaking your spirit and touching your faith in ways that can destroy you."

It had seemed harmless that first night more than five years ago when Anna had been brought into the St. Ann's emergency room. It was the middle of winter, and temperatures were below freezing. She had been found sitting in an alleyway, crying and very drunk. A stranger brought her in, a stranger who disappeared without identifying himself.

Anna, such a tiny little creature, appeared so alone and so vulnerable. Sister had asked her if there was any family she could contact. Anna replied, "No, there's no one."

Sister pressed further. "Perhaps a friend then."

Anna repeated herself, "No, there's no one." What Sister Mary Kathleen had not known was Anna had for some time had been protecting those she loved from learning just how self-destructive she had become.

Sister Mary Kathleen had become emotional involved with Anna from that first moment together. The emotions slipped into her spirit with only a vague awareness. She had seen Anna sporadically for the past five year, and each time she'd seemed alone—that is, until the last two weeks when Anna had opened up to her and Sister Mary

Kathleen had fallen in love with Anna's whole family, including Cayden Jennings.

One of St. Ann's lay nurses entered Anna's room and informed Sister there was a long-distance phone call waiting for her.

"I have to take this call, Anna. I'll check on you tomorrow." Anna suddenly dozed off as Sister Mary Kathleen hastily left the room. She hurried to her office to take the phone call in privacy.

There were four different phone lines into St. Ann's Hospital. Line four was a number that they didn't give out to the public. Sister Mary Kathleen gulped in a breath, tried to steady her shaking hand, and hit the blinking button for line four. "Sister Mary Kathleen here." Her voice sounded shaky, and her sentence came out almost like a squeal.

"Sister Mary Assumpta here returning your phone call. I was surprised to get your phone call, Sister. I just received your monthly written report for the hospital today, and I've only had time to glance at it."

Sister Mary Kathleen breathed a sigh of relief for the slight reprieve. At least she had something concrete to start the conversation without going into the true reason right away.

"The Juneau-Douglas city borough has broken ground for the new hospital just this week. St. Ann's Hospital has a year, maybe two at the most before Barlette Memorial Hospital is up and running. It is estimated that it will have between seventy to seventy-five beds. As you know, Mother Superior, St. Ann's Hospital cannot meet all the community's needs in health care. We're just too small for the present fast-growing population."

Only the slight buzz of the long-distance phone line could be heard as Sister Mary Kathleen hesitated, taking several deep breaths. Mother Superior was silent, waiting. She'd been the mother superior for the two thousand Saint Ann's nuns for more than thirty years, and she was as wise as she was intelligent. More importantly, she had an unwavering faith that had seen the best and the worst of humanity.

As a young teenager, Sister Mary Assumpta had seen what evil truly was, and it had changed her forever. A young girl from a neighboring farm had given birth to a baby girl out of wedlock, a colossal social no-no at the time. The young girl went in the middle of winter into the surrounding forest to give birth. Mother Superior came upon her while collecting pinecones for Christmas decorations. She heard the baby's first cry, and she ran toward the sound and found the mother with her hand over the baby's nose and mouth. The baby was limp in her arms, and it had turned a grayish blue. Then she had taken a razor blade and slit her wrist.

The young woman had bled out by the time the young teenager had gotten help to her. It wasn't the act of murder-suicide by a young girl with her whole life ahead of her that was evil. It was the cruelty, the moral degradation heaped on one human being by a society that condemned her and left her in despair and without hope. That was the true evil.

Sister Mary Assumpta had chosen to become a nun because her faith told her the best way to fight evil was through the power of God's love.

Sister Mary Kathleen stumbled over her words. She explained how she had met Anna, how she had connected with her over the last five years, believing she was all alone in the world, how Anna had signed herself out against medical advice on four different occasions, and how Sister Mary Kathleen had watched her physically and mentally deteriorate in the last five year.

"What you're telling me, Sister, is that you are invested emotionally with this woman and have been for the past five years. Is that correct?" Mother Superior inserted herself into the middle of Sister Mary Kathleen's narrative.

"Yes, it seemed so harmless at the time, and Anna needed someone to believe in her, someone to be her friend." Sister Mary Kathleen continued, "Anna's death is imminent, and her admission three weeks ago has changed everything. I've become emotionally attached to her whole family. I found out she had a family, three children all adopted out and all from different fathers. The first child, a son, was the product of a repeated rape by two different men. The second child was a daughter by the man she married and is still married to, although they have been estranged from each other for the past eighteen years—that is, until the past two weeks. Not only have they reconciled, but both have become born-again Christians. The issue I'm struggling with is my emotional attachment to the whole family, specifically Anna's son, Cayden Jennings." The last sentence coming from Sister Mary Kathleen was almost a sob.

"I see," Mother Superior said, and then she added, "And what do you think God's will is for you, Sister?"

Sister Mary Kathleen replied, "I know that God is a God of order and not a God of confusion, and right now I'm so confused spiritually and mentally. I think maybe my faith is being tested. I need some time to fast and pray, something that is impossible as the administrator of this hospital. Perhaps I could take a leave of absence." Her voice trailed off, and there was another silence between the two nuns.

It took a moment or two before Mother Superior spoke. "You understand you cannot run from your spiritual confusion, Sister, and that you are in a spiritual battle. Let me remind you of God's Word. Ephesians 6:10–17 says, 'Finally, be strong in the Lord and in his might power. Put on the full armor of God so that you can. For out take your stand against the devil's schemes. For our struggle is not against flesh and blood, but against the rulers, against the authorities, against the powers of this dark world and against the spiritual forces of evil in the heavenly realms. Therefore put on the full armor of God so that when the day of evil comes, you may be able to stand your ground, and after you have done everything, to stand. Stand firm then, with the belt of truth buckled around your waist, with the breastplate of righteousness in place and with your feet fitted with the readiness that comes from the gospel of peace. In addition to all this, take up the shield of faith, with which you can extinguish all the flaming arrows of the evil one. Take the helmet of salvation and the sword of the Spirit which is the word of God. And pray I the Spirit on all occasions with all kinds of prayers and requests.'"

"Yes, Mother, I understand, but right now my emotions are keeping me from thinking straight." Sister Mary Kathleen was both embarrassed and ashamed at her inability to resolve her feelings for Cayden.

Sister Mary Assumpta quietly replied, "Let me pray for guidance, Sister, and I'll call you back as soon as possible."

After saying good-bye, the two nuns hung up. Sister Mary Kathleen folded her arms and put her head on her desk. She was physically exhausted and spiritually drained, and for the first time since she'd become a nun, she began to sob uncontrollably.

She called out in despair, "Oh, God, please help me."

CHAPTER 43

J C had spent the last several days thinking. He had a new awareness about himself that he hadn't before known. For one, he'd learned about forgiveness. Forgiveness wasn't about justice. Forgiveness was about a state of mind. All those wasted years he'd buried his anger, unable to forgive ... what? The Russian fur traders who had used, abused, and even killed his people? The United States of America's federal government for buying Alaska from the Russians and then ignoring Alaska's need for financial supplements as well as law and order? For World War II and the people burning his village? For the internment of his people in filthy conditions without enough medical supplies or food? It wasn't just the rage he'd felt when he found out he had a daughter he never knew existed that had triggered a deeper and more profound anger, an anger that had controlled his life for the past twenty years.

The list went on and on. And what had he done? Nothing!

Absolutely nothing! He'd stuck his head in the sand, blocking the painful truth from touching his soul. In reality, he hadn't been living his life. He'd only been surviving, existing in a bubble he'd built around himself to protect him from the deep consuming pain of the near genocide of his people.

He was now aware that in forcing himself to forgive Ahha, he had opened a hidden part of himself he wasn't proud of. He remembered a quote by Edmund Burke. "The only thing necessary for the triumphs of evil is for good men to do nothing." He was done with all that. He would fight for his people, fight for justice, fight to bring to the Aleut nation the pride and dignity they deserved. He was motivated, even driven in the hope he would meet his daughter when she turned eighteen. He wanted to be a man she would be proud to call father.

All his introspection had brought a profound revelation he recognized as truth. It was the reality he was not in love with Anna Hasson. JC loved Anna, but he was in love with Ahha, the Aleut princess. He was in love with a different time and a different place. He was in love with the beauty of an Aleut princess who ran free in their village, bringing with her contagious laughter. He had watched as this sweet spirit grew into a beautiful young woman. With her came the hope for a future that would bring back the pride and dignity the Aleut nation had once had before the Russian traders and white men had come to live among them. Then *poof*, one day she was gone, and with her went the magic of her presence.

There was only one way out of pain, and that was through it. The time had come for JC to share his newfound self with Anna Hasson. Sven had stopped by JC's job the night before and told him that Anna was deteriorating rapidly and that it wouldn't be much longer before they all would lose her.

It was early morning and already light outside. The daylight hours in Juneau became longer each day in the late spring. Low whitish gray clouds hung over the downtown area. The light from the sun tried to peek through and bounced off the Gastinue Channel waters. Surrounded by the high peaks of the three mountains, the atmospheric cocoon felt surreal, leaving its residents with the feeling of safety and security.

St. Ann's Hospital was six blocks uphill from JC's apartment in the middle of downtown Juneau. As he breathed in the fresh air and repeated to himself what he wanted to share with Anna, the only sounds he heard were the familiar noises of an Alaska coastal seaplane taking off in the channel.

JC found Anna awake regardless of the early hour. It was painful to look at her. Anna's thick, long black hair haloed her drawn face.

There was still a light in her brown eyes, but any animation she once had had slowed to the point of nonexistence.

"Hey," JC said.

"Hey yourself," Anna replied and slowly smiled. "I'm so happy you're here. I have something I want give you, something for you to give our daughter when she contacts you."

"You seem so sure that she's going to contact me," JC replied.

"I have to believe that, JC. I have been blessed beyond words these last two weeks. The only fly in the ointment, so to speak, is not being able to see my second daughter before I die. I believe that someday God will see that my three children are together and that they will be proud of their Aleut heritage. Speaking of that, there's something in the closet I want you to have to give to our daughter."

Without a word, JC opened the closet door, and what he saw broke his heart. It was Ahha's leather dress, the dress she'd been wearing the day she had been kidnapped from the village. It was the dress her mother, Annuk, had made the winter of her grief at the loss of her husband and sons, the dress she'd been wearing when she stepped out of playing the role of the young girl into the woman who was the beautiful Aleut princess. It was like a dream, a dream of joy and hope, not only for JC and Ahha but for their whole village.

But instead of a dream, it had turned into a living nightmare that would change all their lives.

Both JC and Ahha were openly weeping, but it was Anna Hasson who spoke. "We have to let it go, JC. There's no going back, no changing what has been done." Then as if the emotions of the moment had exhausted her, Anna Hasson closed her eyes, dozing off.

For just a fleeting moment, JC saw Ahha, the Aleut princess, lying in the hospital bed, and then she was gone, gone from him forever. He picked up the garment, kissed Anna on the forehead, and left. He instinctively knew there was no need to share with Anna all he'd been through in the last few day. Somehow, he knew she knew anyway. His job now was to treasure Ahha's garment until the day came when he could give it to their daughter. It was going to be a long three years.

CHAPTER 44

She was again dreaming. She heard the small gold bells, three separate rings announcing the Holy Eucharist. Faceless people were going forward to receive Communion. Why was the ringing continuing and getting louder with each ring? Something must be wrong. Sister Mary Kathleen forced herself out of the heavy fog. It was the house phone ringing next to her bed. They'd put one in her sleeping quarters for emergencies.

She picked up the receiver. "Sister Mary Kathleen here."

The familiar voice of her night nurse supervisor spoke, "Yes, Sister, you asked us to call you if Ms. Hasson took a turn for the worst. She's running a temperature, and she has mild symptoms of hypovolemic shock."

"Tell me the symptoms," Sister Mary Kathleen replied.

"Ms. Hasson is complaining of a headache, nausea, and dizziness. She is dozing off every ten minutes or so, and she's sweating profusely.

We've had to change her hospital grown twice. There is also some bleeding from her vagina."

"I'm coming. Give me a few minutes," Sister Mary Kathleen answered and hung up the receiver.

There was no predicting the exact time of a person's death. It was always in God's time. She had trained herself to dress in her nun's habit in less than five minutes, and while dressing, she prayed for Anna. She prayed her death would be peaceful without any suffering and with her family around her. Cayden briefly filled her thoughts. She literally shook the thoughts of him away.

The dream lingered, and Sister reviewed her personal belief in the Holy Eucharist. Roman Catholic theology taught that the bread and wine of Communion transcended the natural laws of physics and became the body and blood of Jesus Christ. She smiled to herself, remembering her first Communion. She was dressed up in a white dress and veil, parading down the center aisle of the church with the seven other children who were also making their first Communion. It was one of the most reverent moments in her life.

Over many years Sister Mary Kathleen had witnessed many debates and downright arguments about the truth of the church's stand on the Holy Eucharist. She had come to believe the motif was the heart of the individual receiving Communion. If in the deepest part of a person's soul, the individual believed the Holy Eucharist transcended natural laws, then it was truth for that individual, and that was okay. Just as it was okay if the truth for the individual who sincerely believed communion was "in remembrance."

The problem with the "in remembrance" theology often was that people developed a lack of reverence or prayerful thought when a church taught the ritual of Communion was "in remembrance of the Last Supper of Jesus Christ with his disciples."

Sister Mary Kathleen believed in God's Word, and whatever belief system one adopted, Holy Communion should always be taken seriously and in reverence. First Corinthians 11:27–32 (NIV) said, "Therefore whoever eats the bread or drinks the cup of the Lord in an unworthy manner will be guilty of sinning against the body and blood of the Lord. A man ought to examine himself before he eats of the bread and drinks of the cup. For anyone who eats and drinks without recognizing the body of the Lord eats and drinks judgment on himself. That is why many among you are weak and sick, and a number of you have fallen asleep, but if we judged ourselves, we would not come under judgment. When we are judged by the Lord, we are being disciplined so that we will not be condemned with the world."

Sister Mary Kathleen reviewed Anna's medical chart, noting

that she had stopped eating and that she had taken only a few sips of water in the last twenty-four hours. That was always a sign that the body was shutting down. She also noted that Anna had been in and out of consciousness in the last twelve hours. Sister went directly to Anna's room.

Anna looked extremely frail. She seemed as fragile as a china doll, one that could break at any minute. Sister gently picked up a hand and caressed it, noticing for the first time the wedding band on her left ring finger. Choking on her words, she whispered, "If you can hear me, Anna, squeeze my hand." Anna not only lightly squeezed Sister's hand, but she opened her eyes and said, "Please call me by my real name, Ahha, for it is Ahha who will stand before the Lord in judgment. Anna Hasson was just a pretend person hiding Ahha behind unbearable pain."

"Would you like me to call your family, Ahha?"

"Please," Ahha answered and drifted into unconsciousness again.

Sister Mary Kathleen called Sven and told him he and Ahha's family should come to the hospital as soon as possible. Sven voice was shaking so hard he could barely get the words out. "How much longer, Sister?"

"That's difficult to say, Sven. At the most, a couple of days. Possibly only hours. Let's pray she doesn't suffer and dies peacefully."

As she hung up the phone receiver, Sister was overwhelmed at the depth of love she held for this tiny Aleut princess. It had sneaked up on her over the last five years without any real conscious awareness of it until these last three weeks.

The emotional conflict Sister Mary Kathleen was experiencing was rattling her a little, and she was unable to always think in a rational professional manner. On the one hand, she had told Ahha she would do her best to be with her when she died, and on the other hand, she felt that being in the presence of Cayden and remaining aloof was uncomfortable at best. She had received a phone call from Sister Mary Assumpta and knew she would be leaving St. Ann's Hospital and Juneau in the next two days. Her replacement was already on her way. She was an older nun who could handle the administrative duties of St. Ann's for the next couple of years while Bartlette Memorial Hospital was being built.

Sven arrived at the hospital within an hour of Sister Mary Kathleen's phone call. He had called his daughter, Kimberly, Cayden, Linda, and JC. He knew they would all come within the next hour. Anna Ahha was hooked up to an IV and did not respond to his whispered, "I love you." He sat down at the side of her bed, holding her left hand, twisting her wedding ring around and around. He was heartsick at all the wasted years. Even the joy of revealing his fatherhood to his daughter didn't take away the condemnation he felt for eighteen lost years.

Cayden was the first to arrive. Shaking hands with Sven, he asked how much longer his mother had. Sven said, "Not long," and then he proceeded to tell him about the gift Anna had wanted to give to him herself.

A handmade Aleut basket sat next to the still blooming bouquet of wild Alaskan flowers. Sven explained to Cayden how the boy's grandmother, Annuk, had woven the basket. He handed the basket to Cayden and told him to open it. Inside Cayden found the most intricate bird carving in ivory he had ever seen. The workmanship was impressive. Sven explained to him how Annuk had carved the bird as a young woman. It was a puffin, the artic parrot.

"Do you know what a totem is, Cayden? Sven asked.

"You mean like a totem pole?" Cayden asked.

"Well, sort of," Sven continued. "A totem is always something living like an animal or bird. It's a symbol for a person. It speaks to that person in a spiritual way. Your mother, Ahha, told me that everyone has a totem. It's just that some people don't recognize it. The puffin was your grandmother Annuk's totem."

"Do you have a totem?" Cayden asked Sven.

Seven smiled and said, "I'm not very good at recognizing spiritual things, Cayden. But sometimes when I've been out on the water fishing and I've pulled in a king salmon and the sun is bouncing off the seawater and the silver scales of the fish, I've felt …well, I've felt like the fish was talking to me." Sven looked at Cayden, blushing with embarrassment.

Cayden reach out and patted Sven's shoulder and said, "I know what you mean, Sven. I love walking in the forest, listening to the many sounds of the various living creatures. Every now and then, I'll see a monarch butterfly come to rest on a nearby wildflower. I can't describe the feeling I experience. I just know I feel happy and at peace with the world. I suppose that's a totem in a way." Sven nodded in understanding.

"That carving, Son, is from a walrus tusk. Your grandmother cherished it. It was one of the few items she took with her when she was forced to leave the village she'd lived in all her life." Anna Ahha's voice was weak, a hoarse whisper that could barely be heard. She was once again awake.

Seven jumped up from his chair and began to caress her forehead. Cayden stood to the side of him, not knowing what to say.

Both Kim and JC came walking into the room, and both said at the same time, "Ahha." She reached out her arm, embracing first Kim and then JC, telling them both she loved them.

Sven spoke first, and he stumbled over his words. "Anna Ahha, what are we going to do without you!"

Linda's eyes were red and swollen from crying the whole three-block walk from her house. Entering Ahha's room, she could see that her two children, JC, and Sven were already there. She was surprised that Ahha was awake and talking.

Ahha looked around and whispered, "Every person that I love most in the world is in this room. Well, almost everyone, and she looked directly at JC. "Promise me you'll do everything you can to find our daughter, and tell her I loved her with all my heart. Help her to be proud she's Aleut. Promise me!"

JC stood at the foot of her bed, his eyes welling up with tears, and he answered, "I promise, Ahha."

"Could someone please find Sister Mary Kathleen. I need to see her." Ahha's words were coming slower, and those in the room had to listen closely to hear what she was saying. Linda volunteered and went looking for her.

Cayden said, "I'm so happy you found us, Ahha. I want you to know that both Kim and I are proud to be the children of an Aleut princess and proud we are Aleut. We will do what we can to see that our people get justice."

Cayden could see that Linda was returning, and behind her

was Sister Mary Kathleen. He quickly moved to the corner of the room. He sensed it was as difficult for her as it was for him to be in the same room.

Sister Mary Kathleen kept her eyes lowered, aware that Cayden was in the room. "What can I do for you, Anna? I mean Ahha."

"Sister, I want the last rites." Anna said quietly.

"All right, Ahha, let me see what I can do." And she swiftly left the room.

Then JC asked, "What exactly are the last rites?"

Cayden said that he had seen his grandmother receive them just before she died. "The last rites are a set of sacraments given to people who are perceived to be near death. They are meant to prepare the dying person's soul for death by providing absolution for sins by penance, sacramental grace, and prayers for the relief of suffering through anointing, and there's also the final administration of the Eucharist, known as viaticum. The normal order of administration is first penance and then anointing and then viaticum."

Ahha let out a deep sigh—the kind of sign that only comes from feeling free of a long and heavy burden. She'd done the right thing in giving him up for adoption, and she felt his strength as he reached out and squeezed her hand.

Ahha turned her attention to Linda reaching out to her. Her

voice was weak but still audible. "I don't know what I'd done without you, Linda. You saved my life, and I love you like a sister."

Linda was sobbing. How many times over the past twenty years had she given up on Ahha. Too many to count, and yet she'd always felt responsible, always reconnected with her. "I guess patience isn't my strong suit." She smiled a little at Ahha.

Ahha's eyes lit up for just a second. "Well, I surely tried your patience to the limit." Everyone gave a small laugh. It was a light moment for all in the room, lifting the intense heaviness that came with knowing you are about to lose someone you love. Grief is nothing more than love with no place to go.

An older priest appeared at the door to Ahha's hospital room, a man whose lined face and white hair spoke of the kind of wisdom that came from many years of living. Introducing himself, he spoke directly to Ahha, "I'm here to give you the last rites of the church. I understand you've requested them."

Ahha nodded. Her eyes were heavy. She wanted to close them; however, she knew if she closed them, she might not be able to open them again, and she wanted—no, she needed—to make sure she was right with God. Without words, Ahha's family filed out of the room so Ahha could make her last confession in private.

The priest put on his purple stole over his white collar and black garment. "Have you, Ahha, accepted Jesus Christ as your personal savior?"

"Yes, Father, and in the last two weeks, it has changed me back to the person I was born to be."

"Are you ready to make your last confession?" the priest asked while blessing her with the sign of the cross.

"Yes, Father." And then the Aleut princess, Ahha, began, "Bless me, Father, for I have sinned. I have sinned against God and against everyone I love. I have sinned with a false pride that led to the betrayal of my people and of all those who have loved me." Ahha's voice was weak but firm.

The priest heard hundreds of last confessions during his long life. The sin of pride did not surprise him as nine out of ten of last confessions were often about the hidden sin of false pride.

Ahha continued, "I was proud of being an Aleut princess, so proud that when I was kidnapped and raped, I was so indignant. I couldn't bring myself to accept the help I needed. I blamed God and carried my anger inside of me. It controlled my life up until two weeks ago. That terrible pride and anger led to the betrayal of my people, of my children, of my husband, and of all those who dared to love me. All the other sins I committed because of my poor choices pale in comparison. I am so sorry, so very sorry." Ahha didn't have any tears left. She was tired, weary, and without any strength left in her body. If she could just sleep. Her eyes were beginning to close involuntarily.

The priest began the anointing with blessed oil. He gently made the sign of the cross on the forehead, the mouth, and the cheeks while repeating the Lord's Prayer. "Come on, child of God. Stay awake just a little longer," he softly said. Ahha forced her eyes open, not wanting to come back from the tunnel with the brilliant light. The priest then administered the Eucharist.

"The body of Christ," the priest prayed while placing the wafer on Ahha's tongue, and then he placed a small gold chalice with wine to her lips. He then prayed, asking God to accept Ahha into His kingdom.

She was running free through the village she loved, filled with joy, laughter, and love. Eternity was ahead of her, and she no longer was filled with fear.

CHAPTER 45

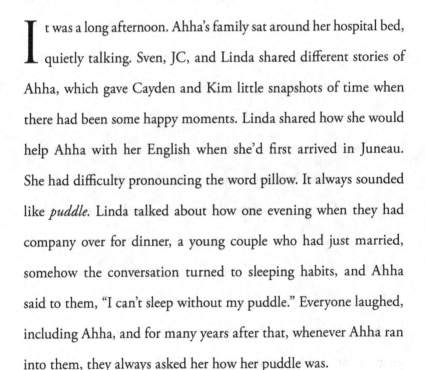

It was a long afternoon. Ahha's family sat around her hospital bed, quietly talking. Sven, JC, and Linda shared different stories of Ahha, which gave Cayden and Kim little snapshots of time when there had been some happy moments. Linda shared how she would help Ahha with her English when she'd first arrived in Juneau. She had difficulty pronouncing the word pillow. It always sounded like *puddle.* Linda talked about how one evening when they had company over for dinner, a young couple who had just married, somehow the conversation turned to sleeping habits, and Ahha said to them, "I can't sleep without my puddle." Everyone laughed, including Ahha, and for many years after that, whenever Ahha ran into them, they always asked her how her puddle was.

Cayden told the story of when they were first married and Ahha decided she was going to bake her first cake. The recipe called for separating three eggs. She had taken three bowls and put an egg in each one. When he'd arrived home, she was sitting at the kitchen table and crying because she couldn't figure out how to finish the rest of the recipe. He smiled and showed her, and they'd both laughed so hard that they couldn't make the cake until the next day.

JC shared a story of Ahha at about the age of eight. Blueberries grew wild in the rolling volcanic hills of the village. One afternoon a group of women were out picking blueberries with the help of their older children. The children had all been told not to eat the berries because they were filled with worms and needed to be first soaked in water. Walking back home with their baskets filled to the top, Anuuk looked at Ahha and asked, "How come you ate the berries when you were told not to?" Ahha couldn't figure out how her mother knew she'd eaten some of the blueberries, so she'd tried to deny it. Anuuk said firmly, "I know you ate the berries, Ahha." JC was with the group that day, and he leaned over and whispered to Ahha, "Ahha, your teeth and lips are blue from the berries." Ahha's eyes said it all, and she immediately covered her mouth with her hand. Everyone in the group that day, including Anuuk, was giggling, and Ahha eventually joined in. Kim and Cayden loved hearing the stories, stories that showed them another side of their mother, the happy, carefree side.

At about two in the afternoon, Sister Mary Kathleen came into the room and asked the family to wait in the hall for a few minutes while she checked on Ahha. She had not gained consciousness since the priest had left. They had medicated her to keep her comfortable, and she looked like she was just in a heavy sleep. Pulling the covers back to change the pad on her bed and put a clean grown on her, Sister could see that both of Ahha's feet up to her knees were mottled. The circulation was slowly leaving her extremities. It wouldn't be long now. She pulled the covers up over her so all one could see was the delicate face with the dark black hair spread out around her. Her small delicate arms and hands laid on each side of her on top of the covers.

Ahha's breathing had changed. Her breathing was shallow. She took quick breaths followed by times when she wasn't breathing at all. Her exhale was longer than her inhale, which was a sign that the process of dying had begun.

Sister Mary Kathleen called the family back into the room, telling them to call her when there was fifteen seconds between Ahha's breathing. Sister didn't dare make eye contact with Cayden, and she directed her instructions at Sven. Cayden stayed in the background, knowing his presence made Sister Mary Kathleen uncomfortable.

Kim had never watched anyone die, and it was a traumatic

experience for her. Both Sven and Cayden quietly reassured her that Ahha was comfortable and at peace. Sven also quietly told Kim that the wedding ring now on Ahha's finger was to be given to her. It was both of their wishes for their daughter. Kim cried silent tears when Sven told her that. For a young eighteen-year-old with her whole life ahead of her, she had grown beyond her years, learning some of life's most difficult lessons. She learned that from the moment of a person's birth, the individual was heading toward his or her own death. It wasn't a morbid lesson. It was a lesson to live life to its fullest. She had learned to use whatever talents a person had for the betterment of the world. She had learned to follow her dreams and to be the person she was born to be. She had learned the key to life was love, and God is love.

In the last week, JC had seen Ahha come back from wherever she'd been hiding for the past twenty years. It had touched his spirit in ways that had changed him. Secretly, he still harbored questions about his daughter. Had it been the best choice for his daughter to be adopted? He knew he had to live with that uncertainty for at least another three years. He would live the next three years fighting for the Aleut nation. No longer would he ignore the sad reality that his people had come close to complete annihilation through genocide.

Sven was filled with regrets. Although grateful for the past two weeks, he couldn't help but regret the past eighteen years. For Sven, he was losing his wife forever, and he couldn't get past that pain.

Cayden was focused on counting the time between his mother's breath, and for the last few minutes, it had been fifteen seconds between her inhaling and exhaling. He leaned over to Sven and whispered in his ear how he thought it was time to call Sister Mary Kathleen. Sven stood up without a word and slowly went to find her.

Sister Mary Kathleen had been present for many deaths both as a nun and as a nurse. It was always a challenge for her to understand the unique dynamics of each family. Who was in denial? Who was angry? Who was emotionally distraught? Who was in shock? Who was unable to forgive the family member because of a poor history in the relationship and even an estranged relationship with the person dying?

Anna Hasson's family would be completely different. Sister Mary Kathleen had to keep her emotional distance. It was going to be difficult, comforting Ahha's family while concealing her feelings toward Cayden.

There was a quiet calmness that filled the hospital room like a gentle wind that spoke of eternal life. Sven was on one side at the head of the bed. Next to him JC stood like a plaster statue, and he softly whispered over and over, "Go home, Ahha. The ancients are waiting for you."

Sven was gently caressing his wife's forehead, lovingly telling her that it was okay for her to let go, that she didn't have to worry about her family, and that all of them would love her forever. He was already grieving, in his own surreal space separate from the others in the room, even his daughter.

Linda, Kim, and Cayden stood at the foot of the bed. Both Kim and Linda were quietly crying. Cayden stood between them with an arm around each of them in an awkward effort to comfort them. It was no surprise to Sister Mary Kathleen to see him manifest his emotional strength in death.

Sister Mary Kathleen stood with her stethoscope hanging from her neck on the opposite side of Ahha's bed, listening every couple of minutes to her heart as it became weaker. Both her breathing and heartbeat peacefully drifting away as the stars in the dawn of the morning until the last light of the last star was finally hidden from the viewer.

Sister Mary Kathleen stood and quietly spoke, "The Aleut princess is gone." For a fleeting second, she made eye contact with Cayden, and her heart broke when she saw the sadness in his eyes.

CHAPTER 46

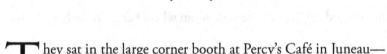

T hey sat in the large corner booth at Percy's Café in Juneau—
Sven, JC, Linda, Cayden, and Kim. Cayden and Kim were
eating a side order of french fries with a side of gravy. Their subdued
conversation centered on how to say a final good-bye to Ahha, the
Aleut princess.

The aftershock when loosing someone you love to death can
sometimes protect a person from the emotional and spiritual pain
that goes with it. One keeps on moving but in a surreal state of
mind. People know it in their brains, but in their spirits where the
real people live, they are sheltered from the reality of death. It comes
to the point when people must make a choice. Do they believe in
eternal life, or do they believe a person just ceases to exist?

Ahha's family believed in eternal life. It was the first time for Kim
to face the death of a human being. Both sets of her grandparents
had died when she was very young. She'd only been about four years

old when her fraternal grandfather had died. All the adults around Kim had told her he had died and gone to heaven.

When her family had talked about how they were going to visit her grandfather, she asked if she could go. In her four-year-old mind, if they were going to visit her grandpa, they would go visit him in heaven. When they got to the funeral home, Kim's father picked her up and carried her into the room where her grandfather lay. The room was small with heavy velvet drapes on the windows. The smell was sickeningly sweet with too many fresh flowers crammed into a small space. Her grandfather lay encircled in white shiny satin in a casket. Kim looked at her father, and in complete disappointment, she asked, "Is this heaven?"

Ahha's family agreed they would only have a graveside service, and Sven and JC would take care of making the arrangements.

The day was one of Juneau's rare days with clear blue skies. The sunbeams bounced off the waters of Gastinue Channel between Douglas Island and the mainland of Juneau. Sven looked out the large picture window of his sister's home and thought, *This is the day I bury the only women I have ever loved.* He could not and would not cry. He was afraid if he started crying, he would never stop. Besides, he had to be strong for his daughter, Kim.

Cayden was taking an early morning walk in the small forests area around his home. His mind was in a swirl. Sven had called him the night before and told him he had dropped by St. Ann's Hospital to see if it was possible for Sister Mary Kathleen to attend the small graveside service. He had been told by the person at the reception desk that Sister Mary Kathleen was no longer at the hospital and had been transferred. When Sven asked where, the receptionist told him the staff did not have that information. Sven then called Cayden since Cayden was the one who suggested they ask her to attend.

Why? Cayden asked himself. *Why did I spontaneously go into her office that day?* He was responsible for frightening her, and now he had driven her off. He was burdened with guilt. He had fallen in love with a nun, and it would be a burden he'd silently have to carry the rest of his life.

There was a small cemetery along Douglas Highway headed into the center of downtown Douglas. That was where the Aleut princess would be buried with a small stone headstone that read, "The Aleut Princess, Ahha." Under the title in smaller print, it would read, "Anna Hasson," and also list the dates of her birth and death.

They all arrived at the grave site together—Cayden, Kim, and Kim's parents, Elaine and Brian, Linda and her husband, Willie, JC, and Sven. The Russian Orthodox priest was there to lead the service.

The priest spoke of Ahha's recent return to a relationship with Jesus Christ. He spoke of her heritage as an Aleut princess and how she'd found her children and reconciled with Sven, JC, and Linda in the last four weeks. Most of all, he spoke of Ahha's belief in her Aleut people, claiming her blood covenant right before she died.

Father Valimar then led the family in reciting the Nicene Creed. "We believe in one God, the Father Almighty. maker of heaven and earth, and of all things visible and invisible. And in one Lord, Jesus Christ, the only begotten Son of God, begotten of the Father before all worlds, God of God, Light of Light, very God of very God, begotten, not made, being of one substance with the Father by whom all things were made; who for us men, and for our salvation, came down from heaven, and was conceived by the Holy Spirit of the Virgin Mary, and was made man, and was crucified also for under Pontius Pilate. He suffered and was buried, and on the third day He rose again, according to the scriptures, and ascended into heaven, and sitteth on the right hand of the Father. And He shall come again with glory to judge both the quick and the dead, whose kingdom shall have no end.

"And we believe in the Holy Spirit, the Lord and giver of life, who proceedeth from the Father and the Son, who with the Father and the Son together is worshipped and glorified, who spoke by the prophets. And we believe one holy Catholic (universal) and apostolic church. We acknowledge one baptism for the remission of sins. And we look for the resurrection of the dead … and the life of the world to come. Amen."

The heartfelt prayer brought some inner peace to Ahha's family because their faith was strong. Hebrews 11:1–3 (NIV) says, "Now, faith is being sure of what we hope for and certain of what we do not see. This is what the ancients were commended for. By faith we understand that the universe was formed at God's command, so that what is seen was not made out of what was visible."

JC draped an ancient Aleut blanket around his shoulders. It had been given to him by his father just before JC left the internment camp to look for work in Juneau. He began to chant. The rhythm of the chant resembled a requiem Mass in the Catholic church. He slowly danced around Ahha's casket and grave.

"Hmmmmm'm. Long ago when the Aleut nation was many, they traveled across the frozen waters searching for a new place to settle. The moon protected them from the cold nights. The wise crow said, 'I will be your spirit guide and go before you.' The great whales said, 'We will give you food,' and the great white bear said, 'I will give you courage.' They came to a land that had many rolling hills because they had been built from the ocean floor by fire. Fire would renew them and cleanse them from the suffering they had endured in the old land. They came to the new land and thrived. Surrounded by the sea, it gave up its treasures, giving them food, clothing, heat, and light. The whales, the walruses, the sea otters, the seals, and the birds. They grew in strength and numbers until they were the people of the many islands.

"Hmmmmmm'm. Then the white man from the old land came in boats, taking their treasures, killing many of the men, and keeping some of the women to themselves for their own pleasure. The Aleut people became their slaves as the trickster raven covered their lands with sadness. They brought with them their God, and the shamans of the villages lost their magical powers. Building many churches over time, the Aleut people converted to Christianity but stayed with some of the old ways, keeping their totems, their spirit guides, and their love for the earth.

"Hmmmmmm'm. Then after much suffering at the hands of the white man, their numbers decreased every year. Then a light appeared in one of the villages, a small baby girl who had only Aleut blood in her veins. She ran through the village free, magically bringing with her hope, laughter, and happiness. Her mother, who was wise in the ancient ways, chanted her people's stories, teaching her basket weaving and carving from the walrus tusks.

"Hmmmmm'm. The hawk that had protected the life force of the animals disappeared, and the trickster raven fooled the little girl's father and two brothers in the sea with many whales. The whales became confused because of the meeting of the two seas, and the father and two brothers went to the bottom of the sea to live.

"Hmmmmm'm. The cold winter brought much sadness to the magical girl, who then took care of her mother. Spring arrived, and the magical girl's mother wasn't so sad. But the time of suffering for the magical girl's people was not over. The otter no longer brought laughter, grace, and empathy, and Agugux, the creator, was silent.

"Hmmmm'm. The magical girl was stolen from her village and taken to the white man's world, where she lived and suffered for many years. She gave her three children away because she was tricked by the raven into believing that she was no longer worthy of being magical and the Aleut princess.

"Hmmmm'm. The loons, as with all birds, are divine messengers from Aguugux. And the loons brought an all-white angel from the spirit realm to the Aleut princess. The angel brought the Aleut princess back to Aguugux. Aguugux was no longer silent and showed the Aleut princess that she indeed was and always would be the Aleut princess, who would through her children bring her people to peace and abundance. The Aleut princess is now in eternity, leaving behind her a family who will always love her."

She was free now, running through the village of her youth. She could hear the laughter of small children playing, off in the distance. She was surrounded in light and love. The Aleut Princess was home.

Epilogue

The Call of the Loons

Echo Cove sits about thirty miles north of downtown Juneau. Its natural beauty is pristine. Coming into the channel from the sea that feeds the cove, one is greeted by a circle of pine and spruce trees with all their wild foliage and flowers. The gray rocky beach is usually filled with various wild birds gliding over the water.

The night would have been pitch black had not the sky been filled with millions of twinkling stars and a full moon shinning in the center of the cove just over the tree line. The water was as clear and calm as smooth glass.

Cayden Jennings sat on the beach, reflecting on the many major changes in his life over the past six month. He had met his biological mother and been with her when she had died. He had found out he had two halfsisters, one of whom he'd meant. He'd become good friends with the father of his sister, Kimberly. He'd also become good friends with the father of his second sister—a sister no one knew yet. JC had also given him a detailed history of the Aleut people. He now thought of them as his people. He was half Aleut and now knew of their severe suffering by the hands of not only the Russian fur traders but also wards of the US government.

Echo Cove logging was shutting down the camp. Cayden's father had reached an age when the necessary physical strength needed for logging had become too difficult. Besides, Cayden's father had earned enough money to retire comfortable. Cayden had no idea what he was going to do with the rest of his life.

Tomorrow Cayden and his father, along with two crew members, would start tearing down the logging camp as required by the National Forrest Service. The site would be left with no evidence there had ever been a logging camp in the area.

For the first time in his twenty-eight years, he was overwhelmed with his life, and he had no idea about where he was going. Besides, he'd fallen in love with a woman he could never have. That was something he was far too embarrassed to ever tell anyone.

Slowly, he stood up from his spot on the beach. All he wanted at this second was sleep. He wanted to escape from the reality of his life. Where had his once happy life gone?

About the Author

L oretta Sanford Cuellar was born and raised in Juneau, Alaska. She presently lives in Goose Creek, South Carolina, where she shares her home with her youngest son, Tom Mayer, and his wife, Debora.

Recently widowed, Loretta lost her husband, Ben, of thirty-seven years on July 4, 2016. She has eight children, two of them from previous marriages by her former husband, Ben. She has twenty-four grandchildren, all of whom she describes as "super special," and fourteen great-grandchildren, the oldest being twelve and the youngest being two months.

Aleut Princess is her second published work. Her first publication was a "different kind of devotional" titled *Truthseeker*, written under the pseudonym Dawn Sanford and published in May 2003.

She has said, "I got sidetracked from writing for a few years with rebuilding a home in North Carolina and my husband being diagnosed with cancer. Because of medical expenses, I went back to work as a social worker full-time, working in Morganton, North Carolina, for Burke County in adult protective services. I finally retired (again), and we moved to South Carolina to be near family."

Loretta is a woman of faith and states, "I'm a bit of a mystic, and I do believe that often God talks to us through nature." She attends Calvary Chapel of Charleston with her daughter Becky Calvert and will be working on the second book of the Totem series, *The Call of the Loons.*

Printed in the United States
By Bookmasters